TIME FOR THE POLKA DOT

Alex O'Connor

Best wishes,

Alex O'Connor.

APS BOOKS
YORKSHIRE

APS Books,
The Stables Field Lane,
Aberford,
West Yorkshire,
LS25 3AE

APS Books is a subsidiary of the APS Publications imprint

www.andrewsparke.com

TIME FOR THE POLKA DOT...

PROLOGUE

They say that drowning is one of the worst ways to die ... now Kevin was about to find out. He had given up, resigned to his fate, thrown in the towel – it seemed ripe for clichés.

That was until he saw the baby bobbing about like a plastic duck at bath time. He knew it was alive because it was crying lustily.

And it changed everything.

1

The five friends had met up in high spirits at Sydney Airport for the usual drudgery of booking in their suitcases, passport control, and the ever more stringent security. A round or two of drinks in the departure lounge, a cursory tour of the shops, the first not-very-witty leg-pulling ... and onto the plane. Loud ribaldry as they worked their way past the posh seats at the front, just to piss off the executive dickheads who were already being served glasses of champagne. And then they were battling it out in cattle class to get hand luggage stowed away, settling into their cramped seats, and craning necks to be first to identify any *fit* air hostesses.

A typical before take-off scene of people wrestling with neck pillows, fiddling with mobile phones, adjusting earpieces, eclectic chatter, kids crying, lockers being shut. The rumbustious babble so familiar to the cabin crew. There would be the urbane voice of the pilot, welcoming words enunciated in the tones of a high society cocktail party. Providing information on the time, the altitude ... come on skipper, get the thing into the air.

Then it was the safety blurb which everyone pooh-poohed apart from the nervous few who hated flying and were twitching in their seats and feeling sick. Airlines were increasingly trying to liven up the mindless dirge by throwing wads of cash at celebrities who earned far too much anyway in the belief that it just might entice a minority to stick with it.

But these were hardly Shakespearian performances and the cattle were far more interested in sifting the list of in-flight movies, how much free alcohol they could snaffle when the drinks trolley came round, and watching with amusement the obese slob two rows up as he tried his darnedest to get the seat belt to fit over a bulging belly.

Was there any point in knowing that your life jacket was under your seat when you were so squashed in like sardines you would never be able to access it? And why would it matter either way given everyone was almost certain to be wiped out in a crash? If your time was up then your time was up.

At last, after what seemed endless taxiing across tarmac, the engines were in overdrive, or whatever the correct aeronautical term, and you were speeding down the runway. Hard back in your seat, hands tensed on the armrest, sneak a look at the taut faces around you ... and, thank goodness, we have lift off.

Not being an engineer, it never failed to amaze Kevin that something so flimsy – wobbly wings, plastic interior, with engines which appeared far too heavy for their supports, all, you suspected, held together with glue along the lines of an Airfix kit, could ever leave the ground with so much freight and so many passengers. One could only hunker down in one's ignorance and hope those paid to know what they were doing really did.

Nevertheless, no sidestepping a long and tedious six hours-plus boredom-fest where however you tried to while away the time – music, magazine, documentary – nothing seemed to suffice.

A routine that never altered.

Except never say never because this flight was going to be different ... very different.

A shudder ran down the fuselage, it seemed like the plane was being shaken about, cabin pressure dropped, and it rapidly lost altitude.

It was mayhem in cattle class. There were terrible screams, people were scrabbling with oxygen masks, personal possessions were tumbling about the cabin, while the buffeting saw the toilet queue clattered to the floor, blows to the head leaving some dazed and others unconscious.

It was panic in its most extreme form. There were people praying to their God, people crying, people sending last text messages on their phones, grown men calling for their mothers. Kevin knew it was the end. He surprised himself by finding a moment to wonder what was happening with the pilots. Their training would have told them to get the aircraft below 10,000 ft. If they were still capable of functioning, they must have been doing all in their power to hang on in there and get off a mayday.

In economy, terror morphed into calm. Many of Kevin's fellow passengers were frozen, incapable of thought or deed.

Then they broke through the cloud, with the ocean seemingly rushing up to meet them and the screams began once more. They were haunting and agonised, as if they came from the beginning of time. Kevin never felt the aircraft enter the water. He was already numb. This then was death … except oddly the more he thought about it the more he became convinced he would live. Under water, he was still strapped to his seat, yet sensed someone or something standing guard over him and distant light above his head. It seemed an eternity before he could free himself. It was suspended animation. Reaching the light became all-encompassing.

Then he broke the surface unable to believe his luck. His lungs ached and he was choking, but alive. It seemed impossible, but it was true. He really was alive.

Lying there floating on his back with the waves lapping his face Kevin wondered if any of his friends had made it: Johnnie the wise-cracking insurance salesman, Jack the sex-obsessed mechanic (dirty by day and, they joked, dirty by night), the lascivious and boastful Alex, and Phil, the quiet and cultured philosophy student. Probably all already dead. His companions on the ill-fated lad's trip for a week in Bali.

Leaving just Kevin on his own in the ocean surrounded by flotsam. Kevin the red-haired outsider with the delicate complexion which burned too easily. Kevin, the Sydney raised boy who strangely never really took to swimming. The young man who could manage a length of the swimming pool or paddle in the sea for ten minutes but for whom water always seemed an alien environment.

And now that lack of swimming prowess was going to drown him.

2

He was a million miles away from positivity as he struggled in the Indian Ocean.

His position seemed hopeless - virtually a non-swimmer in a vast seascape, not a sight of land, hope of imminent salvation non-existent. Easiest to just let go. Nice to have known you. His Mum, Dad, and Vicky his sister would be distraught, but would rebuild their lives in the fullness of time.

Kevin thought back to his upbringing. The family had never been regular churchgoers, attending occasionally, usually Easter and Christmas. Recently he had barely attended at all. Yet there was a residue of belief still within him. The flame had not been extinguished. It continued to flicker. He took a deep breath and said a prayer.

Dear God, I have turned my back on your teachings, I have shut myself away from you, I have transgressed in so many ways, I am a miserable sinner, but please be with me in this my hour of greatest need. Amen.

He thought too of Becky - they weren't exactly boyfriend and girlfriend but they had grown up together, attended the same school, laughed together, cried together, been intimate. She was beautiful, she was bright, she was kind and caring and he had never told her that he loved her. Damn, why hadn't he told her he loved her?

Perhaps because he was still too immature. Stupid, stupid, stupid.

So why had that bloody baby shown up? Now he had no choice … he would have to fight, he would have to suffer, he would have to push his body and soul to the limits, he had to try and survive. He could give up on himself, but not on a baby? It was one thing to rationalise death all alone, forsaken by the world. It was quite another to effectively murder the child by doing nothing

Kevin tried to compose himself.

He surveyed the little mite – it was hard to tell the sex for certain, but a girl, he thought. She was staring at him as if survival was pre-ordained, confident he was her protector. He wished he were as confident.

There was debris – a stove-in suitcase, a remnant of wing. He grabbed at a passing seat, anything that might act as a buoyancy aid – in all the commotion donning a life jacket had gone for a burton.

He winced.

For the first time he realised that his left wrist had seized. There was no strength in it. It was all he could do to hold onto the seat for grim death – maybe it would prove a grim death.

Now he noticed bodies – those whose hopes and dreams would never be fulfilled. Snuffed out in an instant.

The baby was becoming agitated and grouchy. He'd never thought much about babies and their needs before.

Managing to remove the nappy, he wiped its bottom as best he could and hoping that would suffice he allowed the soiled garment to float off and join the rest of the detritus. In the process, he discovered that the baby was indeed a girl.

If escaping death had been a miracle, he now needed another. That the Indonesian air-sea rescue service could find them as the ocean currents moved them further and further from the crash co-ordinates.

Kevin was weakening – the sun blazed down, salt ate into his skin, his hold on the seat and the baby was ever more precarious. What about sharks? Who cared about sharks? If they put him out of his misery then so be it. He had tried his utmost. This was not Hollywood – it went way past sharks.

He must not go to sleep – then the baby would die and almost certainly he would too. Rather like counting sheep, but with the reverse intention of staying awake, he listed all the names he could think of that the baby might be called.

He decided on Hope.

It was surely not her real name – he wasn't a gypsy fortune teller – but he hoped Hope would bring them luck.

She had gone quiet – hard to tell how she was faring. Alive or dead? Every bone in his body told him she was alive. This baby had guts.

But their fate was sealed unless deliverance came soon.

Losing concentration as yet another wave flowed over them, she slipped from his grasp. He yanked her back in. If she had gone he could never have forgiven himself.

Flight lieutenant Hassan Suhendra was closer to the pair than he knew as he and the crew of his military transport stared out at an unforgiving sea that was never to be under-estimated. He had no idea if there were any survivors – only that two hundred and seventy souls were unaccounted for. He recognised it was a forlorn mission. But you had to do all in your power whilst sufficient daylight and aviation fuel remained.

Kevin heard engine noise before he caught sight of the aircraft. Were his faculties playing tricks? He tried to raise his injured left arm but couldn't. He dare not raise his right and risk becoming detached from the cabin seat and the baby.

There was no indication that it had seen them.

Indeed no-one had noticed anything out of the ordinary, and certainly not survivors. The clock was ticking down when one of the crew reported what could be wreckage.

They did a final sweep.

Was that wreckage? Was that a tell-tale slick or simply a natural darker patch? *Nothing to lose*, thought Flt Lt Suhendra, *in dropping a life raft. Just in case.*

On hunches like that human lives depend.

Kevin saw it plunge from the cargo bay and inflate on impact. He wanted to scream his thanks. Summon a resounding hip, hip, hooray. However, it was critical to conserve his energy.

Had they been spotted? He had no way of knowing.

Anyway, it had landed perhaps five hundred metres away, perhaps further. What then use was it going to be? He could not swim to it. The likelihood was it would simply float off, so near but so far.

As time passed, and it continued to taunt, he began to resent their 'meddling'.

Yet it was his impression that the raft was drifting towards them. Was that the case? Or were his eyes deceiving him? Like a mirage in the desert.

Many minutes went by. Now he was sure. Hope really was a lucky mascot. His prayers were being answered.

Many more minutes and it was so close he could almost reach out and touch it.

In what seemed one of the most momentous decisions of his life his blurred brain told him to abandon the seat. Now he had hold of the life raft, found the entrance, and bundled the baby over the lip. He sought to follow but couldn't. Muscles like feather dusters. He tried again and failed again. He felt the last of his being ebbing away.

"No," he told himself. "You cannot let go now. You must get into that life raft. You must."

He dredged up every vestige of strength he had left and crying out in his distress levered himself half on/half off.

Then, inch by inch, the speed of a geriatric tortoise, every movement anguish, was able to squirm all his body clear of the water.

He collapsed, spent, at the furthest reaches of his endeavour.

3

How long was he out of it? Perhaps an hour. Perhaps two hours. Perhaps three.

At least it blanked all immediacy.

No further need to pore over the life or death quandary.

If the latter, maybe months later someone somewhere would find a tiny mummified body and a gnarled corpse inside a tattered life raft ravished by wind and tide.

Then the world would know they had fought as long as they could fight.

If the former, then both could bear witness and honour those who would never return.

There would be times ahead when Kevin would question whether death might have been preferable to life.

By now, the missing plane was leading the news bulletins.

Stern-faced announcers were telling how it had disappeared from radar screens on route to Ngurah Rai International – named after a Balinese leader killed fighting for independence from the Dutch – Bali's main airport and Indonesia's second largest. Close to the main tourist areas, it handled millions of passengers a year.

And now a procession of the increasingly desperate were gathering in the main terminal building.

As is the norm with these sorts of tragedies, accurate news was at a premium, in part because the authorities themselves were largely in the dark.

For public consumption, the flight was still 'delayed', but with a search underway, it was obvious something had gone terribly wrong.

Relatives in both Bali and Sydney were now frantic for information and clutching at straws – this was all fake news, a monstrous hoax, a computer glitch. Refusing to accept the alternative – the aircraft had crashed into the sea. If that were the case, there would likely be no survivors.

Quickly the sentiment turned ugly. The crowd vented their frustration at being told so little. They hurled abuse at airport and airline representatives.

Tall tales were being bandied about; fantasists were laying down poison. It had been hijacked to China so a leading democracy campaigner could be thrown in jail. It had run into an electrical storm, turned back and diverted to Port Moresby on New Guinea, where for some unknown reason a news blackout had been imposed while passengers were being given the once over.

None of it was true.

Instead, freighters, warships and fishing boats continued to make for the crash site.

One was the container vessel, the Sola Spirit, outward bound from her home port of Mumbai. She was on a tight deadline but the law of the sea is universal. Her captain had swung her onto a new course and now she was in the vicinity of where communications with the aircraft had been severed.

The crew knew that sighting anyone amid the swells was a tall order; identifying wreckage remote. All the same, eyes were straining. You had to believe. You could not just casually write off so many lives. And what if they had all died? The families would want to know why. They would want to apportion blame. It was incumbent on the sailors to pick up any clues.

When the slightest lead matters, the ocean delights in fooling you – particularly if the light is poor. What seems like clothing turns into just another lump of weed. A body in the sea is only an old oil drum.

4

They had been at it for several hours when a cry went up.

Could that be a life raft in the distance? To everyone's astonishment as the ship eased closer it was indeed a life raft.

Excitement began to build. A container ship's company is perhaps twenty to thirty strong. Not big numbers. Now they were all agog. This was once in a lifetime.

Would there be anybody inside it?

They put down a ladder from the side of the ship. A rope was tied around the waist of a young deckhand and he swam the few metres to the raft. Pushing aside the entrance flaps, expecting to find nothing, and reeled back in astonishment, extending a thumbs up to his comrades. There was someone there, slumped on the floor.

They pulled the raft close up to the ship and willing hands reached out.

Kevin gave a low moan and stirred ever so slightly. A buzz of anticipation surged through the Sola Spirit's crew – he was alive.

It was incredible.

Cautiously and meticulously they drew him up and onto the deck.

But, to be absolutely sure, the deckhand had poked his head into the life raft for a second look and to his utter amazement there was an infant lying to one side. Shouting his joy, his colleagues could barely credit it. In his arms, he was holding a baby.

Unbelievable!

Was it alive too?

They hurried the child on board.

At first, they could not detect any signs of life and the ship's first-aider took charge. He had boned up on instruction manuals, practised on a dummy, but had never before been called on to resuscitate anyone for real. His recall of what to do in the case of a baby was extremely woolly. Therefore, he improvised.

Tilting the baby's head back, he blew a tiny amount of air into its lungs. Then gingerly massaged the chest.

He did it again.

And again.

At the fourth time of asking, the baby coughed.

A cheer rose from the onlookers.

It coughed again, and now the chest was rising and falling as regular breathing resumed.

They peeled off her sodden top, dried the little one, pinned an old hand towel around her bottom, and swathed her in a blanket. Placing her in a laundry basket, they transferred her into the galley for extra warmth, figuring that despite the tropical climate she might need it after being immersed for so long.

She opened her eyes and another cheer went up.

For Kevin, events were largely ethereal. He felt there were people around him but he couldn't make out who. He knew stuff was going on but he didn't know what. As he later recalled: "Everything seemed vacant, like it was passing me by. It was the most foreign of sensations.

"It wasn't an out-of-body experience the way people close to death describe it. More like being divorced from reality. It was as if my mind and body had never met. I was there but I wasn't."

The debilitating sun was no doubt a contributory factor – it had barbequed his forehead, scorched cheeks, ears and nose…and everything puckered from the salt.

As with the baby, they stripped him of his wet clothes. He was frail, his body was desiccated, but, they reckoned, he was young enough and sturdy enough to come through this. They bathed his face, rubbed soothing cream into his skin, trickled water into his mouth, and laid him on a bunk. Their medical knowledge was limited – sleep would surely be the best cure.

The captain set a new course, this time for Benoa Harbour, Bali's main port. It was important to get the pair to hospital quickly. He radioed in his estimated time of arrival, stating he had picked up two air crash survivors who required urgent medical attention.

Somewhere along the way Kevin was jolted awake, squinted, and indicated that his throat was parched. His rescuers brought a cup to his dried-up lips and gave him more water. He smiled his thanks. Then a crease spread along his brow.

He tried to speak but his throat was just too sore. He tried again.

Still nothing decipherable – they could just work out the letter *b*, but what could it mean? Some couldn't speak any English; others had only pigeon. Then the penny dropped.

The word had to be 'baby' surely.

The baby was fine, they told him. He raised a shaky hand in salute. It was enough. His eyelids were already coming down like metal shutters on a shop front. Within seconds, he was away with the fairies.

And the baby did indeed display every sign of being fine.

So much so it was crying out that it was hungry and thirsty.

They found an old lemonade bottle, gave it rudimentary sterilisation in hot water, boiled some milk, poured it in, left it to cool, tested the liquid on their skin to ensure it was more or less the right temperature, and fed it to the baby.

The baby gulped it down enthusiastically.

5

Word leaked, and then spread around Bali like wildfire even before the Sola Spirit had docked.

Benoa is a busy commercial port – fishing boats at one end of the spectrum and cruise liners at the other. Now there were ambulances and police cars at the quayside. A crowd of onlookers had built up. This was the biggest thing to hit the town in decades.

With the airport situated close to the capital, Denpasar, and only five miles from the harbour, many of the families were dashing down there hoping against hope that a loved one had been plucked from the deep. No one was prepared to trust the scant information filtering out. Perhaps talk of two survivors meant twenty-two.

Soon the police were fully stretched keeping back a swaying, near hysterical throng.

It is the way with incidents such as these.

All the time there were fresh rumours – another lifeboat had been found, full to the gunnels. Sadly, it was not to be.

With several ships on site, bodies had been recovered. So had a small amount of wreckage. But that was it. Not news that families listening to their radios and scanning through their phones wanted to hear.

At last, the Sola Spirit was tying up alongside. The gangway was down and a combined police and medical team sprang into action.

After an initial assessment on the ship, the baby was sped to a local hospital for a fuller examination.

Visualise the chaotic scenes. People scrambling to see. Reporters chasing scraps. Photographers battling for pictures. Curious ghouls with no link to any of it clogging up entrances and exits. A reluctance to part, with police having to force a corridor open.

It took longer to remove Kevin. Awake but very woozy, he was this time far more clued in to people – taking his pulse, checking his breathing, his blood pressure, setting up a drip. His hand was throbbing. So were his ribs, and he tried to indicate this to them. He was just so, so tired. His legs were like jelly. His body felt like a steamroller had run over it. Muttering his name took a prodigious effort.

He thought of his mother and father and whether they knew yet. He assumed not.

The airline was going through the passenger roster to establish identities. Wisely, no one wanted to make any media comment until they were sure. It would be the same when the bodies started arriving. This had to be thorough, it had to be precise, and, if that took time, then so be it. Rough on the families. But they must not be inadvertently put through new traumas because someone, however well-meaning, had screwed up.

Everything needed to be verified – too bad if delay exacerbated the hostility of the mob, fed up with the endless waiting. Albeit, that simply spouted further conjecture layered on top of tittle-tattle – yet another distraction for those on the front line.

A cargo shed became a temporary mortuary. There were no occupants. However, the first batch of bodies was already on its way.

Kevin must have flaked out again because when he next came round he was in a hospital bed. A bandage was around his chest. His hand was in a plaster cast. Like a lead weight. He could barely move it. They told him later it was two broken ribs, a cracked bone in his wrist, extensive bruising and lacerations. There was concern for his spleen – a danger it might rupture. He had, in fact, got off extraordinarily lightly.

He knew not how long he had been lying there.

It subsequently transpired that a combination of sedatives and exhaustion had knocked him out for eighteen hours.

Trying to get a fix on what was around him, he realised that Mum, Dad and Vicky were huddled by the bed.

He was no longer on his own.

Mum was holding his good arm, her face full of love. He attempted to speak, but, again, the words would not form. Dad was shushing him –

it could wait. Mum was saying how precious he was. It was all too much to take in and sleep enveloped him once more.

6

When lucidity returned Becky was there at his bedside too.

It generated within him an amalgam of lap dog and lion. She must love him too to come all that way.

She looked gorgeous. She was wearing a blue skirt and a white top. He marvelled at legs which seemed to go on for ever, her trim waist, and her flowing brown locks.

"Becky," he murmured, hoping he hadn't injected too much 'cave man' into his voice in the presence of parents and sister.

She smiled that so sexy smile which brought out the dimple in her cheek, and then she leant over and ever so gently kissed his forehead.

His heart rate leapt; his loins felt they were on fire. "Becky..." His voice trailed away as his gratitude for her being there suffused with everything she meant to him. He wanted to convey the horror, how scared he had been. However, amidst the jumble of conflicting emotions the ability to frame sentences had deserted him.

Becky was telling him there was loads of time to talk – for now he needed all the rest he could get. "You're going to beat this," she confided. "Everyone's rooting for you. We'll get it done."

Then he had to ask the inevitable.

"The baby?"

The contented gurgles, the dinky smile, even the tiny belches of air...she was captivating. The apple of the eye of all the nurses and midwives. Showing so much devotion to their wonder babe while, like Kevin, trying to guess her name.

Angelique? She was an angel. Storm? She had survived so much at such a tender age. Sandy? Bali's beaches were such a draw.

Physically, having got fluids into her, she was as right as rain. So remarkable that surely there had to be a catch. Someone so young couldn't have post-traumatic stress disorder, could they? Nobody wanted to think that negatively. Especially as she was now an orphan – the powers-that-be had identified who she was and to be ultra-safe had conducted a DNA match. She came from Normal in Illinois in the United States.

It seemed appropriate because nothing could ever again be normal for Suzanne Elizabeth Duthie.

In McLean County, Normal lies adjacent to the better-known Bloomington. The twin centres have a population in the low six figures.

Where father Robert, a lawyer, and mother Rose, a teacher, had chosen to raise children. Suzi was their first-born. Rose had so much wanted a girl and it had come true. Suzi had meant everything to them – until a brother or sister could arrive to complete the family, which was their fervent wish.

Why was she travelling at an age when she hadn't even attempted her first tremulous steps?

They were bound for Dubai where Rose's sister Abigail, a worker in the sports/leisure/hospitality sector, was on secondment.

The sisters were close, it was to be Abby's first sight of her nine-month-old niece in the flesh and she was very much looking forward to it.

It being thousands of miles going east or west, Robert and Rose thought they might as well turn the trip into a long vacation, taking extended leave from their jobs, to maximise what they could get out of the steep air fares. So, they went west and made a first stop in San Francisco. You think you know your own country but there were whole tracts of the United States they had never been. They took sightseeing trips like any other tourist – Alcatraz, the Golden Gate Bridge, a boat cruise on San Francisco Bay, and the proverbial cable car ride. What a city. So long as you turned a blind eye to the drug-ridden seamy side. But then most cities had a seamy side.

Back in the air, next up was Sydney, and they hit locations with which Kevin was so familiar – the Opera House, the Harbour Bridge, and Bondi Beach. They didn't have time to do it justice and put down a marker that they must return some day.

From there, what more bewitching a destination than Bali on route to Dubai?

They were eager to see the island if only to understand why so many raved about it. Did it deserve all that was written extolling its virtues? Or was tourism and plastic waste ruining yet another paradise?

They never found out. Instead they had been taken along with so many others with similar stories to tell.

Stories of human achievement and human frailty.

For Robert and Rose, Normal was the centre of their universe even though the name never failed to produce titters from those with a 'cake in the face' sense of humour. Advertising types were forever seeking to link it with Bland, Missouri, and Boring, Maryland. With the town of Oblong also being in Illinois, a much-quoted headline in the local Bloomington-Normal Pantagraph (itself one heck of a title) had gone down in folk lore – "Oblong man marries Normal woman".

Nobody seemed quite sure whether it was true or, more likely, apocryphal.

And how did Normal get its name?

The Chicago Tribune explained it thus: "Normal is not named Normal out of an excess of Midwestern humility. The town used to be North Bloomington but, in establishing its own identity in the mid-19th century, chose to borrow its new name from the local college." What is now Illinois State University was then Illinois State Normal University, the normal deriving from a French innovation, higher education for teachers and women in what were called *ecoles normales*.

Normal and Bloomington have various claims to fame. Both sit adjacent to the famed Route 66 and there are all sorts of links to Abraham Lincoln, revered sixteenth President of the United States, who owned property in Bloomington, had many friends in the area and, as a travelling attorney in his early years, acted in local court cases.

Then there's steak 'n' shake featuring a combination of premium burgers and milk shakes, founded in Normal in 1934, the brainchild of the gloriously named Gus Belt, a restaurant chain and an ongoing marketing and promotional bonanza.

7

Robert and Rose had met in senior high.

It was in essence an attraction of opposites. He was relatively reserved until Rose and law school brought him out of himself. Like Kevin as it happened, he was into sport, American football and soccer to the fore. They might have got on well had they ever met.

The name Duthie is Scottish in origin. Indeed you will find Duthies all over. Perhaps unsurprising given the Duthie motto in Latin is *data fata secutus,* which translates as follow my destiny.

Great travellers are the Scots. Not always at their own instigation. Rather like the Irish potato famine sent waves of emigrants to the New World, so the Highland Clearances saw tenants evicted from their farms and crofts.

Sheep replaced people.

Taking place mostly in the period from 1750 to 1860, the evictions went against the principle that clan members had an inalienable right to rent land in the clan territory though this was never recognised in Scottish law.

So, accepting that life can deal you a rotten hand, they left for America, Canada and Australia. In the main, resolute individuals prepared to begin again from scratch. Prepared for further hardship in doing so. Full of hope.

Just a handful ever saw their homeland again, but they never gave up their birth-right.

Today, side by side with St Andrew's associations in cities and towns across the United States are a plethora of Caledonian clubs, Robert Burns societies celebrating the acclaimed poet, and Highland Games organisations.

Go to Aberdeen in Scotland and you will find Duthie Park, situated by the banks of the River Dee, forty-four acres given to the local council in 1881 by Lady Elizabeth Duthie of Ruthrieston, in memory of her uncle and her brother. It is noted for the winter gardens glasshouses – tropical and arid, many exotic plants, a sanctuary which continues to draw in around a million visitors every year.

Rose di Matteo was, as her name sounds, of Italian descent. And for the Italians it was not a dissimilar story to the Scots.

Between around 1880 and 1924, more than four million Italians sailed to the United States, half of them between 1900 and 1910 alone – the majority fleeing the grinding rural poverty of Sicily and southern Italy.

Like many in that exodus, Rose possessed a flamboyance, an outgoing nature which sometimes got her into scrapes, an exuberance to make the most of life, a front foot approach and a willingness to try things even if they came back to bite you.

Rose and Robert became friends in the school choir. That she always had her back to him was neither here nor there. It was the proximity that did it. He fell in love with her glorious neck and the silky hair. Her smell was enough to send him almost insane.

Music, arts, dance…Rose participated in it all.

Rosa was a name bestowed on di Matteo women from way back but it had over the years become Americanised with that part of the family which had ended up in the mid-West.

Robert was her rock.

They attended their local church most Sundays and tried to live their lives imbued with moral values and the difference between right and wrong. It was a partnership that could be summed up in the words of the glorious Michael Forster hymn, which includes the lines: "Let love be real, with no manipulation, no secret wish to harness or control; let us accept each other's incompleteness, and share the joy of learning to be whole."

They made a good team.

Cruel in the extreme that they should have lost their lives in so godawful a fashion. And now frantic phone calls were taking place between their relatives.

8

A heart-broken Abby was on route to Bali.

Her first inkling was the doorbell ringing at her rented apartment located in a popular area for overseas workers.

It was her day off.

There stood two representatives of the US Consulate General's Office.

Taken aback, mind racing, what could they want? She had been so busy at work that the disaster had passed her by.

They broke the news as humanely as possible, but there is never a good way to broach such a bleak message. That Suzi was alive, the child Abby had never seen, was at least something to hold onto.

However, in her mental turmoil at first all she could think about was Robert and Rose. Would they have known what was happening in those paralysing last moments as the aircraft hit the water? Surely, they must have been terrified. The thought that their bodies might never be claimed back from the depths pained her enormously.

She sat there in floods of tears, unable and unwilling to get her head around what was a nightmare.

And, of course, David and Nancy from the Consulate had no answer. Nancy put her arm around Abby. Crying was a release; best to let it all out. Nancy, a trained bereavement counsellor was well aware it would be far worse for Abby to bottle it all up, thence to sink into a cesspit of private grief.

Not that it took bereavement counselling for Nancy to know that the reactions of people confronted with great loss could be like night and day. She had started out as a local news reporter but after three years or so had called a halt, realising she wasn't cut out for all that journalism could throw at you. It wasn't quite for her, so push the button and make the break. There was no kick-back – she had made many friends and she had experienced things which would stand her in good stead. Once she had mapped out where she wanted to go from journalism, the career swop worked.

Journalists refer to it as the 'door knock' when they are sent out by their bosses to speak to the bereaved. There was a knack to it and some were much better at wheedling their way into homes than others. And some parents, husbands, wives, in their heartache, needed to talk. They wanted to tell this complete stranger their loved-one's life story. They got out the family album and reminisced. They were anxious that the rest of society should know even as they mourned. Almost a sacred duty. Quite remarkable.

Sometimes it went the other way.

Nancy had gone to the home of a family whose eight-year-old daughter had been fatally injured after being thrown from her pony. Something had spooked it. And wearing the right health and safety endorsed protective head gear, was not enough to save her.

The father loomed in the doorway; Nancy stated who she was and her reason for being there. The husband, desolation convulsing his face, speech measured, said he did not dispute the nature of her inquiry, but requested Nancy take her leave. Seconds later, the mother, out of it, screaming, incoherent, doped up, burst from the house, flew at her, and chased her down the garden path.

The whole business unnerved her. Perhaps it was why she subsequently went in for bereavement counselling.

It felt like aeons but was probably only about twenty minutes before Abby began to think more rationally.

David and Nancy added substance to the crash outline, how it seemed certain there were just two survivors, and one of them was Suzi.

Suzi. Poor Suzi. Both her parents gone. In a strange country. Strange people. Bound to be in pieces. Abby knew she had to get to Bali as soon as she could.

David and Nancy had been acting on the same assumption. Leave it to the Consulate, they would phone airlines and see what might be available, have their counterparts in Bali meet her.

Abby started flailing around in confusion. She would need to pack a case, perhaps two. Where was she going to get baby clothes? Where had she put her passport? She must phone her employers. She must phone her mother and father and Robert's mother and father. What was to be done once she got to Bali? She was in a complete tizz.

Nancy and David told her they were on her side. It would all be OK. Just take it slowly. Sketch out a plan.

For Abby, all that mattered now was Suzi.

The long term could stay long term. Bodies or no bodies? Funeral or memorial service? Nancy and David were right – joined up thinking would eventually come into its own. Things would coalesce. Meanwhile, she must be bold, cleanse herself of the obtuse and inconsequential. This was a mission of mercy.

Generally quite practical, she began to organise herself.

Soon she was speaking to both sets of grandparents back home in McLean County. They were beside themselves. They already knew and were trying to take in the immensity of it – the Sheriff's Office had been in contact and DNA swabs provided.

All were supportive of her decision to fly to Bali.

Abby's relief was palpable. That she hadn't had to explain it all. She had the feeling that she would be doing a lot of explaining to the inquisitive and well-meaning. It would be draining.

Did she need help? Did she need money?

Abby told something of a white lie, promising she had everything under control. All four were getting on in years and you could count the times they had been outside the US on one hand. A trip of that magnitude would be arduous. She was determined not to put them through it.

Anyway, they were more than placated when she told them that, once given the go-ahead, she intended to take Suzi straight back to Normal. Even at the end of a phone she could feel the reassurance of family. It was the responsible thing to do, they told her. They would see their darling granddaughter soon enough.

She rang her employers and briefed them on her dilemma.

They could not have been more understanding and bent over backwards to facilitate. If she needed anything – anything at all – she only had to ask. Her boss said the necessity of getting Suzi to Normal took precedence. Abby would be on leave of absence. She would remain on full pay for the duration. The team were absolutely behind her. Don't fret.

Albeit, while neither said anything concrete, the undertone to the conversation was suggestive of an acceptance that Abby was unlikely to ever make it back to Dubai.

It had been a quality role, but now there was a wider canvas.

Back to packing.

You know what it's like when you are in a dither – you're mind goes blank.

She found her large suitcase and fumbled about for a smaller one she knew she had somewhere – they would have to go in the hold but it would be worth any extra cost, not that cost was a consideration given the situation.

A load of clothes – no clue as to how long the stay might be and it could take days before she had time to think about throwing things in a washing machine. She went round the flat retrieving mementos, photographs, ornaments, jewellery. Her wash things, her makeup, lots more. Her laptop computer would go with her as hand luggage.

What else would she need?

Come on, think, Abby, think.

Nancy was throwing in ideas, ensuring that Abby had her phone, her phone charger, passport, bankcards…the essentials. Forget baby clothes, nappies, wipes and all the rest. That was for the Bali end. People would rally round.

Anything from the flat she was unable to carry could be freighted to her.

David and the team at the Consulate came up trumps – used their influence and got her on a flight leaving that night.

As she waited for the taxi, Abby was biting her fingernails.

She was twenty-seven, three years younger than Rose. There had been men but nobody truly standout had walked into her life. The only babies she had encountered were those of friends, where you could sit them on your knee, bump them up and down, make suitably quirky noises, and hand them back. Now she would be thrust into spontaneous motherhood in a form she had never envisaged. No time to prepare, no antenatal classes, she would have to wing it.

Nancy went with her in the taxi – it was a one-hour drive. But, for Abby, thoughts scooting around her mind like numbered balls in a lottery draw machine, they had hardly left before they arrived.

Nancy put her hand on Abby's – repeating that it would be all right, no point in upsetting herself, stay composed.

Abby smiled weakly.

The taxi was pulling up at Departures – the lights were bright, there was an incessant bustle of people, vehicles, take offs and landings, heat 'incinerated' the lungs…like most big airports it was non-stop.

An airport official met them – designated to look after Abby and smooth the way for her.

Abby and Nancy hugged.

"Thank you so much for everything you've done," said Abby, groping for the right words. It had been less than a day but she felt she had known Nancy for yonks.

Nancy smiled.

They hugged again.

"Look after yourself," said Nancy. "Give the baby a kiss from me."

And then Abby was off, steeled to the usual airport aggravation most of us know so well – checking in, passport inspection, security, waiting for the gate number to come up.

Finally, she and others were being called forward, embarking among the first as the airline, at the instigation of the Consulate, had fixed a priority seat for her.

Nancy thanked her lucky stars and in particular that the media hadn't cottoned on to there being a Dubai link to what was increasingly being billed as the Bali Baby Disaster. She had seen news scrums before with journalists thrusting tape recorders in faces, photographers battling to get the telling shot and TV crews pushing and shoving – hypocrites who were forever claiming the moral high ground while being as intrusive as everyone else. The media pack in full pursuit mode was never an edifying sight.

Nancy would not wish that on anyone. She fervently hoped whoever was her counterpart would shield Abby from their excesses.

9

It was a nine-hour flight to Bali. Abby got a little shuteye, but, so typical of air travel, the turbulent type which never seems to refresh. She felt apprehensive, weary and unprepared, but wheels locked down, runway in sight, it was, she told herself, essential she stepped up to the plate to meet all that was bound to come her way.

The cabin crew had been going through the usual routine, passengers had their seatbelts fastened, items of baggage were secure and there was no one left in the toilets.

It was a smooth landing and soon they were disembarking.

Abby thanked the flight attendant.

"The best of luck."

They both knew she was going to need it.

The local Consulate was on the mark. Abby was met by a tall, lean, angular individual. In his early-thirties, she guessed. He introduced himself as John Munro. They smiled at each other – Abby felt an instant attraction. Explosive even, such as she had never experienced before. But this was not the time nor the place.

He told her that a car had been set aside for her – once they had picked out her cases they would be off, circumventing the standard procedures. It had all been approved.

"That's very thoughtful of you," she said softly. Then, overcome by a heady mix of John and the journey, she almost fainted.

"Are you all right," he exclaimed, taking hold of her.

"Yes, honestly, I'm fine," she said, feeling foolish. And, trembling, added: "It's been a long trip."

At baggage reclaim, she pointed out her suitcases and he pulled them from the conveyor. He directed her away from the milling crowd and through a side door indicated by an airport staffer. They entered a restricted zone and in a jiffy were getting into the back seat of a Buick.

The driver pulled away towards a little used exit gate.

A handful of media had peeled off from the hospital stakeout. All but one were at the front. However, a maverick photographer had gambled on the possibility of subterfuge.

Kerpow! The flash almost blinded them.

The snapper wasn't sure what he had got. He recognised it as a consular car and he recognised one of the consular officers in the back. But who was the blonde? He phoned ahead to tip off a reporter colleague. Nobody had got any live pics of Kevin or the baby so far – deemed still unfit to be exposed to public gaze. Forty-eight hours in and the press corps were walking on hot coals.

"Damn it," muttered John.

They had been rumbled.

He emphasised to Abby the massive interest in the 'story' – it could all get very messy. She absorbed his advice, but nothing could have prepared her for their arrival at the hospital.

The place was heaving and the car surrounded before they could usher her inside. The tumult was scary. People were bashing on the windows so forcefully Abby feared the glass might shatter. And she edged closer to John. Between him and the driver they got a door open and ploughed into the bedlam. She hung onto him as if her life depended on it, thrust close into his body as they elbowed their way through to the main entrance.

It would have been lovely had it not been so white-knuckle.

But they had made it.

Ruffled and breathless, she was glad of his arm around her. He found her a seat, got her a glass of water, safe at last. She thanked him and, unable to stop herself, plunged into the azure pools of his eyes.

Giddy, she inquired whether there was somewhere she could freshen up.

This time it was he who was caught off-guard. Of course this arresting young woman who he already felt at one with would need the ladies after such a hardball encounter.

Fortunately, there were restrooms nearby and he reproached himself for his insensitivity.

Abby took time over her ablutions, tweaked her makeup and faced off the mirror – why do mirrors always zoom in on your imperfections – as if this was the end of innocence. She would show them – no way would she be cowed into that old stereotype, the helpless female, a betrayal of womankind down the ages. She was ready for whatever run-ins were coming; a sojourn which no doubt would leave her thicker-skinned at its conclusion. She just hoped this would not put to the sword all she had sworn to uphold.

John was waiting for her. He was accompanied by one of the hospital's administrators who led them to an office, sat them down and sent out for drinks – John chose white coffee while Abby opted for fresh orange.

The administrator kept to an outline, staying succinct, not wanting to tax her. He ran through Suzi's condition on arrival, the string of tests doctors had carried out; there were no major issues; it was quite extraordinary and he couldn't explain it. She was eating and drinking, and was generally "in rude health". It would be wise to keep her in for another day or two for monitoring, just in case they might have missed something. Then she should be fit to go home, wherever home was.

He assumed Abby would be eager to see Suzi 'as soon as'.

"Yes, that would make my day," responded Abby.

He would find her a room in which to stay. They would bring her belongings up from reception where the driver had deposited them.

Don't be afraid to utilise the hospital facilities – she must be in need of sustenance, the canteen would be at her disposal. He motioned for a colleague to come in, take a head and shoulders photo, and sort out a temporary security pass.

Did she have any questions?

She felt as if she ought to have a hundred and one questions but couldn't think of anything off the cuff.

They would want a more intensive chat with her both about Suzi plus how to deal with all the media attention – but that could hold for morning.

The three of them set off for the ward. It took a good few minutes – all hospitals seem to have endless corridors and a multitude of doors.

Finally, they were there. It was the usual busy scene with nurses scurrying about, children crying, concerned mums and dads.

And there was Suzi …

10

It was a first sight of the girl who meant so much.

They handed her to Abby who fussed over her, kissed her, stroked her hair and tried to reassure the little one.

Suzi was wary.

Abby told herself the poor tot had been through such a battering that she was bound to be bewildered. Here was another grown-up she had never met before in her short life. Who was this? What did she want?

John made his excuses. He said he would wait for her outside and she should take her time.

She smiled happily, at the baby in her arms, and then back to him. As he left John thought she looked perfect. One day she would make a wonderful mother herself. Though it had only been hours, he could feel himself becoming smitten while at the same time circumspect because it would be unacceptable to get involved with someone in his professional charge. It left him conflicted.

Abby was half an hour playing with Suzi as they sought to get to know each other. She told Suzi all about herself, how she was Suzi's aunty, how Suzi was very much loved and that Mummy and Daddy were in the hands of God. Naturally, Suzi would not remember nor understand any of this. It was a start, which both could work on.

Abby handed Suzi back, promised she would return soon, waved and said bye-bye.

Then she was gone.

John was there with the administrator. Her temporary pass including photo were complete – that was fast – and she put it around her neck. The administrator inquired how Abby's first meeting with Suzi had gone.

"Fantastic," she replied, beaming.

Another walk along corridors and then the three of them arrived at Abby's room for the night. Her suitcases were already there.

It was light and airy.

Was this suitable?

"Yes, yes, absolutely. I very much appreciate all you're doing for me."

Now it was the administrator's turn to beam. He told her that, thinking on, if there was anything she required, he was at her disposal. And he gave her a mobile number to phone.

Then he took his leave.

The two of them were alone, of which John was all too conscious. This was inappropriate. Give her twenty minutes to loosen up. Perhaps, afterwards, they might go and sample what 'delicacies' the canteen had to offer?

She said she would very much like to.

He went off, plonked himself down on a convenient bench and frittered away the time scrolling through emails and text messages. When he got back, she was sitting on the side of the bed ready – efficiency and punctuality must be two more of her talents.

They followed knife and fork indicators and were quickly there.

It was like so many canteens – tired décor, difficult to marry up the food with the menu, cutlery in various stages of cleanliness and bored yet impatient staff, all-powerful in their own backyard, measuring out helpings that wouldn't sustain a gnat, as if it was coming out of their own wages.

She chose fish and rice; he opted for a mild curry.

A room full of tables spread out in front of them. One by a window appealed and they sat down.

John skimmed the smattering of mostly sad, drab and self-absorbed souls dotted about – this was not the elegant restaurant he would have chosen for a first 'date'. It turned out he had done the caterers a dis-service as the portions were not as miniscule as first surmised.

Little was said – tough to impress a girl when your mouth is full of food. However, as they sipped water after clearing their plates, they got talking – all a trifle constricted as is almost inevitably the case on first meeting.

Abby told him a little about Normal and contrasted it with the lifestyle in Dubai. He did his best to advertise the delights of Bali. During which 'boy meets girl' prompts established both were single.

She asked about his name, Munro.

Like many Americans, he was a complicated melting pot. As with Robert, he was of Scottish extraction on his father's side. His mother was English though of Austrian heritage. They lived near London. Dad hailed from Texas, in the oil business, and moved around a lot, something of a trouble-shooter, so it had seemed judicious to base themselves where Mum had friends and relatives.

So, from the age of five, John, an only child, was largely brought up in the land of Robin Hood and Winston Churchill, and, at the age of thirteen, he had been sent to public school – the fee-paying independent arm of the education system in the UK – Uppingham, in the tiny, rural county of Rutland, roughly in the middle of the country. It had taken a while to fit in. Yet virtually everything you could think of was on hand – from cricket to am-dram, speech making to carpentry, and much more beside. All under-written by top quality teaching. A period of experimentation and hard work – exams to pass, expectations to meet.

Reminiscing had diverted him from the here and now. He realised he had overdone the spiel because she was nearly asleep at the table – it was time to go.

He walked her back to her room.

"Will you be here tomorrow?" she yawned, worn out and needing her bed. "I could do with a bit of support with everything the hospital seems to have lined up."

John assured her that was a definite – his other work would just have to be fitted in as and when, he told himself. He shouldn't be spending so much time on this one 'project' but he wanted very much to do so. "Until the morning," he said.

"You've been so very attentive," she told him.

They parted, hormones all over the place.

11

Kevin was stronger by the hour and chatting away in his room. He was still getting gyp from the ribs but was avidly collecting signatures on the plaster cast.

Reading some of the hundreds of get-well-soon cards.

From people he had never met and would never meet.

Hopefully he could thank them all via the good offices of the hospital.

Nevertheless, Kevin felt things were pressing in on him.

At some point he would have to run through with the family the wider aspects of his ordeal. At some point he would no doubt have to give statements to police, air crash investigators and others. At some point he wanted to see the baby again and try and build a bridge to relatives. At some point he would need to do something to satisfy the media's agitation for interviews and pictures. At some point he would have to sort out where he and Becky were headed. At some point there would be the funerals of his friends – he ought to be there.

He wasn't up to it. Just thinking about it left him subdued and jittery.

His confidence was shot – curling up into a ball mentally, wanting to cocoon himself away. He felt inadequate – he had never been afflicted that way before.

Becky and the family said it was a natural defence mechanism after all he had gone through. They would nurse him back to health. They told themselves he just needed time, let him recover at his own pace, recharge his batteries.

However, his mood swings worried them.

The hospital's two-strong PR team was swamped and, as soon as the police had named Kevin and Suzi, they were even more swamped. To the extent they had to ask for temporary back-up – two human resources staff were volunteered. They weren't a lot of use but better than nothing.

For the media, the hospital's modus operandi didn't go nearly far enough. Correspondents wanted much more than condition reports, which was all that had been authorised to go out. Being resourceful and persuasive, news organisations had uncovered a variety of shots of Kevin at play. Kevin larking about with mates, Kevin offering a toast complete with large glass of beer, Kevin on the rugby field.

A similar trawl had turned up pics of Suzi. They fastened on to one where she was with Rose, sitting in a paddling pool and slapping water about – it tied in with being snatched from the ocean.

The hunt was on to unearth everything about the pair however obscure. It almost seemed that anybody who had ever known them was having a microphone thrust in their face. Feature writers and teams from women's magazines were interviewing baby experts, child psychologists, disaster coordinators…to draw up a profile of how Kevin and Suzi might be reacting and what it could mean for the rest of their lives.

And all types of mischief was going on in a vicious showdown to get the first interview with Kevin.

It was like a feeding frenzy.

Those back home were being pestered, dizzying sums of money were being bandied about for an 'exclusive'. The more unscrupulous hacks were bribing hospital staff to deliver 'contraband' letters to the family arguing why they should be first in line, a dodgy 'doctor' in white coat was uncovered and thrown out on his ear. Something was going to have to give.

All those in charge concurred that it was time to get Kevin, the baby and Abby in the same room, and, if that worked well, then to formulate a media strategy which everyone could sign up to.

Next day John phoned Abby to see where things were at – just his voice was a thrill. She said she didn't know what was going on – he said he would come in anyway.

There was a knock on her door – it was the same official she had spoken with previously. He presumed she would be keen to see Suzi again. But would she like to meet Kevin too?

Definitely she would like to meet Kevin. This was the man to whom Suzi owed her life. Abby seemed to be forever thanking someone, but in Kevin's case thanks could never even come close to reflecting the family's gratitude.

"I'll go and set it up," the functionary told her.

He made a beeline for Kevin's room and went through much the same parallel procedure.

Kevin didn't immediately answer in the affirmative. He had worked out this had to happen. But was he up to it? What could he say to Abby? Would they get on? Yet he wanted to meet her and he very much wanted to meet Suzi.

An hour later, bounced into it, he and Abby were being introduced and, yes, it was a diffident beginning.

Abby got the show on the road. How was Kevin's recovery going?

Washed out, no energy, but thankful to be in one piece.

He asked about her journey – she told him that Bali was breath-taking. It was just a pity she was there for all the wrong reasons.

"Snap," said Kevin.

She thanked him for what he had done to save Suzi. "You must have been very frightened."

His face cracked like a broken bowl. "In many respects Suzi saved me. I wouldn't have made it without her." His voice dipped; his eyes were like saucers.

This wasn't the moment for a question and answer session. The man had endured enough.

Abby was spared when in through the door came Suzi in the arms of a nurse.

Hovering at the back, Kevin's parents, Becky, Vicky and John had been trying to act unobtrusively, as quiet as church mice, but a host of voices were immediately hailing Suzi's arrival.

She eyed everyone curiously, then, going all coy, hid her face in the nurse's breast, accidentally dropping the white rabbit she was clutching. She lunged towards where it had fallen as if to say 'somebody pick it up, will you'. Abby reclaimed it for her and it proved opportune for the nurse to pass Suzi over.

"Hello, Suzi. Do you remember me from yesterday? I'm Abby, your Mummy's sister. You are lively today, aren't you?"

Suzi panned along the smiling faces.

"And, do you know who is here, Suzi?" went on Abby. "It's Kevin. He's the man you met when you were splashing about in the water. Do you remember splashing in the water, Suzi?"

There was an under-current of amusement from the others – nothing like baby talk to beget unanimity.

Abby motioned to Kevin that he might like to take Suzi. They both rose from their chairs and somewhat tentatively, in case he turned out to be all fingers and thumbs, Abby passed Suzi to him.

At first, Kevin stayed standing, incredibly self-conscious, rocking the baby to and fro in his arms, silently repeating over and over to himself – whatever you do don't drop her!

He looked into her eyes; she looked into his. Was there recognition? He decided to make the most of it.

"We remember each other well, don't we, Suzi? We were playing in the sea forever and a day. I'm so pleased that you are much, much better. I was worried about you. Were you worried about me?"

There was laughter in the room.

He was getting into this; had now resumed his seat.

"Where did you get white rabbit from, Suzi? Did the nurses give him to you?"

He wibble-wobbled Suzi's nose with white rabbit. Big smiles and chuckles from the little one provoked a flurry of sighs and 'ahs'.

Suzi was playing the room – just a natural, he reckoned. Far from being cranky, as she was entitled to be, she seemed to be revelling in the spotlight. Like a lead actress. At the centre of all she surveyed. Performing to the crowd.

As for Kevin he was besotted by this girl who meant so much to him.

All told, it had been a hit.

The baby talk continued until, with Suzi getting a little fractious, the nurse counselled that she return her to the ward – her next feed was due. They all said their goodbyes and, as the door closed, there was another spate of animated conversation.

"Isn't she terrific?"

"Gosh, she is looking well."

"You would never have guessed anything had happened to her."

There was a sudden hush. A baby had brought this disparate bunch together and for a fragment in time they were almost cloned.

12

Their ties evaporated as the administrator 'called the meeting to order'. Plainly, he was bent on getting down to business.

He thought Kevin and Suzi would probably be fit to leave for home in a few days. But there was no hurry. No one was going to frog-march them out!

Kevin gave a wan smile. He was not at all sure he was ready.

The administrator was moving the agenda onwards towards the visceral issue of the media. He had been in these dramas before though nothing as big. The worldwide interest was staggering. He made a phone call and invited the Head of PR to join them.

Thence, they quickly ran through the options – a photo opportunity, a press conference, a statement put out through the hospital, one-to-one interviews.

Kevin went grey.

He didn't think he was robust enough to participate in a press conference; no way one-to-ones.

Abby said she would cooperate on a photo opportunity, just as long as they didn't start firing too many loaded questions at her.

The Head of PR assured her he would lay down 'rules of engagement' to the media, would be there to pull strings, and would step in if things started getting out of hand. He suggested to Kevin that they had a chat and then he would produce words and quotes. A statement, however fulsome, wouldn't satisfy the Press but might provide breathing space. Nothing would be done without Kevin's say-so. Give it a go and see where they got.

Made to sound so reasonable he felt he couldn't fob the oaf off.

It would all be in conjunction with a medical updating of how both Kevin and Suzi were getting on.

Earmarked for 11 am local time the next day.

In the interim, he would sit down with Kevin, then go away and produce the promised draft.

An early afternoon slot was pencilled in.

Given that the meeting had gone on far longer than scheduled, the hospital administrator wound things down smartly.

Everyone went their separate ways.

Kevin's party made for an inner courtyard that offered tranquillity and scented flowers.

Abby and John opted for lunch.

Body-swerving the canteen, John offered to go out and come back with some street food, which he did – Lawar, a Bali dish created from vegetables, coconut, minced meat, herbs and spices…plus a bit of salad for extra appeal. They ate it in her room and it was delicious. She couldn't finish it all and said she would keep some back for her dinner.

They talked about the photo opportunity and how to proceed. Be confident, he told her, pose Suzi sufficient for the photographers to get good shots of her, lots of smiles into the lenses.

But it wasn't all serious – she teased him about the time he was spending with her while he complained about 'needy females'.

It was nice.

John took things further proposing that when the media had plenty of material to keep themselves busy he might have a go at smuggling Abby out and show her a bit of the island and its beaches.

She said she would love that, but perhaps see how the grandstanding went first. She gave him a kiss on the cheek when he departed. He felt a million dollars.

Kevin had dwindled again, thoughts racing as to what he might tell this PR man. As little as he could get away with, he hoped. A contradiction in terms given his background as a sports agent where, of course, good PR is integral to a star's image and earning power.

Becky tried to nurture him, sorting pineapple and watermelon drinks all round, and being relentlessly cheerful.

Yet there was something missing.

Kevin smiled vacantly at her. How could he get across that he felt submerged by the whole process, everything was so OTT, everyone was taking bites out of him. Sacks full of letters and packets kept arriving. He had read loads, his parents were doing their bit, but the volume was undiminished. Women, taken with his gallantry and good looks, were enclosing their knickers and 'come and get me' messages. There were product endorsement offers; charities wanted to sign him up.

It was all on the 'to do' list, a list he didn't want to do.

This was not counting the chatter of technology. His own mobile and laptop had gone down with the plane. A new phone had been couriered to the hospital but so far he hadn't used it, afraid he would be swallowed by a black hole of backed up tripe. Afraid the trolls would be sniping from behind their anonymity.

He made an excuse about needing peace and quiet and returned to his room, which in the interim his mum had artistically restyled. Vases of flowers designed to soothe, the brightest of the cards slung on loops of string along all four walls as at Christmas, set against a backdrop of sedate gardens, the sea and sky...she hoped the karma given off might, as in Buddhism, propagate contemplation and insight, dispelling to a degree the tribulations that engulfed him.

Mum saw the hangdog expression on Becky's face, and moved over to sit beside her. She spoke about how torrid it must be for him. Get him home and hope that on familiar territory, buoyed by family and friends, no pressure, it would all come good. Becky had a key part to play. "I'm sure we'll get the old Kevin back – we need to keep at it."

Becky nodded – it was sound advice and she would do all she could. She thanked Mrs Jackson for her consideration.

Neither was being entirely honest with the other.

Becky was feeling a fish out of water and a bit in the way. Outnumbered three to one. She told herself she was being unduly alarmist. She must shrug this off. His Mum was right – it was bound to take time.

Privately, Kevin's mother felt much less assured than she had led them to believe. Had all this never existed she would have been completely phlegmatic about two young people and a burgeoning amour. But, with Kevin not himself, could he cope with matters of the heart at the same time as regaining his poise and purpose? Would it be too much for him? If it was going to be a choice between mental breakdown and Becky then Becky would have to go. Ruthless but necessary. Maybe they could get back together at some later date. Nevertheless, she told herself, she must be fair to this young woman who so loved her son, and they were a very long way yet from implementing such drastic measures.

Neither did she relish a potentially draconian confrontation.

13

For Kevin, it was coming round towards when he was due to meet the Head of Public Relations.

With every minute that passed, he felt more and more uptight. This is ridiculous – you have to get back in the driving seat, he told the walls in his room. The man was only doing his job. So what was this nervous sweat all about?

It was no good. If anything, he felt more lost than when he really was lost, out on that ocean with the baby.

There was a tap-tap on the door.

Oh God, help. HELP.

The Head of PR was standing there.

"Come in," said a hollow voice, which, Kevin elicited, must be his.

They sat down and for an instant there was a prescient interlude as both men hesitated.

The PR man kicked it off, delving into a pocket of his suit and flourishing a notebook and pen. Just in case there was any nagging doubt about what this was all about.

"My name's Gerry," he said.

Kevin could already see that thanks to a prominent badge which said Gerry Smythies, Head of Public Relations, on it.

"Do you have any objection to me calling you Kevin?"

"No, not at all."

"Well, Kevin, let's work towards painting the picture we want people to see." Treading cautiously, he first lobbed an easy one over the net.

"I don't doubt you would want to thank the doctors, nurses and other hospital staff for all they have done?"

"Too right," agreed Kevin, returning it with relish. "They've been a credit to the medical profession. Their dedication has been stupendous."

"And I guess it would be good to thank the people of Bali and indeed people everywhere who have been offering their best wishes for a speedy recovery?"

"Indeed," said Kevin. "It has been over-whelming. Altruistic. The crew on the container ship too – my life was in their hands."

Engendering the right tone, thought Gerry. A bit of colour enlivens any article.

"Fit as a fiddle soon, I'm sure," he fibbed. "How are you in yourself?"

Kevin fibbed too. "Good, thank you. I've been walking around the hospital grounds and spending time with my family. They've kept things in perspective. It's been rejuvenating. And to think I'd almost given up ever seeing them again."

"And reunited with your girlfriend?"

It startled him. Of course, Becky. He supposed she must be his girlfriend in a manner of speaking. After all, he loved her and he wanted her to love him, yet he was less sure about the level of commitment he could deliver. It was complicated.

He thought for a second. "She's been smashing," he noted. "It's energising having her here." He couldn't find anything else apposite to say.

Gerry had hoped for more. To be told they'd been school sweethearts, she was the only one for him, and he was going to propose to her. Still, must be thankful for small mercies. Should he push further and request Kevin and Becky do a quick photo shoot? But he didn't want to blow it.

He needed to ask about the crash. Did Kevin remember much about it?

42

To buy time Kevin peered into the middle-distance. He could talk about the screams as they prepared to ditch. He could tell how he thought he was gone too. Lungs nearly bursting. There was the self-loathing – all for giving up without a fight. He didn't mention any of these things. These were for the ears of the air crash investigators; he would instead play the "don't want to prejudice the inquiry" card.

"It was over-powering. It breaks me up. But I've been ordered not to go into detail while the investigation is on-going, and I have undertaken so to do." Not strictly true – he hadn't yet spoken to the inspectors though they had signalled they would like to speak to him as soon as he felt able.

Gerry said he fully understood.

Both knew that was a whopper.

"What was it like in the water?"

"At first it was near impossible to believe I was still in the land of the living," said Kevin. "I'm not a good swimmer so I was concentrating on staying afloat."

Time to bring the nip and tuck round to Suzi.

"What about the baby?"

"Yeah, she seemed to arrive out of nowhere. Such a tiny thing surviving such a gargantuan event – so improbable. But she was very much alive. I knew then that I had to show what I was made of, grit my teeth, and marshal every ounce of willpower."

Gerry was scribbling furiously. "How did it feel to have saved her life?"

It was the wrong question, and it had been going so well.

Kevin scowled. "I want it to be crystal clear that I do not regard myself as courageous in any of this. There are many people being put through the wringer. I caught a break. Anyway, it was the baby who saved me, not the other way around. She was my treasure." It was almost a speech and it occurred to him he had got more animated than he probably should have.

Gerry's face confirmed as much.

Another prescient interlude.

"We'll leave it at that for the present. I'll go away and write this up, then come back in an hour or two. We can go over it then, add and subtract as appropriate. Play about with the sense. Twiddle around with the words." He fiddled in a bag and brought out a camera. Would Kevin mind having a photo taken? It would be useful for the media to obtain an 'in hospital' shot. A plug for the hospital at the same time.

Kevin shrugged. He just wanted this over.

Gerry posed him sitting on the bed. Click. A couple more just in case. Click. Click.

Finally, it was over.

Gerry backed away. He had pulled it off. However, it still had to be tied up. A talented ex-journalist who had switched to the 'dark side', winkling out a story remained part of his very existence even though these days it had to be camouflaged in corporate gunk, and, of course, every word cleared.

He hit his computer enthusiastically and the words flowed. This was not a tin-pot quid pro quo for some minor charity gift to the hospital. This called for careful crafting…it brought out his professionalism. Not so tabloid in nature that Kevin might baulk at the whole thing. Not so lily-livered that it would read dull and wooden. He checked and re-checked it so both the facts were correct and the pitch was proportionate.

When satisfied he went to find Kevin.

He found him on his own seated in a waiting area staring into no man's land.

A bit peculiar, thought Gerry.

Even more peculiar that Kevin seemed to look vacantly straight through him as if they'd never met…before there was embarrassed recognition.

The PR let it go.

He opened his laptop and pulled up the requisite document – he'd decided not to print it out because sometimes these things had a harsher tinge to them on a black and white page, less threatening on computer.

An old dog's new trick.

Kevin flicked through it – flick being the operative word.

He could tell the guy to bin it. He could tell him he hated it all. He could go through it for an hour and a half, scoring out and adding in, not that there was anything insanely inaccurate about it.

But his eyes had glazed over. Life was too short (of all people he had come to know that) and it was simply too much bother. He didn't want to be rude to someone who, when all said and done, was trying his best.

"Yeah," said Kevin. "Go with it as it is."

Gerry blurted his thanks. Got out of there fast before Kevin had second thoughts.

Then set off to put it through his bosses.

That would probably stretch his negotiating chicanery. You normally had to drop a line here or there for no good reason, just so the top man was persuaded that due homage had been paid. Maybe add in some blatant PR guff about the hospital's expertise in accident and emergency. Most of the media would likely put red pencil through the flowery passages anyway. Massage the pompous prick's ego along the lines of how it all showed the hospital in such a proactive light, which it did.

Halleluiah, it got the nod. Job done.

He took the final version and printed off a hundred copies – he thought that should suffice. Not everyone wanted to read these things on a phone or tablet especially as, crammed together at a packed press briefing, jostling with the next-door neighbours was a given.

Next, he posted a statement about a statement, plus the photo opportunity, on the hospital's web site. Then tipped off the local media, stringers and one or two particular mates.

The phones were red hot for what remained of the day with media operatives, who had descended on Bali from far and wide, fishing for an advance on what was going to be said.

Gerry talked it up, told them it would be Kevin's frank take on surviving against the odds, how the baby had inspired him to mine depths of endurance he never thought he possessed, but wouldn't give away specifics.

Just enough for the smart ones to wet appetites.

This had to be a success all round.

Gerry left for home. An ex-pat with a Balinese wife, he had had plenty of practice at keeping work and home life apart. He sank a beer then sank into a chair. The next day could wait. Never cross bridges until you come to them.

14

That morning he was in early. There was an enormous amount to do.

Run the rule over the conference room, ensure the TV people with their lighting, sound and cameras were in situ, microphones were working, there was a medical backboard, plenty of seats, all was well with Abby and Suzi, hospital officials knew the programme.

No major snags. Everyone primed.

The venue was soon chock-full, hot and sweaty. The primitive air conditioning made conditions just about bearable.

Gerry produced copies of Kevin's statement – it and a photo were now available to download – and began to distribute them. There was the usual argy-bargy, grapple and groan, but nothing too bad. Some spilled onto the floor in the skirmish. Some journos had taken more than they needed, others were clamouring for one. Gerry swooped up those that had hit the deck. Mollified, the media got down to reading it.

Gerry gave it another five minutes for the sake of any late-comers, took to the main microphone and ran through some administration – location of fire exits, phones to silent, when asking a question please state your name and what media organisation you represent.

Then one of the doctors, using a second mic, detailed the latest condition reports on Kevin Jackson and Suzi Duthie. In summary, they would likely be discharged in 48-hours or so.

He sat down again.

Gerry went to a side door and, with what he hoped was a certain pizazz, ushered in Abby with Suzi in her arms. Flashlights lit up the room; cameras cheeped like birds. Something of the theatrical entrance of a king or queen!

Seated out front, for the benefit of all present, Gerry confirmed who they were – *never assume because the one time you do you'll end up with egg on your face.*

Abby smiled broadly into the line-up in front of her. More flash lights and camera clicking. She cradled Suzi on her knee and made the sort of gooey baby noises that she knew would enchant all-comers.

"Isn't she the one," Abby announced to nobody and everybody. "And such a brave little girl."

Coincidence - Suzi waggling her hands about as if applauding.

Pumped full of adrenalin, the media pack, finally with something substantive to go at, ratcheted up the stakes, scorning such niceties as politeness, restraint and manners, resorting to assertive verbal chaos. Nobody bothered identifying themselves.

Trying to organise the media is like herding cats.

Nevertheless, Gerry was sure Abby would measure up. She motioned to him obliquely. He winked back at her.

"How is Suzi handling it all?" boomed a voice from the rear.

"Brilliantly. She's been ever so good. Touch wood that it continues."

"Might her health be adversely affected?"

"She was dehydrated when first admitted but she's battled back well. We're very relieved."

"How is she taking to hospital?"

"The nurses have been spoiling her and there is so much to absorb. I hope I can take her home to the United States fairly soon, but we don't want to jump ahead of ourselves. Constantly adjusting to new circumstances is challenging for anyone, never mind a nine-month-old."

"Has Suzi met Kevin since the rescue?"

"She has indeed – very moving for all of us. It is impossible to thank him enough. To keep her alive while at the same time keeping himself alive was above and beyond what any reasonable person might presuppose. It must have been so terrifying and who could blame him if all he'd done was try to save himself. I know he won't like me saying this but he is our mighty champion."

"Is Suzi missing her parents?"

"I'm sure she must be but of course being so very young it's difficult to tell. The wider family is united and she will get lots of love. We are keeping our fingers crossed. But being orphaned in this way is devastating."

"Do you worry that in time she could prove mentally scarred?"

Gerry interrupted to say he felt this was unfair, but Abby indicated she would take it.

"That is for the future," she said. "Hopefully not. We will have to address it if and when it arises. I am sure there will be clinicians to call on should that be necessary."

The sweet smile was there again. Cue lights, camera, action.

"Just two more," said Gerry. "We don't want to tire the baby out."

A flurry of shouts from the mass and Abby pulled one out of the air at random, asking who would look after the child once in the States.

"We are still talking about that," said Abby. "In the first instance I'm going to be there to provide continuity, but as to the longer term we'll have to see. However, she has caring grandparents, uncles and aunts, so I'm sure we'll work it out."

What a natural, decided Gerry, admiring how this impressive young woman was taking it all in her stride, thoughts echoed by John who was standing to one side.

"Last question."

He pointed to one of the local journalists – small-town parochialism was always worth indulging because they would be around long after the rest had gone and needed to be kept onside.

"Have you been impressed by Bali and the response of the Bali people."

Abby shone, cameras whirred, yet another flurry of flash lights.

"Everyone has been so kind. It is my first visit to Bali but I would love to come back. It is a beautiful island. The care provided by the hospital has been first class. I must also thank the Consulate for their ministrations and support. People of Bali – we owe you so much. The goodwill and love towards Suzi has been humbling."

She tried to catch John's eye. She hoped he was proud of her.

Abby and Suzi left by the same side door amidst shouts of 'every success', 'all the best' and similar such sentiments.

John realised that the media weren't the hard-hearted beasts they were made out to be. They were only human too, with human feelings. Who could not be touched by such an epic survival story?

Gerry was at the microphone again, for the benefit of the visual media, reading Kevin's statement in full.

At the end there were inquiries about whether Kevin would be put up for interview – the media is endlessly greedy for more. Gerry said Kevin was still fragile, in pain and did not feel he was ready. He would keep them abreast of developments. They would be the first to know should Kevin subsequently be willing to speak.

The room began to break up, cameras turned off, journalists and photographers gathering up their gear and charging for the exits, to file for a myriad of global outlets.

Gerry was full of himself – a bullseye.

15

John was pleased too. Maybe he could spirit Abby off to a secluded beach while they were all distracted. He hoped so. No response when he knocked on the door to her room. He found her in the ward, playing with Suzi. Bound up in what she was doing, she never initially noticed his presence. He stayed still, enchanted by the chemistry. He had only known this girl for a couple of days yet he was captivated. He could not fathom it. Nobody else had ever had this effect on him.

At last she spotted him standing there. "Oh, hi John." That same dazzling smile which tore at his heartstrings. She turned back to Suzi. "Look Suzi, here's John, are you going to wave to him."

She took Suzi's hand and waved. Suzi blew a bubble for good measure. Then Abby was snuffling her nose into the baby's neck to squeals of excitement from Suzi. "This big, bad man is going to take me away from you for the afternoon," she quipped.

And looked back at John.

"Are you going to sweep me off in a gilded carriage led by a procession of Hindu gods?" she joked, Bali being more than eighty per cent Hindu.

"Something like that," he responded, po-faced.

She laughed. Placed Suzi back into her cot, handed her a rattle, told her she would see her soon, and meantime the nurses would look after her.

They left.

Abby's room first stop.

"What's the chances of a swim?" she queried.

"Pretty good, I should think."

She found the bikini she had, as an afterthought, thrown in with all the rest of her clutter just in case. I mean for goodness sake. How could you go to Bali without a bikini? The two went hand in hand. Yes, pangs of guilt at the prospect of enjoying herself, but a break, if only for a short while, was necessary pressure relief.

The bikini spawned flip-flops, a towel, sun cream, sunglasses…

John cogitated not for the first time on how women never travel light whereas men – this was sexist. Mustn't go there.

"Got everything?"

"Think so."

She put a finger to her cheek and pondered – God, she was beautiful.

"Let's go," she announced.

They strolled to the car which was in an overflow parking lot five minutes' walk away. Might it be an idea to hide her under a blanket on the back seat in case any of the media were hanging around?

She tossed her hair and went all shy.

Then shrugged. "Let's just go as we are. I intend to have not a care in the world, and, anyway, the media are my friends now."

Soon they were on the road, driving through lush agriculture, passing exotic temples, rice terraces, birds flitting about in the trees.

It was as idyllic as Abby had imagined until John got his own back, telling her to look out for large water monitors and snakes including the king cobra and reticulated python.

Deliciously, she purported to be shocked.

Beware too of the mountainous terrain, with a number of volcanoes.

"Now you're giving me the heebie-jeebies."

They pulled up at a small, sandy beach far removed from the mainstream, and got out of the car.

There wasn't a soul about.

"Oh, John," she exclaimed. "It's scintillating."

Then squeezed his hand, driving him almost wild with lust. There was no way he was giving that hand back – if he ended up the creek without a paddle and charges of compromising his office were proffered then he would accept his fate. He had to find out where this was leading. They walked onto the white sand hand-in-hand as the palm trees swayed their approbation.

They stood there for several minutes, so picture-postcard.

"I can't resist," she said, and for a split second he got the wrong idea. "I'm going back to the car to get my swimming things."

"Good thinking," he blabbed.

At the uncertainty in his voice, she stopped and turned. "I take it that it's safe to bathe?"

"Yes," he assured her. "I checked with the locals when I first came here. I've swum a few times. Haven't been eaten by a Great White yet."

She raised an eyebrow.

"You shouldn't tempt fate."

Undeterred, she found her towel and bikini, then, pointing very deliberately, stated that she was going behind a clump of tropical vegetation and shrubbery fringing the beach.

"And no peeking."

He put on his trunks in the back seat, and only peeked a bit.

The bikini was a sultry yellow.

His eyes wallowed in her firm breasts, the willowy blonde hair, the slim waist, the sleek legs … wow, those legs. How he wanted to hold her in his arms.

She came over to him, and gave him a playful shove in the chest.

"Last one into the sea is a sissy," she exclaimed, and was off.

They raced down to the water and plunged in.

Well, more like, he plunged in. She was rather daintier, jumping up and down with glee, before pretending to splash him.

He pretended to splash her back.

She pretended to duck him under. He lifted her aloft and spun her around, deaf to her protests.

"Big bully. Don't like you anymore."

Turned away, and broke into a gentle breaststroke.

He let her go, engrossed by the spectre of this feisty woman he had fallen for – so different to all the others.

They swam and frolicked, frolicked and swam. The water was warm, the sun was shining, the setting was hard to beat. Until, the swim at an end, both were drying themselves with their towels.

She put hands through her hair. "I forgot my bathing hat. I must look so bedraggled."

He assured her that she was as glamorous as a film star.

And couldn't stop himself as his hands moved onto her waist as if electronically programmed. He brought her close and they kissed for the first time.

They kissed slowly and tenderly.

Then they kissed passionately and provocatively.

She felt elated. You are supposed to know when it is true love. She knew already.

He felt he had entered a harbour of calm.

A local walking his dog along the beach hove into frame, and the spell was broken.

She put a light top on and rubbed sun block into her arms, legs and feet. She offered it to him and he did the same.

Placed their towels side by side on the sand – they wouldn't be damp for long in these temperatures – and lay down, his arm around her, her face nuzzling into his side.

They were there a long time.

Reluctant to tear herself away until the double stimulus of Suzi and a glass of fresh, cool, cold-pressed sugar cane juice could no longer be resisted.

After sorting themselves out, they returned to the car, tried to shake out as much sand as they could – it gets everywhere – and drove home, both mulling how much they had to give something that beguiled them both.

Until, on the way he had an idea.

"I'll take you past my apartment block so you can see where I live."

"Why, Mr Munro," she declared, as though he had taken things too far. "Are you trying to seduce me?" She looked demurely at him and they were laughing again.

After the detour, he dropped her off at the hospital. He would pick her up the following afternoon.

"Shall we do it all again," he almost implored.

"Yes, let's," she replied.

They kissed, she got out of the car and waved as he drove off.

She held her gaze until it was out of sight, then whistled to herself. Events were moving fast.

16

But the next day … oh, the next day.

It was towards the end of the dry season but there was little threat of a tropical downpour. They stopped at a roadside restaurant, went for a walk up to a beauty spot vantage point and then found a different beach.

Because he didn't know it, they confined themselves to walking, cuddling, kissing, paddling and admiring the panorama.

She told him loads more about life in Normal and her role in the running of a major sports and leisure complex in Dubai. He told her about his route from public school in England, through university in the States, to joining the Bureau of Consular Affairs – he spoke four languages – and how the Bali posting had come out of the blue. If they had told him the world is your oyster, Bali was sure to have been in the top five.

Once more, it was time to go.

They got in the car.

"OK," he said. "Back to the hospital."

"Actually," she said. "Why don't you show me this bachelor flat of yours? The spin by yesterday intrigued me. I'm curious to see more of how you live here in Bali."

"It's a bit of a tip," he apologised. "I would have given it a clean had I known."

"Don't you want to show me?" she flirted.

"No, I'd love to." A quick response.

"Make it happen then," said Abby. She had firmly set her sights on this madly attractive, suave, consummate gentleman, but he would need to woo her.

He parked up – the scheme seemed well kept and maintained. Modern materials interspersed with local stone. A tidy garden with colourful flowers. He put the key in the door and ushered her in.

It was a compact sort of place – kitchen divided off from a lounge/dining area, two bedrooms, one of which he used as a study, toilet and bathroom.

The lounge could certainly do with a tidy – DVDs lying all over the place, magazines dotted about, used coffee mugs.

He showed her the master bedroom. "Is this where I proposition you?" he asked cheekily.

"I don't know," she said. "Perhaps you'd better try your luck."

They locked bodies, they kissed, and they knew that each very much wanted the other. She unbuttoned his shirt and rummaged through the hairs on his chest. He removed her top and then her bra – her nipples were like beacons for his mouth. Quickly she dropped her skirt, stripped away her panties, and slid under the sheets.

At the speed of light, driven by an orgy of longing, his trousers and underpants had vanished.

Their lips gorged on each other, he stroked her most precious gift, her hands swept over his erect penis. Taking this slow was out of the question. She opened her legs wide and he entered her.

She swooned and held him ever tighter.

He oozed pleasure. A coupling that took them to Venus and back.

Finally, they came apart and lay panting on the bed. Neither wanted to let go.

"Oh, John, that was magnificent," she schmoozed in his ear.

He snuggled up to her even more, kissing her neck and stroking her thighs.

They stayed entwined for as long as their bodies allowed, before separating. Both felt utterly fulfilled.

She asked to use his shower. He pulled a fresh towel out of a cupboard drawer and handed it to her.

He followed after and at the point he had finished she was already dried and dressed and had taken a seat in the lounge. He swiftly covered his own nakedness, took a brush to his hair, and then got them a cup of coffee. It had been so good neither knew quite what to say. She laid her head on his shoulder and simply told him how nice it was.

He told her she was special, and meant it.

The next afternoon when he found her in her room in the hospital her temperament had gone from glorious to glum.

Poles apart.

He knew why.

The Consulate had told him that the hospital was releasing Suzi and he was to make arrangements for Abby and the baby to fly to the US.

He tried to gee her up – it would be a fresh start for a child who in all probability should have been dead. Someone who relied on her for everything.

She gave him a half smile, and said she supposed so.

Like raindrops on a windowpane, two tears meandered down her cheek, racing each other, as she studied him with big, sad eyes.

He held her as they sat on the side of the bed and her despair tumbled out – what if they were never to see each other again.

She could not expect him to jack in a great job in a great place for someone he barely knew. But she would always hold dear their bond.

He let her say her piece, all the while caressing her hair and face.

Her tears left a sodden patch on the front of his shirt. "Oh, look what I've done." She reached for some tissues and made a pretence of trying to mop it dry.

He took a firm grip on her arms and made her look into his face.

"Now," he said. "Listen carefully.

"I pledge to you this is no holiday fling. I think we both know that – not a holiday and not a fling. Nor is it the last we will see of each other – the absolute opposite is the case. Right person, place to die for, ropey timing. But we're going to figure this out. Already you mean everything to me. I will not give you up come what may. We're going to write long letters to each other. We're going to speak on the phone as regularly as we can. We're going to connect via video chat apps. All my leave is going to be spent with you, Abby."

It was the words she so wanted to hear.

"Oh, John," she sobbed, the tears those of happiness this time. She threw her arms over his shoulders and dissolved. "Oh, John, do you really mean that? Do you think we could?"

He told her they must strive tirelessly to pursue their dream, must keep telling one another that distance made the heart grow fonder. It would not be easy, it might fail, but if they didn't try they would always lament what might have been.

"I want to make it work," she told him.

"I do too," he said.

A love kiss sealed the pact, now they had promised themselves to each other.

It could have been a prelude to … to … she pulled away.

"We mustn't, or I am going to want you more than I can resist … and there's so much to do."

He smiled.

"Let's go to it," he said.

Abby had that earlier that morning been called into the administration office and given the news about Suzi. Now they discussed all the things she would need on route – as Nancy had presaged back in Dubai, they rallied round. As they had done all along.

Separately, John had been phoning airlines and comparing flights. The choice focussed in on Denpasar to Chicago with just the one transit stop. It would take a whole day and more. A long and tiring flight but particularly so for a wee baby.

John and Abby talked it through, what bags could go in the hold and what could be carried on board. He said he would liaise with the hospital and ensure there was no duplication. They would also need to initiate a shopping trip. A baby carrier attached to her front was a must.

He got out his mobile and booked the tickets.

They exchanged images to put on their phones, and also addresses, emails and phone numbers.

He mucked in with the packing for what would be an early morning start.

Still she was all a flutter as to how she was going to manage. He told her there were mothers with infants doing it every day of the week.

As she had said earlier, there was so much to do that the hours flew by. They managed a spot of supper but otherwise it was all go.

She promised him she would get an early night. He promised her he would take her and Suzi to the airport well in advance of the flight.

A penny for their thoughts? Both were too tired.

He clocked in on schedule in the morning, placed her bags in the boot, while everyone made a big fuss over Suzi, and Abby expressed her thanks repeatedly.

"Run, run, before you're late," they told her.

A quick pose for half a dozen photographers still on the beat and keen to get the bye-bye-baby shot. Some had become so familiar Abby was virtually on first name terms with them.

Thence it was off to the airport.

She checked in. It was VIP treatment similar to her arrival. John smoothed over last minute doubts.

Despite Suzi in the carrier and a bag full of baby gear, they kissed as though it was just the two of them in a tree-lined glade rather than a noisy terminal full of people, neither caring whether any media killjoys were watching or not. As it happened, they weren't.

Then she and Suzi were gone.

17

Kevin had opted not to see Abby off – she was bound to be mad busy. Though not so mad busy that she couldn't find space to supply all the necessary contact details to enable him to keep in touch. Attached was a hand-written note expressing her admiration for him and what he had done. The door would always be open whenever he wished to visit, and the family would keep him in the loop. It was good of her and he felt re-assured. Adamant he would stay connected. Suzi would be a part of him for the rest of his life.

Like Suzi, it was time to head home.

His parents, Becky and Vicky sought to play it down. It was as if the *celebrity status* was destroying him. Constantly on edge, he was dogged by the guilt that tends to afflict survivors – why had he been spared when so many others were dead? How was he to bear such a burden?

Whenever anyone looked directly towards him he turned into a pillar of salt. What were they thinking? Were these the departed returned to hound him? Or were they the Devil's bounty hunters?

Becky had tried to big him up and when that didn't work she sought to flood him with love. One night she engineered it that they were on their own. They kissed but his heart was not in it. And she was dismayed when having made herself as sexy as she could, putting on the flimsiest of flimsy outfits, he shrank away from her, saying he did not yet feel up to intercourse. He had never used that phraseology before and its formality killed everything.

She had badly wanted sex with him – it had been a while.

Before, it had always been good.

Her frustrations began to grow.

Vicky and his parents kept shuffling the pack in a bid to coax him out of the gloom bunker where he was hiding. They talked endlessly about family, things Kevin had got up to when he was young, turned conversation round to his love of sport. But sport seemed so trivial compared to the wider poppy fields of death and destruction. Once more, they told themselves that when they got back to Sydney he would turn the corner. There was no Plan B.

When the hospital announced he was fit to go, they were keen to catch the first available flight.

However, there was still the media.

While the statement issued on Kevin's behalf had been well-received, only his full, unexpurgated story would shake them off, and, failing that, some good quotes out of his own mouth to induce a truce.

The hospital had requested more than once that his privacy be respected, but that could only ever be a holding operation.

Could he say a few words? Might it not be cleansing?

He flatly refused.

The whole world seemed to be ganging up on him. Eating him alive. Feasting on blood. He felt under attack from all sides.

Gerry had sympathy with the media just as he had sympathy for Kevin. Kevin had thrown them one bone, if only he would be prepared to throw them another. Alternatively, Gerry toyed with some stunt to weasel him away from under their noses. But then the media were sure to get their own back to the detriment of the hospital's reputation and Gerry knew who would be blamed!

Might he stand, wave, say a few words, while departing the main entrance. The family needed to talk him round.

Like an angler with a thrashing salmon that had taken the lure, they reeled in, let out slack, reeled in and finally netted his cooperation if only in deference to the hospital staff who had done so much to treat his injuries – the ribs were much improved as was the wrist. No damage to the spleen after all.

Becky offered to take some of the heat by speaking to the media herself.

He caved in.

They would have him stand next to a group of nurses who had played a formative role in getting him back on his feet.

It worked after a fashion.

His parents, Becky and Vicky bolstered him as he came out into an unruly crowd of photographers, reporters, TV crews, flashing lights, hubble and bubble. It shook him to the core and he would have turned back had that been possible. Somehow, he snivelled a comment or three, pecks on the cheek for the nurses, a desultory wave, and was gradually eased to a waiting taxi. He cowered down, physically shaking, as it moved off, headed for the airport.

Becky held back and they converged on her.

She performed like a trooper.

What was wrong with Kevin – even the media had been floored by his oppressed demeanour and sunken eyes?

He was, she said, still hooked into the whole thing, stressed out, and unable to let go. He would need tenderness and love over the next few weeks, preferably staying out of the public eye.

Was he pleased to leave hospital? Yes, he was and the staff had all gone the extra mile. He was in their debt and always would be.

What was the relationship between her and Kevin? She was waiting for that one. There was no way she was going to lie. She might not tell the whole truth but she wasn't going to lie. She said they were close friends, had known each other from childhood and he meant a lot to her.

Were they engaged? No, they weren't engaged.

What were their hopes for the future? Simply to get Kevin comfortable in his own skin again – they weren't thinking past that.

What about the baby? Suzi had captured his heart. Theirs would always be an unbreakable tie.

She cut it short – had to catch the same flight back to Sydney. They let her go without any hassle, acknowledging she had levelled with them.

She got into a second taxi and they were soon making a steady pace down the road.

Becky closed her eyes. It had not been easy and she felt a little drained herself. It had allowed her a glimpse into Kevin's torment. She reasoned there was going to be no quick fix. Was she in for the long haul? She wasn't sure. She pushed the thought to the back of her consciousness and tried to immerse herself in Bali's tourist brochure glories.

Kevin was seated beside his parents on the plane – a waste, thought Becky. She would have liked to have held his hand tight, told him she was beginning to understand. She would hold a candle for him whether they stayed together or broke up.

Arrival at Sydney Airport would mean yet more palaver – first photos back on home soil and all that trash.

It proved exactly so.

18

Bonkers.

People falling over, cameras on the ground, an undignified melee, but nobody ever thinks they might find themselves at the centre of such louche behaviour. Security tried to hold the tide back King Canute-style, but were simply outnumbered. Amidst the cacophony of sound and the barrage of questions, Kevin managed a few grudging platitudes.

Yes, it was pleasing to be back.

Sure, the first thing he would do was open a cold beer.

No, he didn't feel a hero. He did what he could. He wished he could have done more.

Fed up, his father tried to intervene. "Come on, guys, give it a rest. The boy is badly in need of convalescence – this is not good. You've had your pound of flesh. Now let us be. Please."

Nobody took any notice.

He held his temper. But he was seething with resentment.

Kevin, past knowing or caring what he was saying, was sucked dry, then spat out like a piece of discarded chewing gum. His insides and his outside scoured by the media sandstorm.

Didn't know whether he was coming or going.

Father half carried him out of the terminal.

A taxi provided a haven of sorts.

Tears rolled down Kevin's face and a spasm wracked his body.

All three women, his mother, Becky and Vicky, moved to hug him. Mother got there first, trying to soothe and succour.

"Why me? Why me? Why me?"

"It's OK dear; mother's going to take care of you."

He let out a piercing scream, loud enough to penetrate the cosmos.

The taxi driver pulled to the side of the road and stopped the cab. "Is he all right? Is he having a fit? Do you want me to take him to a hospital?"

They told the man to continue onwards to the family home in Manly, one of Sydney's main upmarket suburbs.

Kevin lay sprawled, moaning intermittently, head in his mother's lap as though he were reverting to being a child once more. Vicky was sorrowful, her father was bemused, Becky cringed. Could Kevin be having the breakdown they had all feared?

Not a diagnosis the Jacksons would ever buy. Jacksons didn't have breakdowns. The *b* word was verboten. Australians were hard as nails, weren't they?

At last they were there. The half hour drive had seemed like hours.

They guided him into the house, Mum and Dad with arms around him in case he collapsed.

A crowd which had assembled – a handful of journalists, a few voyeurs who had come to gawp and well-meaning neighbours with banners such as *Welcome Home, Kevin* and *Our Braveheart Returns* – weren't sure what to make of it all. An interweaving of disappointment and concern.

Vicky's turn to go out and say a few words. She thanked them for their warmth and love - there was no intent on Kevin's part to snub anyone, just that everything post the crash coupled with mourning for the death of his friends had left him run-down. He was under doctor's orders. Once fully restored she was sure he would want to pay his respects to the local community.

It produced a murmuring of empathy, the banners were lowered and little groups sidled away, whispering to each other in the way people do when perplexed at a turn of events they had hoped would pan out very differently.

It was a pity for two reasons in particular.

Kevin's parents were well-respected. Brett Jackson, semi-retired, had been a prominent shipbroker. June Jackson had been a midwife prior to her own children coming along. She had taken several years off when they were young – having delivered so many other people's babies she wanted to ensure hers got the best start in life. She had never regretted that decision, was thrilled at the way both Kevin and Vicky had developed into exemplary citizens, and opted for voluntary work rather than resuming her career.

Secondly, Manly was such an attraction. Shimmering beaches, vibrant business community, laid-back, renowned by many to be "as Australian as it gets". Walking trails, almost every kind of leisure activity, the domain of those who sought to flaunt wealth and influence.

With a population of around 80,000, it describes itself as "a must visit destination offering waterfront restaurants, adventure and entertainment for young and old – relax on the wharf, enjoy sensational views and simply take in the ambience of this cosmopolitan resort-style location". In short, Manly prided itself on being a trendy place to live and having a window on the world.

For the first week the world backed off and Kevin was allowed the headroom he craved to grieve for his friends, Alex, Phil, Jack and Johnnie. He tinkered around the house and garden caught up in his own self-doubts, not exactly chilled, but a little less intense. No longer as weighed down. Still largely uncommunicative though, spending hours on an old garden swing, no appetite, guzzling endless cartons of milk.

His mother couldn't make it out though gratified that his manic behaviour had subsided.

Becky had gone back to her work as a beautician but dropped by whenever she could. She found Kevin unresponsive but at the same time needy. He would ask her to hold him as if, rather like in the taxi back from the airport, reverting to the comfort of a foetal position. She would oblige but felt distinctly queasy. She ached for the return of the active, decisive, always-on-the-go boy she had fallen for at school.

He went for a twenty-five minute jog around the locality, something of which mother approved. He went for long walks, but always on his own, which had mother worrying in case he wandered off dementia-like.

And of course the world was bound to intrude before long.

His boss at the sports agency came round to see how he was – he had advance warning of Kevin's vulnerability and took things softly-softly, staying clear of controversial areas, passing on upbeat messages, asking how the firm could be of use, remarking how he was always in their thoughts. He never said anything to the family but it concerned him that Kevin was so hard to engage.

Air accident investigators wanted to interview him – back on Bali his father had asked them, beseeched them, that Kevin be given some leeway. They agreed a deferral, but it could not be postponed indefinitely, they must press on with the probe, the public expected that of them.

Brett strove to safeguard his son, while reiterating how necessary it was that Kevin should find it within himself to open up. There could be things that seemed innocuous which might result in a breakthrough.

Kevin became resigned to cooperating but it put up his anxiety levels and the demands upon him were almost too much to bear. He wasn't being bolshie. Why couldn't others 'get' that all Kevin wanted was to put two fingers up to the outside world. What was wrong with them?

When it could not be put off any longer he found the interviewing process took an enormous amount out of him. It felt like he was being hung, drawn and quartered. OK, they had a job to do … but it was brutal.

Like pulling teeth without an anaesthetic.

Several times Kevin crumbled as he told of the screams, the grizzled faces, which all too often kept him awake at night.

Each time they had to suspend for fifteen minutes or half an hour, drink a cup of tea, take the air, and wait until he was able to go again.

This was not uncaring officialdom but simply that it seemed prudent to concertina the interview into a single day, driving it relentlessly forward until conclusion. All could then be put behind them. No good starting but never finishing.

It ran into the early evening but at last the investigators were satisfied they had all they needed.

19

Kevin emerged suicidal. He went straight to bed, talking vaguely of topping himself.

Mrs Jackson called the family doctor.

The doctor seemed preoccupied, and, after a cursory examination, concluded there was nothing physically wrong with him.

They already knew that!

He prescribed antidepressants and bailed out. Kevin wouldn't take them.

Becky's next visit found Kevin in bits.

She dragged him out for a walk, insistent that shutting himself away was the last thing he should be doing. She talked to him about anything and everything, her work at the beauticians, friends asking for him, the weather, politics, sport. She forced him to interact, continually seeking his opinion. An acquaintance walked by – Kevin would have blanked him but Becky made a point of saying hello, prompting a conversation. At a bridge over a stream, they played Poohsticks and they bought ice creams at a seaside kiosk.

After two hours, they were back at the house. He said it had cheered him up, and, for the first time since the accident, he kissed her as a woman ought to be kissed.

It built her hopes but by the next she came round the improvement had receded – he was switched off. Feeling down herself, she gave it ten minutes, made an excuse and left. And felt a she-devil for doing so. She would remain involved but she knew she couldn't do it for him; he had to help himself.

It was around then that the letter writing started, and that was seriously weird. They all went to the same address – Suzanne Duthie in Normal, Illinois. However, confusingly they all began, Dear Hope. Obviously, Suzi would be unable to read them and there was no attempt to use baby-speak. They were written as though to an adult.

They were long letters too.

Kevin told how he thought about her often, she was his motivation, yet every day was just full of inanity. He could not be doing with it.

And there was more.

What meaning was there in the accident? Why had the two of them been spared? Were they destined for some sort of higher purpose? All too often he found himself morbidly conversing with the dead – were they trying to point the way ahead? He was sure he had entered a void where Becky, Vicky and his parents were peripheral figures. Perhaps, he said to Suzi, she would understand when she was older.

They kept dropping through the family letter box roughly every two months, and they found them disturbing.

Was this man mentally ill? Were they expected to respond? Should they phone Kevin's parents and voice their concerns for him? Should they shred the letters or keep them?

Presumably, Hope was a kind of pet name for Suzi?

There was a lengthy discourse about what to do and, because opinions differed, the most sober outcome was to kick the can down the road. The letters built up into a bundle which was secreted away at the back of a drawer. Except that as the years went by there was another bundle, then a further bundle, and gradually the drawer was taken over. Meanwhile Suzi was growing – toddler, playgroup, schoolgirl.

But first, flashback.

When Abby had alighted at Chicago O'Hare International Airport sleep-deprived and wilting with Suzi in her arms, family members were there to meet her - Robert's mother and father, Anne and Ed, the sisters' mother and father, Sara and Jeb, plus Suzi's two uncles, Harris and Luke. It was quite a reunion or rather it would have been in happier times. All the more as TV crews, reporters, photographers, the usual onslaught, had pitched up to mark Suzi's homecoming.

Abby, who was getting something of a pro at all this, sparked into life – turned on media mode, lit up the glittering smile, tickled Suzi into cooperating for the cameras. Abby reckoned she now knew how it must feel to walk the red carpet at the Oscars.

Everyone wanted a shot of them and Abby tried to oblige.

"Glorious to be back in God's own land," she avowed. "I love you, America." Suzi had been *as good as gold* all flight – in fact, far from it she had been irritable and stroppy.

Nevertheless, the centre of attention once again – from both the family and the media. Amidst this sea of faces, the little one simply clung to Abby like a comfort blanket. Had Kevin been there he might have described it in Aussie twang as like a koala joey to its mum.

The media were pacified and the family set off in convoy for Normal.

They pulled up at Sara and Jeb's home, it being rightly deemed far too morbid for Abby and Suzi to stay at Robert and Rose's house – sacrilegious for anyone to enter. Too early to even consider doing so.

Sara carried Suzi out of the car – Abby had kept nodding off and in case of accidents the babe had been transferred over.

Like at Kevin's it seemed the whole street had turned out.

We Love You, Suzi banners, applause, car horns hooting, apple pie, even fireworks – the latter being somewhat over the top to say the least.

The family thanked their neighbours profusely, showed off Suzi to all and sundry, and members of the media delighted in putting it on record.

When they finally got inside and closed the front door Abby slumped into a chair, took two sips of a cup of coffee and promptly crashed out. Suzi, she knew, was in good hands. Anyway, Abby couldn't keep her eyes open one iota longer.

Sara and Jeb had been busy while Abby had been collecting Suzi. Rose's old cot, which Sara had never been able to bear throwing out, was unearthed beneath a dustsheet in the garage and given a wash-down to remove years of dirt. Now re-assembled, though tarnished and scratched, also a bit old-fashioned, it was spotless and structurally sound, well up to taking a new hammering. Harris had supplied a high chair which they placed Suzi into and tied up the straps. Baby food had been purchased from local stores while they had been inundated with kids' clothes from well-wishers.

They tried her with a chicken concoction and a peach affair.

She seemed to approve albeit plenty was splattered about for good measure.

Sara and Jeb smiled knowingly at each other – it had been years since they were wiping baby mess from the carpet, not something they ever conceived would be coming their way again. It harked back to how flawless were the young, as seen through the prism of one-eyed parenthood. And yet more tears were shed for Robert and Rose. Their bodies were not among those so far recovered though Sara and Jeb had not given up. Perhaps the sea might yet relent.

The priority was to give the devoted couple a proper funeral, a grave to which the family could return, be still and *talk* to them. A memorial service seemed a poor substitute but one they knew they might have to endure. Time would no doubt make the decision for them.

After the feed, a few burps and a good clean of face and hands, they put Suzi down in the cot and she too went out like a light. Her grandparents watched over her in the Land of Nod, then found a duvet to put round Abby who was still out cold in the chair. Then they retired to bed themselves.

Everyone slept in next morning, even Sara and Jeb who were always up early. The family would take it slow for a few days while Abby got over the jet lag, Suzi became re-acquainted with home base, and the constant stream of callers were treated with politeness and civility.

Over Sunday lunch, a calorie-rich roast, there was another family conflab, with Suzi once again at its epicentre.

"Interested parties wanting a cuddle should form an orderly queue," joked Abby.

Later in the afternoon all were partaking of the sunshine in the back garden when the chin-wagging returned to what would be best for Suzi. Nobody wanted to sound dogmatic but everyone pitched in.

Sara and Jeb said they would happily look after her.

But, being in their late fifties, might it prove all too much for them.

Luke and his wife Amanda had young children, Jimmy, aged four, and Jane, aged one. Suzi might be a good fit with their two.

Abby felt it vital that she be there for Suzi in the short term. She said it was unlikely she would return to Dubai and she would probably look for a job locally. She hesitated, but then dropped her big news about how she had met John. She did not want to go overboard this early - they had known each other for less than a week, but would like to see where it might take them. He hoped to come to Normal in the next few months.

They were overjoyed for her appreciating that John meant a lot. Her body language said so in spades. Tempered too, though they didn't tell Abby. While it sounded like the real deal, whirlwind romances were sometimes too good to be true.

So, of Suzi's future, nothing was set in stone. But then did that matter? Let all the close family play a part in her upbringing.

Social Services would no doubt want a say, rightly. But they were willing to make any accommodations the professionals laid down.

Sara and Jeb stuck with Granny and Grandad while for Anne and Ed it remained Grandma and Grandpa.

20

When Becky next went round to see Kevin she found him composing one of his letters to Suzi … except she did not yet know anything about this growing obsession. Her first reaction was to be pleased that he was communicating, and her see-sawing hopes rose once more.

"Who are you writing to?" she asked.

At first he didn't hear her, caught up in what he was doing.

"Sorry," he said. "Did you speak?"

She smiled, he didn't, and it registered as a rebuff.

"I was wondering who you were writing to – you seem very focussed."

"I'm writing to Suzi – I write to her regularly."

At a loss as to why he should be writing to a child not even past its first birthday, she could only reply: "How interesting."

A bland response but she had become inured to disguising her true emotions – in this case bafflement – because any chink in the façade held the capability of opening a new chasm.

For Becky, all too difficult.

So, she let it go and approached from a more acute angle. "Have you spoken with any of your friends recently?"

"No," he screeched, with such hostility it effectively stopped any further discussion of the subject.

"Oh," said Becky, stung by the vitriol.

But, reluctant to give up, came at it from another direction. "What about a holiday, somewhere here in Australia, Cairns and the Great Barrier Reef maybe – it might do you good?"

"No. I don't need a holiday and I certainly don't want a holiday."

He glowered at her – Bali was meant to be a holiday and look how that had turned out. What was she thinking?

Thence retreated back to his letter.

Becky felt like blubbing. "I think I'll go and make a cup of coffee." She didn't ask if he wanted one – she didn't think she could take another rejection.

He never even noticed as she made for the kitchen.

Mrs Jackson was there.

Becky looked as if she had walked into a wall.

"Oh, Becky," his mum commiserated and passed over the tissues.

Becky dabbed at her eyes and sighed. This wasn't how it was meant to be but Becky was past caring about getting into a state in front of what she had hoped might one day be her mother-in-law. "However hard I try, I can't bridge the gulf," she ventured between sniffs. "I don't know what to do or where to turn."

Such that Kevin's mum found herself entranced by this tender-hearted girl who had such a soft spot for her son.

It was not the moment to tell her that the family felt she and Kevin should have a sabbatical, at least until he could regain his health. Instead, putting an arm around her, she steered her to the kitchen table, sat her down and said everything would seem better over a cup of tea.

By the time the tea was poured, Becky was more herself.

They sipped the hot brew.

"He's been through something beyond our understanding," opined Kevin's mother. "This may take very much longer than we first thought."

Becky said she presumed so but once started her worries poured forth. Kevin had transitioned into a different person and she wanted her Kevin back. The writing of letters to a baby seemed … seemed … well, plain odd.

Mum put on her most charismatic voice. The girl cared, she cared, they all cared. However, none of them, and not just Becky, knew how to reach *the Promised Land*. Mum had thought about whether they should get mental health services involved, perhaps even pay privately to see a psychiatrist. But, if that got out, it could stigmatise him. Whatever, unlikely that Kevin would play ball. Therefore, she gave Becky the honest truth. That she had no magic wand either. She had no idea if or when the *real* Kevin would be returned to them. Becky must decide for herself how much she had to give without putting her life on hold. *You only got one life and you needed to live it*. She must do what her head told her rather than her heart.

It was all said with a fondness that addressed Becky as family.

Becky kept committing but gradually her energy faded.

Kevin's mum could see the tiredness in her eyes and the love gradually dissolving. So sad was this that she made it her business to have words with Kevin – one final go at saving the spark which had united them. She said Becky clearly adored him, he could do far worse, he was treating her abysmally, and he should make up his mind if only to set her free.

But Kevin said something bizarre; "There's only one woman in my life now … Suzi."

His mother told him that was ludicrous, to grow up, stop acting like a baby himself, re-connect with his old life, and, by the way, the world didn't owe him a living. Indeed, she got positively cross.

He simply went and sulked. Back communing with the gremlins.

Becky came round less and less, the fire dimmed, and it all petered out as she concluded she was effectively single again.

21

The last time there was even an ember was when the families of the missing four who had travelled with Kevin on what should have been a golden getaway said they could wait for bodies no more.

The joint memorial service for Alex, Jack, Johnnie and Phil was traumatic. Five hundred crammed inside the church and perhaps the same again outside. The hymns were sombre but stirring and there was a reading from Psalm 23 including the immortal words: "Even though I walk through the valley of the shadow of death, I fear no evil, for You are with me; Your rod and Your staff, they comfort me." Mothers broke down and had to be supported, members of the congregation sobbed.

The wake was reserved – given the awful events of the air crash, laughter and bonhomie would have been intemperate. Friends and relatives fondly remembered, spoke of four lives cut short in their prime, the unfairness of it all. What had they ever done to deserve such a fate? People paid their respects but didn't linger.

The media caught the mood and were equally adroit in their coverage.

Kevin was there with his family … just. At first, he had objected, saying his presence – the sole adult survivor – would be an affront to the bereaved. It was a previous life to which he could not return.

Father lost the plot, grabbed the lapels of his son's jacket, got in his face, said the gibberish and bollocks had to end, and told him he was attending the service be it kicking and screaming, come hell or high water.

It produced pandemonium in the household as the two were separated, Kevin's father crimson with fury, Kevin as white as a sheet.

Reluctantly he agreed to go, a sullen presence amidst an outpouring of grief.

Becky, wearing a black suit, black hat, black shoes, said hello to him, took him by the arm, inquired as to his welfare. He acknowledged her. Yet there was no hint of what they had shared.

Neither said another word to each other.

Kevin did not attend the wake, limited though it was. He could not face the intrusion. He could not look people in the eye. Instead, he walked down to the sea and spent an hour catching the wind, seagulls soaring, skimming pebbles, idle beachcombing, and doing everything he could not to think of the crash.

Of course, he could not escape it – he never would.

Many in the congregation felt for him in his isolation; others viewed him as malign and disrespectful.

Just once did his cares fall away – the New Year fireworks display for which Sydney is famed. Wide-eyed children, cheering crowds. The harbour lit up, the bridge mystical in the darkness, explosion after explosion, and the nursery rhyme-effect of the swirling smoke clouds.

But that was a one-off.

22

Babies grow up fast and Suzi was no different.

Walking unsteadily, saying her first words, knocking over ornaments and shedding tears whenever she fell over.

Sara and Jeb had gravitated into looking after her, relieved by Anne, Ed and Abby.

Abby ring-fenced time for Suzi despite having landed a similar job to Dubai as assistant chief executive of a luxury sports and leisure hub.

It was a dream position, but, she told herself, Suzi was a dream girl.

They did not pick up on what was to come, though in retrospect perhaps they should have done. If only, if only …

Her manners were non-existent, still slopping her food about, declaring it to be *pig poo*, referring to Granny as *stinker* and branding Abby *ugly*.

She and the family's collie Lady hated each other. As she grew up, Suzi took every opportunity to pull Lady's tail and kick her. The normally mild-mannered dog growled, bared its teeth, and barked angrily. Suzi responded by throwing her toys at the poor thing. Lady developed such an aversion to Suzi that she went out of her way to avoid the child.

It didn't stop there.

When she was four, she tried to drown a pet rabbit in next-door's pond. When she was five, she hit a boy at a children's party so hard he had to be taken to hospital. Whenever she was thwarted, she screamed the house down at volumes which scythed through your brain.

Conversely, there were times when she played the innocent to perfection. Just a cherub when the media came round to see her blow the candles out on her birthday cake.

Before, in Jekyll and Hyde vein, mutating back into Miss Nasty.

All this was put down to a highly-strung nature, a short fuse, and her being an orphan.

Jeb and Sara found it stressful, toiled with discipline, and were visibly ageing.

Abby could take whatever Suzi threw at her – often literally.

But her attention was elsewhere.

Because by then, she and John, the remarkable love story, were headed to the altar.

He had made it over to Normal after about six months – he had hoped it would have been sooner – fired up by long phone and internet sessions and lots of letter writing.

Encouraged by the family, Abby had moved into Robert and Rose's house. Lying empty, it needed some TLC. Abby hadn't been sure, concerned she would be trespassing on the 'grave' of her sister and brother-in-law. Walking with ghosts and the bad vibes it might bring. Nevertheless, she was persuaded that it was exactly what Robert and Rose would have wanted. Make a new home there, be that temporary or permanent, and honour what they had begun.

So when John rocked up it was all spic and span.

He was aware she could not take loads of days off from her job having only recently started it, but said he was coming anyway.

And when they fell into each other's arms the loved-up aching was as torrid as before. The magnetism alive and gushing, and, like in Bali, the sex was ecstatic.

Work let her have a long weekend incorporating the Friday and they locked and bolted the door, salivating in the thrill of exploring every nook and cranny of their existence.

The visit lasted for just ten days but felt like ten weeks … no, it felt like ten years. They had known that what they had was unique to them, but they had taken it to new vistas.

When they weren't in bed she gave him a spin around Normal – her pride in the town, its many parks and civic amenities, shone through. He observed straight-away that it seemed a nice place with nice people.

She introduced him to the family and they were impressed. Like with any young suitor, meeting her mum and dad was daunting. However, they were very welcoming. There was some gentle probing into his background and prospects – did the cut of his jib befit their daughter? But he was polite, respectful, and it was clear to everyone that he and Abby were head over heels in love.

So parental sixth sense was appeased.

When she saw him off at the airport, they could barely tear themselves apart.

She cried – again!

"Oh, no," she told him. "Not for the first time, I'm soaking your shirt with my tears."

She was laughing, crying, unsure whether to be happy or sad.

He kissed her lovingly, then bags in tow departed for *Departures*.

She returned home and slept for eleven hours straight, worn out but in a land of milk and honey.

She owed it to her employers to give it her all and that is what she did. Spent as much spare time with Suzi as she could, still startled at the little one's attention deficit.

In-between there was courting by phone, web and US Mail.

Between work and the mounting concerns over Suzi, she found her hopes of visiting him in Bali foundering. It wasn't deliberate, she yearned for him … and she told him so. In the blink of an eye, nearly a year had gone by and a part of her was jumpy that she might lose him.

Hence, when he told her in one of their telephone love-ins that he couldn't wait any longer her head was swimming.

She should never have doubted him. He said he had requested some further leave and would arrive the following week. She put in for annual vacation and it was granted.

It was decided they would go away for a short two-centre break, seeing the sights of Chicago, then moving on to Niagara Falls.

They took a stroll along the Riverwalk, which hugs the main branch of the Chicago River, restaurants, bars and offices at every turn, and a skyline of the city's most illustrious architecture.

She showed him Soldier Field, home of the Chicago Bears football team.

Next, onwards to Niagara.

23

Did you know that more than six million cubic feet of water goes over the crest of the falls every minute? Well, you know now.

Awesome, stand out, spectacular … a genial giant.

They did what every tourist has to do and took a Maid of the Mist boat cruise, which has carried passengers into the rapids immediately below since 1846.

They clung to each other as the craft bobbed and weaved, soaked by the spray, the thin plastic rain jackets provided of little practical value. At the benign mercy of one of North America's natural wonders – up there with the Rockies, the Grand Canyon and Yellowstone.

Later that evening, the sun going down, a fading red orb mottling the heavens, sitting in the garden at the motel where they were staying, he proposed. As is tradition, he got down on one knee, produced a ring from a little purse in one of his pockets, and asked her to marry him. It was how she had dreamed it might be when a little girl.

"Yes, yes, yes … a thousand times yes," she shouted aloud, and flung herself into his arms.

This was the man she loved, this was the man she wanted babies with, this was the man with whom she would grow old. Women in love the world over say the exact same thing and it doesn't always pan out. Abby knew it would.

The ring didn't fit and she playfully told him he was hapless, but of course that could easily be rectified.

Then admired the delicate array of stones.

Their lovemaking that night hit new orgasmic highs.

They would always remember that quaint motel in Niagara.

Indeed, when they got back to Normal she knew that, like Suzi, her life would never be normal again.

Abby went straight to her parents, and announced the news. She hugged her mum, she hugged her dad, she hugged John, John hugged her mum and was given a resounding handshake by her father. Amid gasps, John formally asked her father's permission, which he graciously gave.

Champagne, lots of it, was uncorked and there were toasts to the engaged couple.

Uncles and aunts fetched up seemingly out of nowhere, the neighbours were invited round, high fives, and it turned into a party, many an admiring examination of the ring and lots of advice on where to get it sized.

Eventually, tipsy but elated, they poured themselves back home, clutching a full Champagne bottle … because there had to be one last toast – to Robert and Rose.

That night there was no lovemaking – both Abby and John were far too smashed.

Somehow, Suzi had slept right through. Next day Abby and John, slightly worse for wear, called by to tell her of the engagement and show her the ring.

There were no smiles, she was sullen, pulling tufts of fur out of a small teddy and scattering them all over the room.

Abby was disappointed but accepting. Marriage was a difficult concept for a little girl to get her head round.

They telephoned John's parents in England. They too were thrilled for them and expressed a natural desire to meet Abby as soon as it could be arranged. Abby said John had told her lots about them. She would do her utmost to live up to being their daughter-in-law. They told her she would be received into the bosom of the family.

Abby felt enriched but it brought them back to earth.

They sat down to thrash out how their peripatetic lifestyle, thousands of miles apart, could be turned into the permanence they craved.

She offered to hand in her notice, leave Normal, and join him in Bali.

Knowing how hard she would find it to be away from those so dear to her, and continue her guardianship duties towards Suzi, he ruled that out. Instead, he would speak to his line manager and try to get a posting closer to the United States. Once that came through, they could set a date for the wedding.

Deducing this might prove difficult to achieve, she asked him whether he was sure. Might it not put a black mark against his name? Adversely affect chances of promotion.

He joked about how indispensable he was.

He would lay the circumstances on thick. Hopefully, they would be sympathetic.

It was bound to take many months and, in the interim, they would just have to cling on to their dream, get those phone lines zinging, and hit the letter-writing trail once more.

And, she pledged, if it rumbled on then as soon as she was due more holiday she would be on a flight to Bali.

When he left the next day there were fewer tears because both knew their destiny was to shine like the stars.

24

Somewhere along the line, happiness to sadness, it was agreed with the church, as with Kevin's four dead friends, that a memorial service should be held for Robert and Rose. Their bodies hadn't been found and it was time to accept that they may never be.

The family were dignified – they wanted a simple service lauding two ordinary lives.

Their wishes were respected.

On the day, the place was wall-to-wall. Every seat taken. Standing around the sides and the back. People spilled out into the church grounds amidst the gravestones, though this had been anticipated with speakers set up to relay the service to those unable to fit within.

The tributes were touching. Robert and Rose as toddlers, pride in passing school exams, the high standards they set themselves, a love affair that glowed, marriage, parenthood.

By the end, there was barely a dry eye.

The family filed out feeling at peace. They were sure Robert and Rose were at peace too.

Members of the congregation who chose to do so made their way to the house where a spread of food, home-made lemonade, cups of tea and coffee had been laid on. No alcohol – it didn't seem appropriate when it was two young lives, different had it been, say, an elderly person whose full span could be celebrated in all its richness.

Many did go back, talked about the good times, came up with anecdotes, met with friends and acquaintances, and expressed their condolences.

There was solace that so many cared.

People left in their own good time.

Languid and patient was the *theme*.

Soon a lot of other people were also having to be patient as Suzi entered pre-school and threatened to cause chaos. Paint would be sloshed about, there would be screaming and spitting, kids were pushed and pinched and, while teacher was trying to read a story, objects would be thrown at other children.

Her first nursery asked Suzi to leave, saying she was too disruptive.

Sara and Jeb knew her behaviour left much to be desired but it was surely harsh to expel someone so distressed, someone with no mother or father to set an example.

The place refused to reconsider.

They tried a second playgroup and she lasted longer there. However that came to an abrupt end when Suzi was caught trying to stab another child with a pair of scissors.

At home, it was much the same – the dog was still getting it in the neck and everywhere else on its body. Garden flowers would be pulled out. Creepy crawlies would be battered with stones. Crockery was being smashed.

Jeb and Sara tried kindness, they tried infinite good humour, they tried verbal discipline and, at their wits end, they tried corporal punishment. However, smacking Suzi prompted even worse behaviour along with outright defiance.

They took her to a child psychiatrist but butter wouldn't have melted in her mouth during the entire consultation, and the woman couldn't find anything wrong.

Abby sought to take the weight off her parents. She would chivvy Suzi out on nature rambles, to parks, sit with her in front of the television, read books galore to her. It took its toll especially when abused in public and private by this little minx. Poor Abby was constantly being told by Suzi that she was a 'cow' and she 'hated her'.

Of course, Suzi didn't always understand what she was saying, Abby accepted that, but it nevertheless got to you. Like the drip, drip, drip of Chinese water torture. Yet there was an intelligent child somewhere in there. If only her energies could be channelled.

And, all the while, regular as clockwork, the letters from Kevin kept arriving. Jeb and Sara always read them – just in case. Nothing had come up which required their intervention, but you could never be sure. The letters outlined the experiences of a self-ostracised adult male, a meaningless existence – no ambition, adrift from those around him, out of kilter with society.

Sara accepted there were uncanny similarities between Suzi and her rescuer but revolted at the connotation – preferring to put this down to coincidence. Perhaps, thought Sara, she was making more of it than was there. She hoped so. Yet the two of them, Suzi and Kevin, in their own ways both seemed estranged from the rest of humanity.

Maybe when Suzi started full-time education she would turn the page. That school routine and organised lessons would shift her onto the straight and narrow.

Sara didn't want to think about the alternative.

There were no such tantrums from Kevin – his parents might have preferred that there were.

He pulled his weight around the house – doing the dishes, making his bed, putting washing on the line. Yet he had become so subdued, introspective, almost reclusive. He showed no signs of wanting to go back to his job and no signs of returning to the flat they had bought him when he first joined the sports agency.

The first anniversary of the crash was looming.

If they could just persuade him that employment would be therapy – keeping him sufficiently busy with the minutiae of daily existence that he could no longer spend his days fixating on *his woes*. After all, worse things happen in life.

Indeed it was beholden on him to pull his finger out as his boss had been incredibly generous, job mothballed, paying his wages. Everyone knew that couldn't continue ad infinitum. So when the office submitted he do two days a week initially and see how it went, it raised the bar.

The family played it low key – or rather that was what they sought to convey – while surreptitiously beavering away at his psychology.

Work had been ever so encouraging despite little reciprocity, sending chocolates and flowers to the house, and mocking up a video revolving around a spoof hunt for the missing Kevin.

Even Kevin could not but fail to find it a laugh.

At last, he was talked into making a comeback.

However, the big day found him a quivering wreck, simpering in his bedroom and unwilling to come out. His mother phoned in, said there had been a hiccup, it would be short-lived. Keep the faith.

For the next month, they pummelled him.

There were jaunts to bars and barbeques, a whale-watching cruise, a cookery course, and they took him to their local church on Sundays hoping that the love emanating from the congregation would stir his dynamic.

It paid dividends.

He seemed to become less aloof. There were spells of jocularity and joviality. For his part, Kevin appreciated that the family were pulling out all the stops. Their devotion was selfless. He could see where they were coming from, to resist would be a poor show, and gradually he accepted his 'fate'.

Somehow, all over the place, he forced himself through the office door.

Several years later he compared it to what it must have been like to 'go over the top' during World War I. The likes of Passchendaele where so many Australians died. Such temerity and irreverence was indicative of his shallow thought processes.

All the guys and girls made a fuss of him – being as tactile as they could.

The prodigal son had returned.

25

That first day he didn't do much. Back to where it all started – making the tea! Ploughed through emails. Read up on new clients added to the roster during his absence. Generally tried to catch up. Much the same the next day. Like returning to school after missing half the term through illness.

That was his week done – he had survived the crash and now he had survived this.

In part because all had been given instructions on how to handle it. Sufficient to enable them to put on an act to conceal their shock at the dark torpor of someone who had faced such a wretched roll of the dice.

He was gaunt, he was pallid, he was careworn.

On the Friday, there was a get-together of management and staff to talk through what they might do to boost his spirits. It was obvious to everyone that they couldn't just shunt him on to normal duties.

Delicate.

Front-facing tasks would have to be on hold while he built up his capacity. Perhaps purely office-based for the first month, tidying up CVs, running errands, answering the phones. Maybe after that shadowing others at client events and marketing opportunities. All the time talking to him, involving him in office bluster, chewing the fat over a pint after work.

They weren't social workers, but Kevin was a fair dinkum bloke and his predicament plugged into the corporate philanthropy of sheltering the less fortunate. What he had gone through – it could have been any of them. It could have crippled any of them.

Increasingly, mental health was a big issue.

Should they try to set him up with a girl, mooted one optimist? That got laughed down amidst claims that the perpetrator should sort himself out first and gags about the sports agency morphing into a dating agency. What was wrong with that, said a joker. Dating agencies probably made more money than sports agencies.

Soft porn was the thing, said another wilfully.

Howls of derision, and the meeting broke up amid amusement and insult.

They would muddle through – Kevin would surely come round.

And indeed he did.

Gradually they gave him extra bits and pieces to tackle and over a six-month period he was doing more and more while graduating back to a five day week.

Albeit the bouncy, full of ideas Kevin was not back. It was a more plodding Kevin, a Kevin who was reactive rather than proactive, a Kevin who did not seem to have his heart in the job and certainly did not wear it on his sleeve. The chutzpah was missing. Interaction with clients lacked the Midas touch. The final product was not quite there.

He moved back into his flat but gone was the happy-go-lucky lad whose love of life shone through. Out socially, which wasn't often, he would be first to make his excuses after a hesitant couple of drinks. He was awkward with the opposite sex when once he could charm the birds out of the trees.

Things had plateaued and it was unrealistic as the years rolled by to think one day he might be rid of the shadow hanging over him.

There was the one-year anniversary, the five-year anniversary, the inquiry itself seeming never ending.

It had become a disability though the family were thankful that the depression and melancholy had been assuaged if never far from the surface.

He was with a sports agency yet his love of sport had virtually evaporated. He never returned to playing rugby, didn't get along to watch the cricket much either. He worked out on a static cycle in his spare room when he felt the call but that was about it. From a peak of fitness, he had become a couch potato.

This all spilled over into his employment. Even being generous, you would call his performance merely adequate. There was no advancement. He was marooned on the lower rungs of the ladder.

His thirtieth birthday passed with just a modest family celebration – mum, dad, Vicky and that was it. He had insisted he didn't want anything out of the ordinary, no big party, no presents. They bombed out the no presents rule … but acquiesced on the party front.

Old friends were fixing themselves up with partners, getting married, having children. Some invited him to stag celebrations, at home and abroad. He told them it wasn't for him. Since Becky nobody had sprinkled him with stardust. Or rather, he had never allowed them to.

Nights in the flat with a book, TV, film, listening to music – that was the level of a typical week.

In short, he seemed to be missing out on much of what life offered.

26

Abby too feared life was passing her by.

Weeks turned into months; she was still in Normal and John was still in Bali. Yes, they were in contact all the time but Abby was eager to become a wife and hopefully a mother.

Becoming grumpy in her work, with the family and even with John who was every now and then an outlet for her bile. So much so that she found herself picking faults in him – where was the spontaneity, he didn't send her flowers, he did serious rather too well, was he trying hard enough to bring this exile to a swift conclusion?

The doubts appalled her. She told herself she had her Mr Marvellous, someone with a good job and salary, up-standing, loyal, and who loved her. Stop this drivel, Abby, she told *squirrel*, the cuddly toy she took to bed with her as a child and which these days stood in prime place on the chest of drawers.

John too was frustrated. His superiors had taken on board the reasons for his transfer request but were reluctant to let him go and certainly not without having a successor lined up.

The diplomatic machine grinds interminably slowly. There were days when he felt like screaming at them to get their arses into gear. Not something of course *a chap*, in English public school parlance, put into practice – that would scupper everything.

To his shame, his conversations with Abby were sometimes testy. Having to wait was in some ways a vetting – were they truly right for each other? Not that he wanted it that way. He didn't do quarrels – that was not in his makeup. His inclination was always to deflect confrontation and he accepted this was both a strength and a weakness. But there was little he could do to expedite things and there was nothing else for it but nose to the grindstone.

Both of them were almost tearing their hair out when ten months on from him first raising it his boss called him aside one day. Would he like to go to Toronto?

He almost leapt in the air – he knew it was the closest he was going to get, and 'thank you, sir'. It sounded ideal.

The first thing he did was tot up the distances between Normal and Toronto – nine hours by car, one and a half hours by plane to Central Illinois Regional Airport at Bloomington-Normal.

Next, he phoned Abby.

Abby was having a bad day. Things had gone wrong at work, Suzi had been frightful when she visited, and she was in the middle of her tea. She felt a mess and she wasn't in the mood.

What did he want?

And instantly regretted her brusqueness.

He overlooked the sideswipe knowing his news would transcend whatever it was which had riled her.

He almost shouted it out – a posting to Toronto.

She screamed, started blowing kisses to him down the line, and couldn't get the stream of words out fast enough. "Oh, John, I love you, I love you, I love you. When? What about the wedding? I'm going to have so much to do. Darling, that's wonderful."

They knew Toronto was a splendid city – on Lake Ontario, an international centre of business, finance, arts, and culture – and how fortunate they were.

"Eat your tea – it will be going cold," he scolded.

She couldn't care less about her tea. She only wanted to digest this fabulous news. It meant they could at last be together and yet in relatively easy reach of Normal so she could continue to play a role in Suzi's life. She owed it to Robert and Rose. Suzi was hard work, but keeping on her case was non-negotiable. Sure, once she had children herself it would be a challenge to maintain the same closeness. She would do what she could.

John didn't yet know the Toronto timeframe but once a decision had been taken there was a tendency to get it done quickly.

Abby wanted to know what was 'quick'.

Maybe three to four weeks.

She freaked out.

But what about the wedding, she asked again.

He laughed and told her haughtily: "Well, get on the case and organise it pronto."

She screamed again … and now they were both laughing.

On a high, pogoing towards being re-united at last, combined with the likelihood of a mad rush to get married, she was in a complete flap. They broke off the call in loving raptures to enmesh themselves in the solemn commitment they were about to make and all that revolved around it.

Abby went in search of her parents, dancing gaily as she went.

She found them distracted.

Sure enough, it was Suzi again.

27

It was the hurdle they knew was closing in on them and they had no idea how they were going to front up.

Suzi was asking about what had become of her mummy and daddy. Everyone else seemed to have one so why not her?

The first time it cropped up Jeb and Sara ducked and weaved, with Suzi drawn off by a game of hide and seek. Subsequently she seemed to forget all about it.

It was weeks later that the issue was revisited.

"Granny?"

"Yes, dear."

"What's happened to my mummy and daddy? I can't find them anywhere. Are they lost?"

Sara was thrown, but, thinking on her feet, replied: "Well, Suzi, in a way they are lost."

She wasn't ready for the response.

"Why can't we find them?" asked Suzi.

Then, she tugged at granny's arm.

"Come on Granny – let's look in the garden. They might be there."

Sara was stumped by this purest form of child logic, but thought she had better go along with it.

So they went out into the garden and began to search for Robert and Rose.

They searched behind bushes and trees, no one in the garden shed, and nobody hiding in the garage.

"I know," said Suzi. "Let's get Lady. The police always have dogs when they are hunting bad men."

Gosh, thought, Sara, how had she ever learned that? A troubled child but a bright child.

Suzi went into the house. There was much calling of Lady's name and banging of doors. No doubt, Lady was trying not to be found as usual. Eventually she burst out the back quickly followed by Suzi.

Lady ran to Sara as if for protection, her baleful eyes asking what all this was about. But Suzi was calling the shots.

She pointed at Lady. "Go and find mummy and daddy."

Lady looked again to Sara for guidance.

"Go and find mummy and daddy, you stupid dog," ranted Suzi, waving her arms.

Lady shot off all over the place, charging about aimlessly, darting here and sniffing there, with Suzi trying to keep up but failing.

Until Lady was back at square one with Sara.

Suzi was quickly becoming fed up.

She berated the poor thing. "Shoo, shoo, find, find." She aimed a swipe of her hand at Lady who yelped and sped away.

Another mad circle of the garden ensued.

In the pursuit, most undignified, Suzi landed on her backside, levered herself up, took a couple of steps, fell over again, picked herself off the ground, spotted Lady and on went the chase.

Before Lady thrashed around in the plants and emerged with a smelly old tennis ball, depositing it at Suzi's feet with a *perhaps this is what she wants* expression.

"Bad dog, bad dog." She threw the tennis ball at Lady who caught it in mid-air thinking perhaps Suzi wanted to play a game.

But it just made Suzi ever hyper.

She bent down, garnered some soil from a flowerbed and hurled it towards Lady.

Disgusted – what did this infuriating child-human want – Lady espied the still open door and bounded back inside.

Sara had been watching this whole piece of theatre, chuckling to herself – surely something of an early Charlie Chaplin caper.

Suzi didn't see the funny side. Got the hump big time. Indeed, she was almost apoplectic. Sara received short shrift. "I hate you," shrieked Suzi. "I bet you've stolen mummy and daddy – you pig."

That set off Sara into another giggling fit, which in turn infuriated Suzi even more. She ran into the house shouting, swearing, screaming, with Sara hot on her tail. It took many conciliatory words and two bribes, a favourite cartoon on the television accompanied by a Hershey bar, to scrape her off the ceiling. Suzi eventually relented, hands, face and top covered in chocolate, trying to take in the cartoon characters' antics. However, it left Sara on notice that the big question was becoming unavoidable.

When Abby revealed her news about Toronto, her mother and father said they were so pleased for her, but it didn't come through as expressive as it normally would have done. She could see this whole Suzi thing was having an effect on them and she was no longer going to be on the doorstep. Now she was able to pop round when they needed her. Soon, she was going to have to plan her trips carefully. Was she doing the right thing?

They assured her she was. Told her much as the link with Suzi was central to them all she could not compromise her happiness. John was made for her and theirs was a partnership that held such promise. Otherwise, she would regret it for the rest of her days.

How Abby wanted to be curled up in his arms once more.

Nevertheless, the imponderables were building. They had to provide some sort of explanation for Suzi. She would also have to break it to her that she was going away, and then there was the whole hectic wedding.

Not so hectic after all as it turned out.

Toronto got pushed back – some hitch over John's replacement in Bali and when he could take up the position – and the marriage ended up being delayed for a year. It was a choker and a let-down but on the upside it meant they could make it the best ever.

Must however guard against the uncertainty destabilising Suzi yet again.

And all this coming as the youngster was closing in on school age.

To meet this triple bill head on, Abby was fervently of the view that Suzi too could rise to the occasion. But would she?

A strategy was agreed.

First, cautiously make mention of mummy and daddy and why they weren't around. At the same time getting Robert and Rose's picture albums out.

Next, Abby would reveal to Suzi that marriage to John was on the horizon at last.

They would then talk Toronto with her, hoping that Suzi could be coaxed into being happy for Abby rather than taking the view that she was being deserted.

It was going to be a huge ask.

How much would she take in? Would she lose it? Certainly too it would be just the start. She was bound to get even more inquisitive as she got older.

Sara, Jeb, Abby and Suzi had been grocery shopping. Suzi had assisted in putting all the goodies away in cupboards, fridges and freezers.

"Wo," Sara told Suzi, "You have been busy. You've been a great help. I don't know what we would do without you. Let's get you a glass of juice and have a sit-down."

When everyone was comfy they got going.

Sara took the lead. "Suzi, you know we were talking the other day about mummies and daddies."

Suzi, who for some reason was unusually amenable, remained still, waiting for whatever was coming.

"Well, sadly, very sadly, very very sadly, your mummy and daddy had an accident and have gone to heaven. That's why Granny and Grandad look after you."

Sara had planned to say a lot more but prematurely ground to a halt.

Suzi eyed them quizzically. As expected, uncomprehending.

There was one of those silences which last seconds but feel like hours.

When Suzi spoke, it took them all by surprise. "Can I visit them in heaven?"

For all three adults it was the same reaction – lump in throat and hearts melting for the little one and her bravery.

Sara racked her brains as to how to respond. Nothing came to mind that would cover it. So she said: "Heaven is where God lives, Suzi. He takes great care of all those who go to heaven, but I'm afraid visitors are not allowed."

"Why not?" said Suzi.

Abby took over. "Suzi, we've got lots of photographs of mummy and daddy here." She opened up an album. "Would you like to see some of them?"

A curious Suzi got up and went to sit beside Abby and they began to go through the snaps.

She saw Robert and Rose as young children, playing, kindergarten, learning to swim, in school uniform, singing in the choir, as teenagers, university students and getting married.

Abby finished off with Suzi in the arms of her parents. It had been a fast spin through and missing loads out, but it had still taken some thirty

97

or so minutes. Abby had tried to make it lively, something of a game even … so as not to overwhelm her niece and it degenerating into a classroom lesson.

Abby closed the album. "Was that interesting?"

"Yes," announced Suzi. "It was jolly interesting. I wish mummy and daddy could be here now." Then she was off, skipping and jumping. "When is lunch ready? My tummy's empty."

They were all thankful for Suzi changing the subject.

How remarkable that children can seemingly compartmentalise these things. Albeit for sure the topic had merely been allayed while Suzi took in the mass of information.

She had done so well.

28

For Kevin, it began to dawn that the job at the sports agency wasn't going anywhere.

He should have been mortified because this was the position he had coveted and been good at. Now he was treading water and to be frank couldn't give a monkey's. He definitely wasn't getting the same satisfaction – it had turned into a chore.

He had become an embarrassment.

Yet more or less bomb-proof because no company would want the public dishonour of sacking the people's standard-bearer.

In a way that made it worse.

Kevin knew he wasn't pulling his weight and he knew that his colleagues knew he wasn't pulling his weight.

He was letting them down.

But might he be pawning his future were he to sack it off? What would he do? How would he pay the bills? His self-esteem could take a fearful hit. He was getting a reasonable salary. The money just rolled into his bank account. Why disturb the arrangement? Yet, argued his alter ego, if it ended tomorrow something would surely turn up. Perhaps it was time for a fresh start.

By coincidence, as this *should I/shouldn't I* contortion was bugging him, it turned out to be the week for office annual appraisals. Down the years Kevin had rarely met anyone who thought annual appraisals were worth the paper they were written on. Lies and bullshit – that was the general appraisal of appraisals. It was a charade, an annual word game, with only the vaguest correlation between assessment criteria and the actual job itself.

Generally, people knew full well where things were going wrong, but these were forbidden avenues because it would inevitably point the finger at those over-promoted imbeciles who frankly weren't up to it – the management lackeys and yes-men who had clambered up the greasy pole by keeping their nose clean, never querying anything, doing it by the book, heaping praise on the dead-wood ahead of them until it came to stabbing them in the back, and robotically imposing the official business creed. Creeps who never thought out of the box, showed no originality and disavowed individualism.

According to the management handbook it had value as an instrument for galvanising the workforce but in reality it was worthless, box-ticking veneer – demeaning, loathsome, and contemptuous.

Typically, no one believed in it, not even the management.

The sort of cosy set-up which once in a blue moon got blown apart by a whistle-blower or economic crisis. Which normally resulted in gross cost-cutting, eroded pay scales, the departure of those who were good, cynicism, resentment, and wholesale change introduced by consultants and bean counters who knew nothing of the business concerned, saw no purpose in knowing about the business concerned, and operated through algorithms and computer predictions.

So much for appraisals, albeit in a small set-up like the sports agency much looser ties tended to exist.

There are always exceptions to any rule of thumb.

Kevin presumed little from the exercise apart from a wasted thirty minutes to an hour as both parties circled around facets into which neither dared delve.

The meeting was being conducted by the assistant managing director Rick Ronda, one of those plastic-faced gnomes who played a dead bat. Didn't give praise; didn't give grief. Hard to like but nothing to dislike.

Yet, for once, the discussion bumbled into areas of mutual interest where neither had intended to go. Not caring either way, Kevin said he wasn't getting as much out of the job as previously. Ronda said management felt he was perhaps not contributing to the extent he had before the plane crash. Kevin acknowledged his enthusiasm had waned. Ronda said Kevin was well respected, but perhaps there were other scenarios.

It took all of Kevin's will-power to keep a straight face. They both knew this was management-speak for *do you want out*? Kevin muttered the usual claptrap back along the lines of the only certainty being change and the meeting ground on with vague reference to *alternative solutions*.

To cover his back, Ronda emphasised that this was purely exploratory. Nevertheless, times were tight and the management were postulating whether there might be scope for staff to put their names forward for redundancy – no guarantee they would necessarily be accepted of course. They both knew this was more management-speak, this time for *we'll give you a pay-off to quit*.

Somewhat startled at how far down the line this had gone, they resolved to re-convene in due course once both parties had had time to reflect.

Now, by pure fluke, Kevin had shortly before the appraisal meeting bumped into a one-time school friend, David Sako – they hadn't met in years. There had been an amicable chat over a cup of coffee. Sako said he was in property, selling and letting houses. It was easy for anyone with a bit of flair and the gift of the gab. Lots of money to be made. They were always after good people – might Kevin be interested?

Kevin, wholly unfamiliar with the ins and outs of estate agency, flattered the fellow by saying it sounded enthralling, but then never gave it a second thought. Parting, they swopped business cards, and agreed to keep in touch – though with a casual insincerity.

However, in the wake of the appraisal, it was plain as a pikestaff that he ought to give Sako a ring and explore matters further.

I mean – how hard could it be? Conducting a trawl around the internet, it had its merits. Varied. Person to person. Sounded down his street.

They met up at the same coffee house and a serious discussion ensued. Sako proposed Kevin try it on a probationary basis and see how things went.

Kevin said he thought he would like to take up the offer, indicating in generalities what was going down at the sports agency and the likelihood of him moving on.

It was left in Kevin's hands. If his answer was 'yes' then he could start more or less immediately. Subsequently, if the trial proved a success for both parties, then his recruitment would be confirmed.

By the time the appraisal resumed Kevin had pretty much decided to take the money and run. He and Ronda sat down again – the venue being the usual spartan meeting room where bars on the windows were the one missing accoutrement. Might as well take the bull by the horns – *had the company a standard package for anyone who might be inclined towards redundancy?* He sat back chuffed at such back-to-front garbage – management-speak wasn't simply the preserve of management.

Ronda said it was usual for anyone stepping down through ill-health and the like to get two weeks' pay for every year of service. It was the first time they had alluded to ill-health and Kevin got the message – they believed the crash had turned him into a nutter.

Yet he didn't much care what they thought. Perhaps he was a nutter – admittedly the whole thing still seemed to fog his senses, like being disorientated in rain and mist atop a mountain in winter, not that living in Australia he had ever found the need to be up a mountain in winter. So, OK, they could make him out to be a basket case, just as long as the package was so nuts it would be impossible to decline.

But Ronda still held the floor and continued to speak. In the truly exceptional circumstances that were Kevin's the company would agree one month's pay for every year of service.

Now thirty-two, Kevin had been there for fourteen years – that meant he'd get more than a year's pay buckshee, plus recompense for any holiday entitlement not taken up by the due date.

In addition, there would be a goodwill bonus.

All in all the offer came to a highly appealing and hefty sum. There would be no requirement on him to work his notice. Ronda advocated he go away and think about it. They would pay him to speak to an employment lawyer should he wish to take that up.

Kevin said a cooling off period was definitely a good idea.

"Take the rest of the week," said Ronda. "Come back on Monday and let me know your decision."

Kevin retrieved his jacket from the back of his seat and set off to the flat.

Perhaps, he concluded, Ronda wasn't the total twat he had him figured for at the outset. There was some compassion there after all. He was just another grunt trying to turn a dollar.

The deal was decent, but then, to give them their due, the company had generally been decent to him throughout his career there.

29

He went back to his parents' place for the weekend and told them he was thinking of leaving, outlining what was on the table.

His mother was against it – he was in a secure job, they had always looked after him, and it could be a big mistake.

His father was of the opposite persuasion. A new career; a new Kevin.

Sister sat firmly on the fence, saying only he could decide whether it felt right or not.

Kevin said he would sleep on it.

It was a lazy Sunday and nobody said anything about it until, while seated on the patio, drinking glasses of wine before lunch, Vicky could no longer resist.

Had he come to a conclusion?

Kevin said he had.

He would first try bluff, boxer Muhammad Ali's rope-a-dope tactics, and tell them he would take the package so long as they threw in the office car he used when he had to do outside meetings and client visits.

If they said *no* then he would take the package anyway.

That produced scorn, with everyone talking at once, the thesis being that Kevin was a total chancer. They'd never give him the car too, surely.

"Well, we'll see," chimed a jaunty Kevin.

It wasn't directly mentioned but he must surely be back in business if he could come up with a bare-faced wheeze like this.

The atmosphere lightened completely, there was laughter, merriment … it was a good day. Such that Kevin hadn't known with his loved-ones since before the crash.

The next morning he sat opposite Ronda like a poker player going for the big one. He'd never played poker but felt like a cardsharp.

He showed his hand.

Ronda went away and consulted.

Ten minutes later he came back into the room. The car was his.

However, the guttural, no nonsense, turn of phrase in which it was said meant that was it. They wouldn't be pushed any further. It was take it or leave it.

Hey, how badly did they want shot of him! It said something about the encumbrance he had become.

It was agreed. They shook hands.

It would entail a day or two to get the paperwork in order and a week after that to pay the money over.

But, they noted, Kevin was at liberty to take the car home that evening.

The office telegraph was at work – everyone knew something was up though they weren't sure what. After all, Kevin hadn't done a stroke for several days.

"Come on, what's this all about," demanded one of the brasher ones.

Kevin said he was sworn to secrecy – they would find out soon enough.

He was elated … getting the car too was a coup. He was also cautious – like a hermit crab exchanging shells, switching jobs could leave you open to being eaten by predators.

In due course they dotted the i's and crossed the t's. He signed; they signed.

And, with what seemed indecent haste, as though they felt they were ridding themselves of a millstone around their necks, it was his leaving day.

To be fair, they gave him a fulsome send-off. The office came to a halt for three quarters of an hour late afternoon, some wine and nibbles had been laid on, they presented him with a card autographed by everyone complete with piss-takes, plus a laser measurer for working out the size of rooms – it had got about that he was toying with estate agency.

The MD had the usual *urgent meeting* to attend – not wishing to demean himself by supping with the plebs, it was presumed – but Ronda offered a nominal pat on the back along the lines of *long-serving Mr Reliable, thank you for your contribution, wish you well* … blah, blah, rubbish, rubbish.

Shouts of 'Speech, speech' shamed Kevin into replying.

Would miss them all, wished the company every good fortune, sorry to whoever would now take over the mantle of office dunce, joked he was leaving with the best tea-making skills of anyone in Australia, and free-wheeled to a halt amidst much mirth and rapport.

The wine was drunk, some tall tales were told and it was off to one of the local bars. Most stayed a respectable length of time before moving on, a handful hung around for an hour and a half, a trio of mates kept him company in a minor pub crawl … and then home.

All told, a reasonable way to go out.

He sat down in the flat and not for the first time dwelt on where he was headed – not a good idea. Beware over-philosophising – it can take you to dark places. Sometimes simpler to get on with life, accept there will be ups and downs, good and bad, success and failure, rich and poor.

30

Back in Normal, after being messed about for so long, the day of the wedding had come and Abby was in a spin.

Not all the flowers had been delivered, the 1950's Lincoln they had booked was going nowhere thanks to a blown tyre which was being mended at the side of a road somewhere in the back of beyond, and rain was pouring down instead of the promised sunshine.

A dozen of John's side of the family were attending from various parts of the US and England and Abby was desperate to put on a good show for them every bit as much as she wanted it to be perfect for her and her betrothed.

Then someone spilled a cup of coffee and it splashed onto one of the bridesmaid's dresses.

Finally, Suzi was in a frump, dancing in the rain outside, then refusing to have her hair tied in a bow. "I don't want to – it's yucky," she insisted for the umpteenth time.

Jeb and Sara were stalwarts. There was still two hours to go and a lot could happen in two hours. They'd seen it all before – things had a way of working out.

They felt sure of getting her to the church on time.

Jeb was on to the car hire company, Sara was getting coffee stains out of the dress, and, according to the local weather forecast, the rain would soon be replaced by sunshine and light cloud.

John was blissfully unaware.

He was just nervous, plenty nervous.

Geared up and hanging about aimlessly. Easy for men of course, except a trifle more complicated because he was resplendent in a kilt – the Munro tartan is a pre-eminent criss-crossing red, the bee's knees – sporran, plus a dirk hanging ferociously from his belt, all in tribute to the Scottish arm of the family.

Making small-talk, drinking cups of tea and praying nothing disastrous would impinge on proceedings, like having a coughing fit all of a sudden just as he prepared to kiss the bride.

"Take it steady, breathe in and breathe out," said best man Tommy, an old university friend. But Tommy had to make a speech at the breakfast so he wasn't in great shakes either. He pulled out a packet of fags. "Want a smoke?

John had never smoked in his life, yet his fingers hovered over taking that first cigarette.

"Go on," said Tommy. "One won't do you any harm. It'll calm you down."

John resisted. Smoke clung to your breath and your clothes. He didn't want to spoil it for Abby.

"Is my tie straight?"

It was the fourth time in twenty minutes he had parroted the same hogwash. Had he been in his eighties they would have tested for short-term memory loss or maybe even Alzheimer's.

"Yes," insisted Tommy. "Relax."

One hour to go and Abby was afraid her hair still wasn't right. Wrong, said Sara, not a hair out of place. Now, mum's the word.

The florist had been rounded up and was on the way with a second drop of flowers.

"Have the orders of service made it to the church?"

"Yes," said her dad.

Was he sure those leather shoes he hadn't worn in years were going to hold up?

"I went out last week and bought new ones."

Where were the flight tickets for the honeymoon in Hawaii?

"In my pocket."

Half an hour to go and the missing flowers surfaced.

The hire firm phoned to say the tyre was fixed and they were making good progress.

Twenty minutes to go and John and Tommy were walking into the church with an air of confidence which they certainly didn't feel.

Fifteen minutes to go and the rain had stopped.

Ten minutes to go and the cars drew up.

Carefully, ever so carefully, Abby, Jeb and the bridesmaids manoeuvred themselves into them.

Suzi, hair in a bow after all, tried to splash in a puddle and was bodily picked up by one of the chauffeurs and placed in the specified limousine, much to her chagrin.

The cavalcade left for the church and now there was a new dread.

They were going too slow, Abby told her father, as the fleet took it sedately through the town amid applause from bystanders and acquaintances.

Fashionably late by five or maybe ten minutes was one thing – all brides were fashionably late – but to be twenty or, God forbid, thirty minutes late would be mortifying. She could not do that to poor John – doubts would be kicking in; was she ill, had there been an accident, had he been jilted?

Nearly there, insisted dad.

And as the words came out of his mouth, the church came into view.

They were on time. Just as Jeb and Sara had predicted.

Exiting the vehicles there was a lot more kafuffle as they sorted themselves out, brushed down dresses, and made tiny adjustments.

Five minutes later Jeb was walking his radiant daughter down the aisle as the organ music rang out and shafts of sunlight danced through the stained glass windows.

John thrust out his jaw, said a silent vote of thanks, and snuck a quick glance towards his oncoming bride. She was indeed radiant.

She arrived alongside him, they smiled, the minister offered reassurance, and then led them through it.

For the two of them the service passed in a blur.

The minister extolled the vows they were exchanging, marriage was a wondrous institution beloved of God, marriages faced many obstacles, but he was sure theirs would be a loving and fulfilling union.

For both, when he pronounced them husband and wife, it was the most beautiful feeling. John and Abby kissed, goose bumps running down her spine, cheers from the congregation.

Sara shed a tear – mothers were allowed.

So the di Matteos and the Munros were joined on United States soil. Definitely a portrayal of the American Dream.

The reception struck the right note – a multitude of congratulations for the new Mr and Mrs Munro, carefree dancing, some high jinks…

The speeches were serious and frivolous, nothing too outlandish.

Tommy's was nearest the knuckle. A line about how he hoped their marriage would be like the chicken that had proved such a delightful main course – a bit of leg, a bit of breast, and lots of stuffing! One of those that hovered between hilarity and opprobrium … before falling just the side of hilarity.

Phew!

They let him off.

Guessing she could probably get away with just about anything for a day, Suzi hid under the table drapes, discovered she liked wedding cake, her face smothered in it, and took a sneaky taste of champagne from a half-empty glass when nobody was looking. It was grotty, and she spat it out. She jigged around the dance floor like a big person and eventually, shattered, Sara carried her up to the room in which they were staying and put her to bed.

31

Another new experience came just a year later when she started 'big' school.

Mostly she was OK with it.

Being an orphan, the teachers kept an eye on her to ensure she integrated with the rest of the class. She was the sort of kid who needed goals. Get her to respond and state her case. When it came to reading and writing, she got on with her learning, picking it up quicker than most.

Yet there was no love for school. You would probably say she was inured to the whole institutionalised fait accompli.

Simply waiting to rebel.

Her interaction with other pupils was decidedly dicey. There were times she was playing happily and other times when chairs were turned over, faces scratched and kids traduced. To the extent that her classmates saw her as a loose cannon who could explode with no warning. It made making friends difficult.

The staff sought to lay down the law on how to behave. Their interventions were cold-shouldered. Suzi always knew best and she could be a right little madam.

You would see boys crying in corners, complaining their toes had been stamped on. Girls would be howling, their pigtails pulled viciously. It was always Suzi and always she was nowhere to be found. And when the reckoning came the *charm tap* allowed her to talk her way out of so much.

As for lessons, she liked history – the birth and rise of America as a nation – music, and English. Yet overall, she treated school as a bore, which frustrated both her teachers and Jeb and Sara. They tried to elucidate how vital learning was, providing a foot up the ladder, a chance to better yourself ... but found Suzi impassive and unimpressed. And when into her orbit came computer games, social media, and all the rest of the tech slough of despond, then her road ahead was set.

Work and lessons were relegated down the list of priorities in favour of trolling and hip-hop.

It was the start of her disaffection for school and authority generally, a travesty given her intelligence.

Bullying the swots who did want to do well became category one. She had turned into one of the bad girls and she began to revere her hard nut image.

There were staff pow-wows about what to do with her. A group-think with Jeb and Sara. Nobody was able to come up with an answer.

At the age of ten, she began playing truant.

Jeb and Sara would cajole her into school and at the first break she would just walk out. She was done for shoplifting – it started with sweets, cola, jeans. Then it moved on to stealing purses and wallets, pocketing the money and dumping the rest in creeks, bins, drains – anywhere it was unlikely to be discovered.

Which is when the local police started taking greater interest.

Suzi and sidekick Molly Goodright were lifted from the streets, waste ground … anywhere they could get up to no good.

It was something of a game for Suzi. There was the kick of stealing and getting away with it. Running rings around grown-ups was funky. Not so funky being caught but all you ever got was a smack on the wrist. Aghast at what the neighbours must think, Sara and Jeb implored Suzi to put a halt to this counter-productive behaviour, and warned her she would end up in prison. Did she want that?

That wasn't how Suzi saw it.

She had never known her parents – stolen from her by adversity. Then Abby had cut and run, absconding to Toronto. Suzi felt betrayed. She felt rejected. School was a prison camp. Nobody understood her. Nobody cared. Therefore, nobody should expect her to care. She would please herself. She would wage war on society.

Much older, she would be able to look back and identify the flaws in those arguments. People did care. Sara and Jeb cared very much. Abby cared. The school cared. You don't always see it that way when you are young and impressionable.

How to reconcile that the underlying subliminal wounds from the plane crash and losing her parents had left an imprint on Suzi which could never be erased.

Just like on the other side of the globe nobody could relate to what Kevin was going through.

Suzi harshly treated; Kevin shredded and scarred.

Abby was shocked at the way Suzi was disintegrating.

32

Toronto had been humongous as had marriage.

Hawaii had been extraordinary. Neither of them had ever been there before. But, as the guidebooks state, the scenery, warm tropical climate, abundance of public beaches, oceanic environs, and active volcanoes give it X-factor. That is why they had decided to honeymoon there and they were not disappointed.

They took a number of trips, consumed by the islands' beauty. Like that first meeting on Bali. They reconnoitred each other – their bodies, their hopes, their foibles and their love.

Setting up home in Toronto was a new chapter. The embassy had found them an apartment to rent and they had invested a lot of themselves in the way they had decorated it and fitted it out. Much of that had been down to Abby as John's duties meant unsocial hours.

She had given herself eighteen months to make sure this marriage and the new home worked. There was the odd spat like with all newly-weds but they were very happy overall.

It was time to start applying for leisure/hospitality jobs – the practicalities meant reluctantly she had resigned the Normal one. Then a *stomach upset* proved anything but – she was pregnant.

They hadn't planned it but both of them were thrilled as were their families. Gosh. They were going to be parents. Everything would be transformed – first marriage, now parenthood. In a way not ideal – meeting, marriage, maternity. You wait ages for a bus and then three come at once. But, hey, they weren't thinking that way at all. They were very much absorbed in all that the future held.

There was one downside – circumstances dictated that Abby had been unable to get back to Normal and Suzi as much as she had wanted. Morning sickness had latterly knocked her for six. It hadn't sat well with Suzi and it hadn't sat well with Abby either.

It was back to being a "cow" and that was wounding.

Calling people names was mean, said Abby. Suzi wouldn't like it if the shoe was on the other foot.

But that was just weakness.

So she got called a "cow" all the time.

She tried to brush it off but these things gradually wear you down.

Abby gave it everything. What about going to the movies to catch a Disney film? Could she lend a hand with school work? Let's go strawberry picking. The response was as standard – "Go away, cow. I hate you."

Oh for goodness sake! Why did Suzi hate her? What had she done? Had she done something wrong? If she had, she was very sorry and would never do it again.

"Go away, cow. I hate you."

It was impossible.

Abby went back home again.

She sought the affirmation of her mother. She wanted to impart how much her baby was wanted. To inhale Sara and Jeb's joy at a second grandchild to dote over. John came with her for the weekend, leaving her in Normal to fly back to Toronto early on Monday morning for the start of the working week.

Sara and Jeb found both of them in sparkling form. Abby was blooming. John had a near permanent smile.

The conversation swung back to Robert and Rose. Sara and Jeb reminisced – a bit like at the memorial service – about Rose as a little girl, the fun times, getting through the terrible teens, her kindness and how she blossomed into a daughter of which they could be very proud, met Robert, got married, became a mother … and then … and then …

"Don't go there," said Abby. "Not on this day."

They went back to run of the mill – Normal's latest new roads and buildings, news about Abby's childhood friends, the weather, where they might go on holiday.

Suzi was out in the garden, unsuccessfully trying to throw stones at next door's conservatory. The neighbours had got used to her peccadillos and didn't voice their displeasure openly. Sarah and Jeb, they knew, had enough on their plate.

Abby sat down on what had been her favourite patio chair. "Suzi," she said. "Come here, sweetie, I've got something to tell you."

Suzi gave her one of those scathing looks.

This time there were no insults – John was around and Suzi was still trying to figure his personality and status in the family.

"Please Suzi," said Abby. "It's important."

There was something in the way she said it – an appeal to Suzi's better nature. Propelled by what it might mean, Suzi sauntered over.

Abby took her hands. "What would you think if I said you were going to have a little cousin?"

Suzi rubbed her eyes.

Abby tried again.

"I'm going to have a baby," she told Suzi. "That will be nice, won't it?"

However, Suzi still wasn't on the page.

"Where's the baby?" she asked, and spun around as if it should be behind her.

Abby sought to get on the same wavelength.

"We won't get the baby until near Christmas," said Abby.

"Christmas," said Suzi dreamily. "I like Christmas."

Suzi had worked out that Father Christmas was Grandad suited and booted. She hadn't let on. That way you got more presents.

"Is Father Christmas bringing the baby?"

A test for Abby.

"Well, not quite, but sort of," said Abby.

Suzi wasn't at all sure what that meant. She scanned her shoes. Watched a bird, its beak probing for worms in the grass. "Where's the baby now?"

"In my tummy," said Abby.

Suzi was nonplussed. There was a pregnant pause.

"What's it doing in your tummy?"

Abby realised this was all too much for her niece. "Babies are safe there when they're very tiny. When they're a bit bigger they pop out into the world. We'll have another chat when you are older."

Now bored of babies, Suzi left it there.

Instead, she chased the bird, which flew off smartly.

Abby laughed. Suzi laughed.

Abby hoped it wouldn't be the last laugh. As she had previously inferred, once the baby was born it would be nigh on impossible to return to Normal with any consistency.

The baby arrived on time but not without incident.

The gestation was routine. Lots to do – parent classes, going to the hospital for scans, preparing a nursery, getting a cot, a pram. The list went on and on. It kept Abby busy.

John did what he could – a loving father for sure but most likely to be uncoordinated when it came to babies' bottoms. She could not imagine that stinky nappies would ever be his thing. He insisted he would do his share – she gave him the benefit of the doubt.

Massive, uncomfortable, as her due date neared, she just wanted to get on with it.

When the day came and her waters broke John dashed back from work, got her to hospital and tried to be strong.

She had evinced one of those natural deliveries you seem to constantly read about in women's magazine where personalities – film, TV, music, sport – emerge from childbirth with not a blemish and back to a svelte figure in a week or so.

Yoga, birthing pool, no need for pain relief, seamless.

It's rarely like that in real life away from the showbiz bubble.

Hours went by, baby wasn't showing, Abby's blood pressure started rising, the infant was becoming distressed in the womb … and it all ended in an emergency Caesarean. A throng of doctors and nurses, medical equipment everywhere, all a bit scary, touch and go, but they got it out and averted catastrophe.

It was a boy; they had sifted through names, and had chosen Edward. Then, if desired, it could be shortened to Ed or Teddy.

The aftermath wasn't smooth either as it isn't for many first time parents. The baby always seemed to be crying, there were midnight feeds, sometimes it took 'til kingdom come to lull him back to sleep.

All this on top of how much the operation – because it is a major operation – had taken out of her.

John sought to weigh in but there was only so far that went – men don't breastfeed!

It all became a bit too much for Abby who began acting out of character and then off her trolley. She started *hearing things*. There were sudden panic attacks. Next came screaming fits that someone was intent on kidnapping the baby. She turned on John – he was a psycho who was casting spells on Edward. She became hysterical.

She wouldn't go to the doctor – he half cajoled and half dragged her there. The medics logged her haggard appearance – they knew a bad case of post-natal depression when they saw one.

When a nurse tried to take Edward to be weighed there was a near tug-of-war. Which ended with Abby sprawled on the floor. For a second John thought she was dead.

So many emotions flooded through him – shock, heartbreak, guilt, fear.

Fear for his wife and her health, guilt that somehow he should have done more, shock at the unseemly and frankly disturbing tussle he had just witnessed, heartbreak at Abby's distress, plus concern for the baby not least that he might be taken into care while his mother was so ill – thankfully it didn't come to that.

Abby was ten days being treated by mental health services as an in-patient. Baby with her so he could be fed and she could re-establish the maternal bond.

John visited whenever he was allowed which wasn't that often even though work were trying to be good – he had told them what they were going through.

She improved and they let her out, but not without misgivings and not without monitoring. They wanted to be sure she was fully adjusting to motherhood, and caring for the baby appropriately. What if she harmed the baby – mothers, unhinged, not knowing what they were doing, could be very devious? There must be no relapse.

Leaving Jeb to do what he could with Suzi, her own mother flew in from Normal. Taking the strain if Abby needed a break. Setting an example. Acting as a sounding board.

She left after three weeks, confident Abby was restored.

Yet it took a year to get the real Abby back.

John bent over backwards, slaved over cooking, cleaning, washing, submitted to indignities galore. And, yes, became adept at swabbing a bottom of poo.

He was rejected at every turn.

Nothing he did was right; she was always berating him.

By now, as knackered as her, a stone lighter, the ear-bashing was wearing him away. Their marriage was at times hanging by a thread. He dug in, kept taking it on the chin, downed a surreptitious whisky and ginger ale on nights she went to bed early, surely the fire and brimstone would subside.

It did.

At length she was her perky self, they were a proper family once more, and had reverted into loving conformity.

Many things had been jettisoned during this oh so destructive period … one of them being Suzi.

Abby's sole focus was Edward; there was no time for her niece. Abby theorised that Suzi was at an age where she should be becoming more responsible, not less – she couldn't look after both Edward and Suzi. She would pick up the pieces when she could; she hoped Rose would have understood.

When Jenny came along three years later, the birth had been scheduled in advance.

It was an elective Caesarean – Abby had learned, there were no airs and graces, she was an experienced mother, she knew the score.

This time, no post-natal depression.

The family were now well versed in coping and, as soon as Jenny was home, everything clicked into place – boosted by a move to a bigger apartment, purchased rather than rented.

All was good.

If John and Abby had at times taken their partnership for granted, the notion was long gone. They worked at marriage – that way you got the most out of it.

Suzi was still just about on the radar and, out of control as she had become, Abby felt awful. She had made those promises to herself to look after her sister's child. Yet, what else could she have done? Edward's problem birth – no apparent long-term health consequences when he could have ended up with learning difficulties or worse – had turned her life upside down. She didn't feel she could offer to look after Suzi in Toronto – it would have been simply too much to take on someone fast becoming a juvenile delinquent.

Abby instead vowed to catch up with the Suzi enigma as soon as the demands on her own self lessened.

33

Now entering his mid-thirties, Kevin's new career was going well.

He found he had an aptitude for flogging houses and was glad that he had run with it and the gamble had paid off. As long as he could maintain a divide between his work and his shaky personal life then he would be able to keep the balls in the air.

It was a period where the housing market was going through the roof as it were. Sydney was progressive and much-admired, and who wouldn't want to live in a place which averaged seven hours of sunshine daily?

A draw for migrants; demand exceeded supply.

As Sako had prophesied, he was making plenty of dosh and, while the ethos at the estate agency was competitive, everyone got on.

With no mortgage on the flat, no wife and children to support, low outgoings, not one for the flash car, designer clothes or bling jewellery, Kevin's bank balance shot up by leaps and bounds.

Life outside work could be trite – too often he found himself sitting in the flat on his own. His own fault of course. He had failed to maintain his network of friends, the whole sports thing had lapsed, he wasn't one for clubbing … in short, he had grown used to closing the shutters.

That way you didn't get hurt.

Being on his own was the norm.

There were side effects. Loneliness could sometimes sweep over him.

Few are able to master how this can be in a Greater Sydney conurbation of more than five million people, but isolation is not confined to remote regions. In our cities today it's far more common than you might think.

It let in the old depressive tendencies.

He would keep seeing the faces of his four dead friends. It was the same old bad dream – there was no way out, he was drowning, it was the end.

Sometimes he was shaking so much he was sick.

Work was a blessed distraction.

The estate agency was unaware, meaning not that they were unaware that he was the plane crash survivor – all of Australia were aware of that. Simply that they didn't know anything about the rest of it. They just saw someone working his socks off for the company – long hours and, in footie parlance, always showing for the ball.

After a year and a half Sako, who was a director, and the senior partners Daniel Cobb and James Jones, called Kevin in, told him how satisfied they were with his performance, and offered him a minority stake in the business and hence a small share in the profits.

He thanked them, said he wanted to remain at the sharp end, and his only reservation would be if he were to get bogged down in administration and paper work.

They assured him that wouldn't be the case – they employed book keepers and conveyancers on that side.

So he accepted and felt good about it.

One day he bumped into Becky in the street – they hadn't spoken for five years or more. They said hello, smiled, made small talk. He told her she was still the Becky of old. She expressed surprise at his change of career but said she was pleased for him. It was a reluctant and insipid exchange.

Hands were trembling and neither spotted it.

Becky scanned his face for remnants of their one-time tie. But Kevin wasn't giving anything away.

He restrained an impulse to kiss her. He must have been out of his mind to have given her up – but then he probably was out of his mind at the time.

Was she with anyone? She said she had got engaged but they broke up and there had been no one serious since.

And him? No, said Kevin, no one.

"Right pair we are," she jested.

There was nothing more they could find to say to each other. It was that woebegone.

They went on their way.

He found a bench, sat down, held his head in his hands and cried.

He should, he told himself, track her down, invite her out and try to re-kindle their love. Couldn't do it – the night sweats would get worse, the evils might resurface, *the black dog* would be harder to shake off. He was a coward. No other word for it.

When he got back into the office they noticed how subdued he was for the rest of the day. But next morning he was himself again and they thought no more of it.

Kevin had jolted his way out of the downer by writing to Suzi once more. In it he told how living on the margins was bloody difficult. Kevin the Good pre-crash; Kevin the Bad and the Mad post-crash. While doing so he mused on how old she would be. About fourteen, he reckoned. Surely not. He recalculated and it still came to fourteen. Then found a mirror – the first grey hairs were confirmation that he was no spring chicken anymore.

He tried to conjure up what she might look like, how she was getting on in school and whether she was into boys yet.

He had never gotten (in American English) a reply yet from any of the letters. It didn't matter – they served a different purpose.

34

Having introduced Suzi to why she was an orphan, the family had gradually expanded on it as they hoped the portents were propitious.

When she was ten, she knew there had been a harrowing plane crash. From there, already highly computer savvy, she found out for herself exactly how harrowing. She felt intense sadness reading about how many had perished – her mother and father and all the others. She hoped most were unconscious as it hit the water and spared the worst. Perhaps this was why she felt so alienated from everything and everybody. She had been shafted and it was all the fault of those bastards, society, God, authority and the rest.

"I hate them all," she shrilled.

The one intriguing element was this Kevin fella who had saved her from drowning. What sort of character was he – extrovert or introvert?

There was no getting away from the fact that she was in his debt.

She did not dwell on it.

Here was someone else, like Abby, who had abandoned her.

Someone who had made no effort to stay with it – she would have liked to have asked him things, many things, but he was just a name and a face.

She couldn't hate the man – he did after all save her life.

Wherever he was, whatever he was doing, she was not his concern … and why should she be?

Yet, however indifferent, she could never seem to put him behind her.

By now, her truancy from school had become more sophisticated – she would go in at the start of the school day, pay disguised diligence to teachers and work, have lunch and then do a flit. Alternatively, she might depart in the morning and resurface mid-afternoon. There were all sorts of excuses – diarrhoea, sick relatives, migraines (she didn't suffer them but could act like she did) and so on and so forth. Cynically, she didn't shoot a line every day – some days she went to all her classes.

Her teachers were not hoodwinked.

Here was a girl with known problems who could be as bright as a button when she wanted to be but whose grades were so poor. Because of her attitude.

Of course there were lots of other children who did want to learn and you couldn't spend endless hours trying to motivate those who didn't.

They tried remedial classes but being "locked up with the grots" was, for Suzi, simply another provocation.

Sending her to some sort of corrective centre for malcontents was assessed in outline. But they were afraid of the bad publicity were it to leak out that the plane heroine, who in the eyes of the public could do no wrong, was being treated so shabbily.

So, in essence, she did virtually what she liked.

Sara and Jeb were being trampled on, the school had given up, and the authorities were afraid to act.

Something of a magnet, several of the school "awkward squad" had joined her on the street corners and down the amusement arcades. Fags and booze nicked from local stores was the norm. It was both a laugh and a means of blotting out the scumbags. One day someone produced a bag of cocaine – ask no questions tell no lies – and Suzi tried a line. It brought her into a dreamtime where she felt anything was possible, taking her to a level of *enlightenment* she never knew existed.

This was the spectrum to be on and soon various tablets – it was known what they were alleged to be but not whether they were de facto as described, what strength and hence the level of risk in taking them – were being handed around.

They started getting zonked … and then zonked some more.

When you're young, the peril in which you're putting yourself doesn't always register. You are indestructible.

One day the state's Child Protective Services staff picked her off the floor and brought her back home. Sara and Jeb were overwrought – it was the first time, discounting the wedding and the memorial service, Suzi had seen grown-ups cry in earnest. Knowing she might be taken from them, they remained firmly set against accepting they could no longer cope.

That would denigrate the memory of Robert and Rose.

It would be admitting defeat.

They begged for another chance and they got another chance. But they were told emphatically that they were running out of chances.

Suzi was feeling sick, spun a sob story about mending her ways, and crashed out.

The next night she walked out of the front door and was gone for several hours. On her return, she stubbornly refused to say where she had been. She simply laughed at her grandparents.

The dismay etched on their faces zeroed into Suzi's psyche but, come on, she wasn't going to be ruled by a pair of old codgers way off the pace when it came to today's youth culture.

As a sop, there was a spell as a dutiful schoolgirl, but playing goodie two shoes was countered by evenings spent in her bedroom listening to rap music and posting a picture of *her bazookas* on social media outlets. She keenly noted that the number of her followers multiplied correspondingly – she was getting inquiries from men promising all sorts of shenanigans.

For now she resisted – she wasn't quite there yet.

However, that had to be next, she told herself.

So far, her so-called sexual activity had been restricted to snogging sessions and body massages with lads she half fancied, mostly older than herself from the other side of the tracks. It was all a bit poxy and amateur.

Soon some serious shagging was due. She wanted it big time.

The media portrayed it as the be-all-and-end-all. Sex had long ago replaced religion as the ultimate god.

Would she be any good at it?

School had taught them about human sexuality, age of consent, contraception, and sexually transmitted diseases. Those were classes that Suzi made sure she did not skip. Taking in her stride things like periods and the changing nature of her body. Sara had pulled out the stops to take Suzi through the whole process and had provided a concise pamphlet, which had proved useful and instructive.

At fourteen, Suzi summoned up the bravado to go to a clinic on her own and asked to be put on the pill. She was given counselling and handed literature to read. Was she sure?

She said she was sure and started taking it.

Now she felt completely ready to have sex for the first time.

When it happened, it was a bit of a fumble and a rumble. Doug, who she chummed around with at school, though he was a year older, had invited her to a movie. It wasn't up to much and the two had spent most of it down each other's throats. They left arm in arm, stopped at a liquor store, where he went in and bought some shots and beer. It was a hot, humid, night and they went out into a local park and lay down under a tree. They drank a bit, giggled, kissed lots, she took off her top and allowed him to unstrap her bra and play with her melons. His T-shirt had long been shed and she basked in his toned body.

They tossed back more shots and she felt her appetite for this boy rising. He was good-looking, he wasn't pushy and he made her feel she mattered. When he pulled down her jeans – she didn't resist.

They were eager for each other and in no time pants and panties had been discarded. Bring it on.

She opened her legs, he moved on top and, after a bit of prodding - when it struck her that this was probably his first time too - he was there and they were both taking each other's virginity. It was a bit rushed though she didn't yet know that, there was something defective on both sides, but this was definitely what life was about.

Yes, yes, yes.

A eulogy of pollination.

Then it was over; they had done it. Ring out the bells; throw down the tickertape.

It was everything it was cracked up to be and she knew she would want more of it – lots more of it. They broke off, told each other they were the ones, and kissed loads and loads. They got dressed, toasted their prowess in beer, hung-loose and took in the songs of the night, an insect choir that seemed to serenade their becoming one.

It had been naive, she felt sore, but she was exhilarated.

She told herself next time would be better and the time after that better still.

He walked her home – both were walking on air.

She was asleep in a trice and next day was hours in the bath imagining she was doing it all over again as she wallowed and writhed.

When she next caught sight of him at school they exchanged a knowing smile which spoke of a dual connection for all time – you were my first. You always remember your first.

They left it a week and then did it again. This time he was a long time inside her and it was lovely.

The time after she gave him a blowjob – they were learning about pleasure. And when it came to full sex she was on top, taking the lead.

After that, she lost count.

Weeks passed, it was still good, but she was ready to try someone else who might offer greater expertise and finesse.

When the opportunity arose it was stark, absolutely no finesse, and life-changing.

35

Kevin used to be turned on by the prospect of sex.

He had always attracted girls. There were girls before Becky but that was more lust than love. Then there was Becky, which was more love than lust. Since Becky had been out of his life he had turned celibate.

Sex, like sport, seemed nothing in the wider scheme of things and with all his issues he didn't want the problems which girls brought. They might claim to be concentrating on their career, they might insist that a long-term relationship wasn't in the script, but like the rest of the animal kingdom it was all about finding a mate. Well, for ninety-nine per cent of girls at any rate. Feminism was just a masquerade.

He couldn't face the duties and demands a new full-on girlfriend would bring.

Gone was his old habit of giving women marks out of ten. Once, he would be undressing them with his eyes. Not now.

True, there was this new bird, Alice, in the office. She was, like him, a redhead. Delicate paps and a model's grace – a real looker.

At junctures he thought he was getting the come-on – she would drop a sheet of paper, reach down slowly to pick it up, thrusting her breasts forward as he sat at his desk unsure whether or not to avert his gaze. She would *accidentally* brush against him as they passed. She would put a pen to her lips and pout. Unless that is he had the wrong end of the stick – he'd never been able to 'read' women.

Either way, he didn't let it get to him.

She was clever and he guessed she knew she was having an effect.

However, office liaisons were never a good idea and could cause headaches and bitterness whenever they ended. He'd seen it before. There were plenty of reasons to keep his distance, and that's how it stayed. Kevin concentrated on his work – it was continuing to go well and by now he was several years into it.

Women and sex – no.

Until the day when one of the crew was leaving for pastures new.

It was the end of the week, sales targets had been met, everyone was upbeat, so the farewell moved to the local pub where occasionally they met up after work. There was probably a dozen of them, it was a good laugh, a few drinks were downed and onwards to a nearby curry house. By then a handful had dropped out and it was down to eight.

Typically, Kevin had tried to make his excuses but the others refused to take no for an answer, with Alice regaling somewhat ponderously how it was going to be a *hot* date.

It was a divine meal, lots of posturing, more drink, a lazy scene-setter for the weekend. Heading towards midnight, with old-fashioned courtesy, the boys split the bill, it was to be their treat, the girls added a generous tip, and all prepared to go their separate ways.

At which Alice, who hadn't contributed anything, borrowing her share with the promise of reimbursement after pay day, not that anybody was making a point of it, was at Kevin's side and seemingly in a bit of a mess. Unburdened the real reason for her lack of funds – her purse was missing. She must have left it, with her money, cards and keys, in the office – would he mind coming with her, and opening up, so she could hunt for it.

His initial reaction was caution – he wasn't sure about out of hours protocols. Yet on the face of it a reasonable request.

And, being well brought-up, you don't turn down a damsel in distress – so, to some degree against his better judgement, he obliged.

Within minutes they were nearing the office when she half-tripped. He caught her and they carried on with her nestling into his side.

That should have set alarm bells ringing – it didn't.

He pumped in the code, the lights went on, they entered and, rather than continue to her office station, she pushed at the door to the client-visitor area, part formal, part informal, with table, chairs, settees, drinks cabinet, which, because management also sometimes appropriated it for meetings and functions, and you were expected to 'jump' whenever management wanted anything, was colloquially known as the *Kangaroo Club*.

What would her purse be doing there?

Then she put her arms around his head and pulled him towards her, nibbling his neck and espousing how much she had long admired his body. They kissed. She was bringing him on, the beers were a relaxant, and, with the innate weakness of the male gender, he couldn't hold back, contemplating what she would be like in the sack.

Then it finally dawned on him – there was no missing purse. This was a set-up.

Oh, blow the consequences, he was well into it. She was voracious. Jacket, shirt, bra, panties were soon littering the floor. They were all over each other.

By now naked as the day she was born, shunning the more comfortable option of a nice leather sofa, she deftly jockeyed herself onto the table and told him to take her. Primeval instinct kicked in and Kevin was on that table like an athlete responding to a starting pistol.

She was as randy as a sow introduced to a boar; he was a gorilla on the rampage. Rampant with each other, she proved a shouter. "Screw me, screw me, more, more. Fuck me 'til I fart." That supercharged Kevin into ever more titanic efforts.

It was perhaps the best sex he had ever had. She was amazing. Ten on the satisfaction gauge. When it was done, she told him he was astounding and she had wanted him from the first day she had set foot in the office.

Sweat and sex combined in a jungle aroma.

Then it was time to gather themselves – what would the management have made of it – get their clothes back on, clear anything up that needed clearing, laugh at how naughty they had been. Like a crime drama, sweeping the room for fingerprints and forensically removing evidence. Well, not exactly, but you get the drift. Endeavouring to ensure there could be no trace of what had taken place.

They left, careful to turn off the lights.

He hailed a taxi and took her home, closely fused, inhaling her delicious perfume. It pulled up outside a block of flats – a cad would have waved her goodbye but he would have been too ashamed. And after such great sex he didn't need any persuading to join her.

He paid off the taxi, she took out her security pass, the front door opened, she stuck the card in the lift slot, and up they went. It stopped at the eighth floor and she led him hand in hand into the flat.

A one bedroom apartment, lounge, kitchen, bathroom.

Bijou – the single girl's hangout.

A coffee and to bed – both too satiated for more hanky-panky. He contemplated her pert boobs one more time; she turned her back on him.

Sometime in the early hours of the morning he was having this delicious ever so sexual dream when he awoke to find it was no dream – she was caressing his privates with a professional's technique, sure to turn any man into a hot rod. No red-blooded male could have held back. The lovemaking started again and soon they were at it like donkeys.

God, she was good.

Afterwards they just held each other, overcome.

Sleep must have taken over once more because the next he knew was light pouring through the window and the sound of a shower being run – her side of the bed was empty.

He lay there, trying to take in all that had gone down. It seemed surreal.

The shower cut out.

A few minutes later, the door opened and she walked in, towel around her head, bath robe around her body. "Oh, you're awake," she purred. She sat on the bed, kissed him, then swayed away enticingly, took off the robe and pulled on a pair of panties.

It sent him ravenous – there had to be a next-time, whatever the office politics.

She smiled at him – men were so easy to manipulate.

"The shower's free – make yourself at home."

So he did.

He wished in a way he could stay this horny and sticky for ever, but the water was reviving. He soaped himself all over.

She made him more coffee, buttered him some toast.

He went down the road feeling ten feet tall. In tune with the world in a manner he hadn't been for many moons. Suppressed a lunatic urge to sing to the birds and twirl with old ladies. It was good to be alive on such a euphoric day.

36

That week he sought to maintain his professional dignity and she did too. It stayed their secret. Though not something you could keep a lid on for ever. So easy to twig the tell-tale give-aways – over-familiar eye contact here; a hurried chat beside the photocopier there.

They arranged via text to meet after work the following Friday.

Eschewing the office local, they went to a bar in Darling Harbour intending to merge into the crowds. Then got themselves a drink – so serene gazing out over the armada of expensive yachts and cabin cruisers, lights twinkling across the anchorage and casting mythological shadows.

He was edgy, but you couldn't be hung up for long in such an exalted arena.

They clinked glasses, a quick kiss, he stroked her knee.

She started on him. "Wait until I get you home tonight, big boy. I'm going to tear those tight trousers off your arse."

He told her he was going to lick every scintilla of her hedonistic body.

Then they burst out laughing and were soon scheming and giggling like teenagers, inhibitions cast aside.

A nearby fish restaurant appealed.

There would be a twenty minute wait for a table – would that be acceptable, sir?

Yes, that would be in order.

They got themselves another drink and pretended to be grown-ups.

"So, tell me all about yourself," he said, adopting a serious tone. It set her off into fits of giggles again which got him going too. "What's wrong with that question?" he queried, in mock derision.

"That's a lamentable chat-up line. I thought you were the great lover – great lovers don't come out with playground piffle. Besides I saw you reading my file the other day so you know all about me." She had him fazed – he thought he had been really sneaky. "You're going red."

Then she moved closer to him, gave him a steamy look and surreptitiously twiddled his crown jewels. He nearly fell off his stool – how dirty and dangerous she could be. This was the slut from heaven … or was she from hell?

Before he could respond the waiter came up.

Were they ready?

They were, and he showed them to their table.

"I'm ready for anything," she tittered, raising an eyebrow.

"I'm going to have the grouper," he told her.

She hid behind the menu while working out the grouper-groping feeble play on words. "That was dreadful."

"Most of my jokes are."

The fish was fresh – as it should be with a whole ocean out there – washed down with a carafe of wine … had to be Australian.

They left the restaurant arm-in-arm, walked out into the night air, and stopped for a final view of the harbour front. She pushed erotically against him, and they kissed.

"Your place or mine?" He was almost slobbering, the hots for her nearing boiling point.

She placed a finger and ran it slow and filthy along his lips. "Well, you've seen mine," she smirked, pinging a double-entendre back at him. Then she playfully dug him in the ribs. "Anyway, I want to get an idea how the other half live!"

"OK," he said. "You might be disappointed."

"I already know there's no chance of that," she responded saucily.

They held hands and walked the ten minutes to his flat. It was in a trendy neighbourhood, had two bedrooms and a balcony. She told him she was impressed. Nice things mattered in life.

They entered and she took in the ambience. There was the bachelor's dirty cups and plates in the sink waiting to be washed, but it was classy – leather suite, expensive lighting, and tasteful furniture.

Impulsively he picked her up and tossed her onto a sheepskin rug, she bleating like a lamb and faking a protest. She had no intention of faking anything else that night.

Next, they were lying there kissing hungrily. She put a hand inside his trousers and fooled around with him. He mimicked Incey Wincey Spider on a breast. Then they broke apart.

"Let's do it right here."

"But you haven't seen the bedroom yet," he retorted.

"We've got all night to arrive at the bedroom," she asserted, fondling his face and looking pleadingly into his eyes. "I know," she announced, a plot forming. "Let's do it on the balcony."

Her lashes fluttered. His dander was up. He let her go.

"I'll get something to put on the floor." From a cloakroom cupboard, he pulled out an old Li-lo, cushions and some towels, which he spread on the concrete. Practical if unromantic.

Not to be put off, by then she was naked bar some spellbinding blue chiffon panties with purple edging. Draping herself provocatively, her boobs seemed to shimmer under the glow of the moon above and street and car lights below.

Panting for this siren, he was on her in seconds. Writhing as mad things an errant foot struck a pot plant which went sailing down to smash on the slabs below.

In his ardour he missed a gear; she smiled to herself, clasping his hot body ever closer and wanting every inch of him. She moaned loud and long.

"The neighbours," he mumbled.

Until he came within her in an explosion of solar flares. Her body saturated in the Milky Way.

A light came on somewhere below accompanied by a harsh-sounding voice in the blackness demanding they cut the noise. Neither of them stirred, still in raptures and utter contentment. A door slammed shut outside.

Time to investigate the bedroom she hadn't yet seen.

Soon they had sunk into pillows, twee smiles, dancing dreams, he swimming in her feminine oils, she reeking of his earthy outpourings.

No early morning rendezvous this time – they had taken too much out of themselves.

Next day, shamefaced, he hurriedly brushed up soil, shredded plant and broken pot and hoped nobody saw him.

37

In Normal, Suzi was particularly belligerent.

There had been yet another row with Sara and Jeb and she had stormed out, hitting her mobile phone and rendezvousing with the 'awkward squad'. She was sounding off about how shit it was living with grandparents when ear-splitting sounds scrambled their hearing.

Around the corner came thirty or so bikers – leathers, tattoos, gleaming machines, many with poster girls holding tight onto their men. It was intimidating, it was fierce, but it was strangely seductive.

These were the *Bastards on Wheels* and for nothing more than a laugh they had ridden into town, shooting up the centre, tail-ending drivers, touching up any female they could assault – from straight-laced executives to prim and proper housewives – and duelling with cops. Now they were pulling out.

They aspired to join the *Big Four* who have been competing for territory throughout the United States for years. The *Outlaws* the oldest, founded on the outskirts of Chicago in 1935, and still based in the Great Lakes region. The *Hell's Angels*, the largest, with chapters in more than fifty countries, their peak of infamy, when they became a by-word for violence, arguably the 1969 Altamont Speedway Free Festival where a concert-goer was stabbed to death as the Angels conducted security in their own inimitable fashion. The *Pagans*, claiming most of the eastern seaboard, and the *Bandidos*, holding sway in the South, primarily in Texas. All regarded as *outlaw motorcycle gangs* by the FBI, riddled with criminality, and associated with widespread drug and financial racketeering activities, extortion and prostitution.

The Bastards on Wheels weren't in this league … but had designs on getting there one day.

Suzi was still finding herself but you would have had to be closeted in a nunnery not to be in awe of their reputation. On that day she was up for a wild time.

One of the gang pulled his Harley Davidson alongside. "Ever been on a bike, honey?" he drawled. He was big, he was bold, quite a catch in a ferocious sort of way.

"No," she croaked. It was the truth – she had never been on a motorbike. The Harley throbbed with raw energy; Suzi's arousal levels started throbbing in tandem.

"Well, get on."

She wasn't sure. She put on what she hoped was a mean expression and acted as if she was sizing him up.

"Don't do it," said her frequent accomplice Mitzy.

The biker's face splintered. "Ignore that slapper. We ain't bandits. What've you got to be afraid of?"

She tried to lay down a red line. "I need to end up back here – have you got that." She knew, even as she said it, there was no way it was ever going to be.

"Yeah, no problem. We're going to eat up some road – you're going to have plenty of kicks. What's your name, sweetheart?"

"Suzi."

"Honcho," he replied, and patted the seat behind him in a gesture which questioned whether she had the bottle – was she the daring babe she thought she was?

What the heck …

She walked into the street, opened her legs to bestride the metallic monster, and put her hands around his waist. Up for the ride, there was every likelihood she would end up giving him a ride. But that held a spell-binding anticipation in itself.

Then they were off and running, wheelies, whoops, no laws applied, life on the open road, kicking off the traces. Wind in her hair, power under her vagina, she was in the zone.

They lorded the highways, sneered at the populace, cut up cars – they were the rulers. This was her era and she was going to make the most of it.

The lead bike, ridden by a sun-burned red-neck with Gonz stitched across his jacket, turned off onto a side track and soon they pulled up at what seemed a giant bomb shelter in the middle of nowhere. There were bars on the windows, roller blinds on the doors, spikes and barbed wire on the roof, and security cameras (actually fake).

Suzi felt apprehension for the first time but shook it off as quickly as it came. After all, she was now a Bastard on Wheels.

They filed in.

Honcho had a hold on the nape of her neck; part intended to show he was a big shot, part telling the rest that this was his.

But before sex, before all else, it was about getting a beer.

He handed her one and took a long and thirsty slug. She was more particular with her mouthful – it had a twist to it all right.

He downed his, took another and then eased her into the inner warren away from the others. They entered a tatty room – it was block concrete with just one high-up roof window, dimly lit, scruffy, an old armchair, a big bed, nothing else apart from a heap of junk in a corner. He locked the door, pulled her to him and snogged her until she was gagging for air. Next minute, her feet off the ground as she wrapped her legs around him and devoured his kisses she knew just where this was going.

He put her down, had a further swig from the beer bottle and told her to get undressed. This was a man who knew what he wanted and, unlike with any of the others she had dallied over and rejected, she had an all-embracing need to be dominated.

She stripped to her knickers as he slowly divested his cumbersome leathers.

He pointed to her pants. "Off."

This was going to be basic sex. She was ready (sort of), willing (just about) and able (absolutely).

He cleared his underwear and she went goggle-eyed at his impressive manhood. She didn't wait for his command but lay on the bed and acted as though she wanted him – she half did and she half didn't. He joined her on the bed – foreplay at a premium, they kissed and he entered her, all at the same time.

Her uninhibited reaction was one of euphoria, as it seemed to fill her entire body.

She gasped, she panted, she groaned.

It was like nothing she had known before – so different from fumbling about in the park.

And as soon as it had started it was over.

He got up, shook it around as though showing off a prize marrow at an agricultural show, and began getting his clothes back on.

She just lay there ravaged at an action so outlandish and beyond her comprehension. She had crossed a line into becoming a right-on sexual animal.

By now fully dressed, he gave her a half-smile, told her he would be back, unlocked the door and went out.

The key closed in the lock from the outside.

She stayed on the bed and jousted with her conscience.

Jeb and Sara would be getting anxious about her but there was nothing to gain in getting worked up on their account. They would just have to stew. This was biker life – no more school and no more nagging grandparents.

She had satisfied this man, an achievement in itself.

Not only that, she wanted more of him.

Slowly, feeling slightly soiled, she collected her things and waited. Still tingling all over.

Half an hour later, he was back. There was no explanation as to where he had been. "Time to eat," he grunted, with the aura of an absolute monarch.

She asked timidly whether she could wash first.

He took pity on her – gang molls weren't expected to be particular. Then held fast to her as if somehow she might make a break for it.

139

She shook him off, the first sign that she had spirit. "There's no need," she told him, fire in her eyes. "I'm not doing a runner."

He let go of her – it was a tonic to have claimed a tiny victory – and he brought her through another part of the maze to some sort of communal block. There was a line of showers – he probed in a cupboard and found her a towel. Then motioned her on while holding his ground to ensure she was unmolested.

Unisex. A biker was drying himself and a biker's girl was shampooing her hair.

Suzi took her clothes off, got a kick out of telling Honcho to watch over them, and let the water cover her. The other girl offered her some shampoo. She washed her hair, she washed her body, and at last she felt clean. She sneaked a glance at him looking at her – his mojo was working overtime on her figure, which was exactly how she intended it.

Dry and dressed, she uncovered an old comb, a few teeth missing, and slung it through her hair – it would have to do because he was agitating for food.

She was hungry herself.

Next, they were entering something resembling a mess hall – almost a bit like school! Except there were no teachers here.

There were bikers on benches munching stolidly, bikers and birds on dilapidated three-piece suites in various degrees of debauchery, the usual background hum you got in a typical canteen.

Honcho heaped food on his plate from a large bowl filled with a concoction that seemed to be rice and beans based, with a smattering of meat. He lunged at some cutlery with a big, brawny hand, and sat down. Though somewhat sceptical of this odd gruel, she spooned it on thick, reasoning that there would be no knowing where or when she might next eat.

Nothing was said. He was a man of few words notwithstanding his chat-up routine back in Normal. He threw down the grub with alacrity.

She found it adequate without being what you would call tasty. She wasn't sure she could eat it all. He told her to get it down her. No waste here. He waited for her to finish, then indicated that you were expected to wash your own dishes, and that was definitely women's work. She wasn't about to complain of chauvinism in this setting.

She did as she was told while he homed in on another beer. No bottle opener handy but he had a trick up his sleeve – insert into a door hinge, apply the correct amount of pressure, and the top was gone – then slouched into a spare armchair.

She followed him over, curled into his body and directed a love-bite at his neck – she was making an impression. Literally!

With others too. Eyes were on her. Who was this Lolita?

He passed her the beer and she drank from the bottle.

She must have dozed off because the next time she looked around her the light was fading. He smiled at her with what she interpreted as a degree of sensitivity. It was time to leave the now much-diminished assembly and return to the room.

They got undressed – this regular on-off of clothes was almost therapeutic.

Now it was he who waited for her in the bed.

Women! A law unto themselves.

She shaped her hair, freshened her face with her hands. She would have liked a dab of perfume but she hadn't any.

She didn't take long and came to him like a gazelle.

In complete contrast to what had gone before he turned into a cool dude – if rough and ready.

They played it out, they kissed, his hands caressed the length of her body, she massaged him. When they were both needing each other, she told him to 'wait', rolled from under him and he let her 'take the top bunk' as it were. She wiggled her body to make it as sensual as possible for both of them, he hit the jackpot, and their pay-out was mutual delectation.

It had taken just a few hours but she had already half-tamed this big, bad, Bastard.

38

Next day he allowed her to use the toilet and wash, he fed her, but then he led her back to the room.

There was some 'big shit' heading down and there was no way she was going with them. Anyway, they only took fully-fledged members of the gang and she had plenty to prove to be allowed membership – she would first need to get used to their ways.

"I'm going to lock you in – for your own safety."

She argued, said she could look after herself, but he was adamant.

"What about if I need the loo?"

He pulled a large plastic container from out of the junk pile.

"Use that," he said.

And was gone. The key turned in the lock. She was effectively a prisoner.

Apart from anything else, it was going to be a very dreary few hours.

She paced around, grumbled to herself about this unfair confinement, and thought once more about her grandparents – the balloon must surely have gone up by now. They were bound to have reported her missing to the police. But the police were probably inundated by run-aways, many of which often turned up again a few days, sometimes just hours, later. She didn't think they would do much initially, routine inquiries only.

Suzi tried not to think about it.

That lunchtime the 'big shit' hit the fan.

The Bastards on Wheels took on one of their local rivals in a violent brawl in a hick town eighty miles from Chicago. Up to seventy-five bikers knocking seven bells out of each other. The Bastards on Wheels came out of it badly – four left bleeding on the sidewalk, three arrested, and a lot of ego mulched.

When they got back to base, Gonz was in a foul temper. He ordered them into the mess hall and started ranting and raving at the "fucking insult" meted out to them. They were soft, they were weak, they were just "a load of fucking poofters." His fists were smashing down on tables, cups were shattering on walls, anything that could be kicked was being kicked.

No one said a word.

Eventually he ran out of obscenities and just stood there glaring at them. Then, he singled out Honcho and snarled: "Give me the keys to that room – it's my turn to have the bitch."

Honcho flinched. "She's mine. I found her. You leave her be."

Gonz went ballistic at this challenge to his authority. He ran at Honcho and tried to nut him – the proverbial *Glasgow kiss*.

Honcho fended him off and pulled a knife.

There was a giant intake of air around the mess hall – this was getting heavy.

"Right," said Gonz. "So you're the big man, are you? Well I'm going to see your knife and raise you …' He took a revolver from a side pocket and aimed it at Honcho's head. "… one gun."

Honcho backed off, disdained all pretence at playing the white knight, and threw his knife on the floor. "Don't shoot," he said. "You can have her." He held out the keys.

Gonz took them from him, got him by the throat, and put the gun to his temple. He spoke slowly and menacingly. "Don't ever cross me again Honcho or you'll be a dead man. Do I make myself clear?"

"Got it," gurgled Honcho, shaking like a leaf. "You're the boss, Gonz."

"Say it again but louder."

"YOUR'RE THE BOSS, GONZ!"

Gonz swung around 360 degrees. "Have you got the message?" he roared.

There was general assent.

"Who's the leader of this fucking outfit?"

"You are, Gonz."

"And don't ever fucking forget it."

Coldly he left the room.

Of course, Suzi knew nothing of this so when the key turned in the door a frisson of excitement running through her – Honcho was back. Except it wasn't Honcho; it was Gonz.

"Get your clothes off," he bawled.

She shrank from him and did nothing.

"Get your clothes off. I ain't telling you again." And he whacked her in the face with the back of his hand, sending her spinning to the ground.

Picking herself up, she raced to take off her clothes. Then made another blunder. "Where's Honcho?" she insisted. "I'm Honcho's – you know that."

The punch caught her a glancing blow but was still powerful enough to leave her in a heap by one of the walls to her cell. He picked her off the floor, flattened her against the concrete, pulled down his trousers and wrenched her legs apart.

Bang, her body thumped against the wall.

Thrust. He hammered into her.

Bang, her body thumped against the wall.

Thrust. He hammered into her.

The rape lasted no time but felt like forever.

Weeping uncontrollably, finally realising how stupid she had been not to think a dalliance with bikers might come to this, she pleaded with the animal. "Please, please, you're hurting me. You're hurting me."

"Hurting you," he repeated. "Hurting you. I'll show you what hurting is all about." And he removed a truncheon from the wall, pinned there as a prize following a previous altercation with the police, and showed no mercy.

The screams were so graphic they could hear them from the mess hall.

The place went quiet. Nobody moved.

They sat there with their thoughts – if they hadn't been sure what sort of fate awaited them for angering Gonz, they knew now.

Eventually the wailing stopped.

He left her bloodied and broken.

She was never sure how many hours she lay there, rolling in and out of consciousness.

Gonz was happy to see her suffer.

The inhabitants of the mess hall went about their business normally – in reality as abnormal as you could get – while Gonz's stare dared any of them to say anything. When he had taken enough perverse pleasure, he turned towards Honcho and muttered icily: "Go on, you can have her, what's left of her anyway." And, leering, threw the keys at him and turned away.

Slowly, wary of provoking another outburst, the biker made towards the door, turned the handle and almost crept out.

He found her on all fours amidst a small but gradually extending pool of blood. He reached down to her, repelled at the state she was in. "I'm so sorry – it was never meant to be like this."

His face a portrait of disgust, she grasped at the lifeline. She was trying to say something and he strained to hear her muted words. "Get … me … to … a … hospital … or … I'm … going … to … die …" Her voice faded away.

A death had the potential to attract mega-trouble from the authorities. The last thing he needed was to be fitted up by Gonz on a murder rap. But he also cared about this girl. He gathered her up – she couldn't stand – and sat her on the old armchair while he found a towel which he tied round her in a primitive attempt at stemming the bleeding.

He collected what was left of her things and carried her in a fireman's lift to his Harley. Placed her on the bike and let her drape across the front handlebars. The engine roared, he turned on the lights, and drove as fast as he dared towards Bloomington-Normal. He turned the bike into the first hospital he came to, pulled up at the Trauma Center and Emergency Department, carried her as far as reception, little blobs of blood in a trail along the corridor, and hollered for some action.

Alerted to Suzi's ransacked body, gobsmacked at the presence of this swarthy thug in their midst, people came running, a trolley materialised out of nowhere, and he carefully deposited her on it – she was passed out.

He went back to his bike, returning to sling her stuff on the reception desk. Then, as they scurried about, he slipped away into the night, turned the bike around, and was gone.

Running away; tail between legs. Hated it.

39

She knew nothing of the first day, under-going blood transfusions as they fought to stabilise her condition.

146

The second day was a complete blank too as they took her to surgery and sought to patch up her insides.

Days three and four were equally off the radar as they kept her in an induced coma to rest her violated body.

By then they had at last worked out who she was.

Hardened medical staff, sick to the stomach at what had been done to her, had called in the police at the outset. They came up with a missing girl who seemed to match her description – a Suzanne Duthie, aged sixteen, from Normal.

The cops ran Jeb and Sara round to the hospital to see if they could identify the mystery female in the critical care ward.

Sara howled in anguish at the sight – it was Suzi.

There were monitoring machines around the bed, tubes sprouting out of different parts of her body, a ventilator was controlling her breathing, she looked like death. It could yet come to that if infection set in, they were told.

She was being pumped full of antibiotics.

Sara had sworn she would keep her composure whatever greeted them but that went out of the window. She stood there with a tissue, watery eyes, more than a little faint, as Jeb sought to console her. But his stomach was churning.

A thoughtful nurse brought chairs over. She was non-committal about Suzi's chances. Officially her condition was *serious* although that didn't begin to cover it. Doctors would be around later to assess her again, after which it was hoped they would know more and might be able to brief the family in greater detail.

Could they hold Suzi's hand?

"Probably wise not to," said the nurse. But they could talk to Suzi as much as they liked.

They spoke about the garden flowers, the bees buzzing as they collected nectar, a bird's nest in the fir tree. They told her everyone in the family was concerned for her and asking after her.

Abby was stunned at the news and packed a travel bag.

Edward and Jenny were now seven and four so Abby felt safe enough leaving them for what was going to be several days if not a week or more. John took time off work – fortuitously his parents were on their way over from England and would be able to muck in. She hugged the children. Kissed John while at the same time ignoring Edward's cries of "Gross!". They waved her off in a cab bound for Toronto Airport.

Next stop Normal and then the family home. She got out, raced into the house, deposited her suitcase in the hallway, locked the front door again, and thence to the hospital via some nifty shortcuts – taxi drivers always know the rat runs.

On arrival at Suzi's bedside, she had intended first to embrace her mother and father, but Sara was catnapping and Jeb held a finger to his mouth indicating not to wake mother. She noticed that they were both drawn. More so than she ever remembered. She worried for them these days – handling someone as volatile as Suzi was trying enough but they were now in their seventies.

That evening, departing, with Suzi still out of it, she contrived a route that took them past a fast food restaurant. It filled a hole

Then straight to bed. Poor things were gone the moment their heads hit the pillow. Nevertheless, it was back soonest the next morning – they must be there when she first wakened, they insisted.

Day Five and doctors decided to bring Suzi out of the coma and have her breathing under her own steam.

Consciousness gradually returned.

It started with that halfway house when your eyes are 'doing their own thing' – a little like emerging from a bad concussion and having no idea what planet you inhabit.

Flickered open and flickered closed.

Her insides were aching; she could just make out the family's presence.

She faded back into dreamland.

Her inner self in flames, and, in contrast, her nose twitching at the whiff of disinfectant – she must be in hospital. When next she awoke, it was back to not knowing where she was. A white-coated apparition was at her side. Either this was heaven or he was a doctor.

"Hello Suzi. How are you feeling? You've been asleep a very long time."

She tried to smile – it was more of a grimace. Enfeebled, she managed a wavering hand as if to bring him closer.

He moved his head down to hear what she was labouring to say.

"Will … I … still … be … able … to … have … children?"

Bang, straight in his face, a sucker punch … he hadn't expected it. He hesitated – the way you do when there are so many permutations to answering a question. You don't want to lie but neither do you want to set back a courageous young girl's chances.

He pulled up a chair. "It's far too early to say Suzi – we need to get you well. Then we can see where we are. We can talk again when you are more yourself. Meantime, you mustn't worry. Fingers crossed." It was a clever answer, intended to be as realistic as possible, and aimed at bringing calm to a mixed-up adolescent.

But Suzi was no fool.

She lay there cloaked in abject misery.

That set Sara off, but Abby demanded her niece dig deep. "You've always been a fighter – if ever there was a time to fight then this is it. Listen to me, Suzi." She stroked her hand. "You know we love you lots. Everything is forgiven. We just want you right. You must espouse a future that can be anything you want it to be – promise me you'll do that."

The faintest acknowledgement.

She didn't press the point. Suzi would be on the mend soon. And she was – the young have a capacity for healing.

Tubes out, sitting up in bed, starting to take normal food once more, far more alert, a tapering off of the drugs. She had cheated death for a second time.

They transferred her onto a general ward, tucked her up for long spells in a seat beside the bed, got her walking slowly up and down. It had taken so much out of her. Muscles wasted. Shuffling about like the old bags whose purses she once robbed.

However, she had the bit between her teeth now and showing true grit.

The family were delighted and so was the hospital.

So were the police.

40

They made contact, sending an infinitely patient, mother hen-type officer to speak with her. In half hour slots, with gaps between, they talked through the sordid story.

Others, afraid of reprisals, might have preferred keeping schtum. Not Suzi. This wasn't ratting on a pal. It wasn't even much to do with bikers per se. What had been meted out to her was so outrageous that she was prepared to spill the beans. Gonz had it coming. This was mutilation. He was an utter arsehole. He would have been an arsehole whatever the walk of life.

Her signed statement was detailed but she left Honcho out. That was consensual and anyway she owed him. It gave the police plenty to go on. They were talking rape, sexual assault or maybe even attempted murder against Gonz. Senior officers had long sought to turn over the Bastards on Wheels headquarters. Now they could. They had a witness prepared to testify.

Yet, for Suzi, revenge was best served cold – first, she wanted home.

Eventually, the day came when she was well enough to continue her convalescence there – the bed was required for others. Clutching pain killers, a bit doddery in the fresh air, but she walked to the car unaided.

It was a consolation to be back at the house, her own bedroom, somewhere secure. Sara and Jeb were solicitous. Suzi felt bad for treating them so abhorrently – her obnoxious contempt for an elderly couple who only showed unilateral devotion. They faffed about, building her up with home-made foods and bought-in treats like chocolate, ice cream and blueberry muffins, refusing all help with the chores.

It left her plenty of time to think.

She received notification to return to the hospital for the surgeon's handiwork to be assessed and went with trepidation – might he have to go back in with the knife? Sara accompanied her.

A typical hospital appointment – you report in at a cubby window, then find a seat among many others who didn't want to be there either, and wait in line, masking your anxieties and your inadequacies, until way past when you were due to be seen they at last call you through.

They gave her a thorough examination and deemed themselves satisfied with the outcome. But they could not or would not answer the million dollar question – would she be able to have babies? It depended on how her body adjusted. It would be one for the gynaecologists.

Left in limbo but what could she do?

Were she ever to meet her dream lover, someone so right that, just like Abby and John, she would single him out as the father she wanted for her kids, then it would be crunch time.

Would she tell him of her injury, that children might not be possible, and risk him taking off? It would surely be his right to know. He wouldn't back out if he was truly in love with her.

For the present, she would blot it out.

151

Over and above her physical injuries, the biker bestiality had left a mental mark. It was finally dawning that there were consequences for being a wayward child and despising authority.

She span it around her head … and decided to reform. Getting shot of the chip on her shoulder would be a start. She wasn't alone in being an orphan, life wasn't always fair, there were no free lunches going – if she did not get a grip she would never leave her imprint on society. And if you don't do that what's the point of being on this earth?

It was about then that the police hit the HQ of the Bastards on Wheels. They went in mob-handed. They went in tooled up – explosive charges to blow entry, battering rams to smash down doors, crowbars and monkey wrenches, super-sized cutters to rend padlocks apart. No messing and no concession to political correctness. They turned the place over in a frenzy of evidence gathering.

There was plenty to find – drugs, offensive weapons, an illicit still, stolen property. Several guns, suspected of being used in crimes, were in the haul and they even found the truncheon Gonz had used on Suzi – he had put his capture back on the wall. So confident was he in his own invincibility that he hadn't even washed the bloodstains off it – complementing its evidential authenticity.

The Bastards on Wheels had foreseen that were it to come to a showdown then it would likely turn into an OK Corral shoot-out.

It didn't.

So well planned was the raid that they were caught cold. With Gonz taken down before he could get a shot off, cuffed and thrown into a paddy wagon, resistance disintegrated. Half got banged up, destined to head through the legal process. The rest – how to put this delicately – were *encouraged* to take a walk into the sunset.

The Pantagraph put it more explicitly – they'd been run out of the state, it asserted. And good riddance. The paper gave the story big licks, billing it as a throwback to the 1880s Wild West, responsible citizens standing up to evil men, sheriffs and their deputies rampaging through the outlaw hideout.

Suzi soaked it up – Gonz was due everything he was going to get. The courts would send him down, plenty of years in the penitentiary. No word of Honcho in the coverage – Suzi was secretly glad. Had he got away? She never did find out. She assumed he must have done.

In fact, it proved to be a stark lesson for him too.

It forced him to take stock and decide whether he really wanted to ride with tossers like Gonz. He broke with motorcycle gangs, moved to the West Coast where nobody knew him from Adam, opted for small town California rather than the big city, found a job as an air conditioning engineer, got married, had kids, turned into the model family man.

Though he kept the Harley – on occasion dusting it down, giving it an airing, helmet on, the smell of leathers, a beat-up down the road. Such rare excursions kept him sane when things were getting on top of him, a release valve, and that was when he would ask himself what had become of that pretty little thing from Normal whose bloody memory he could never expunge. One of those blots on your life where you so wish you could have your time over again.

41

Back in Sydney the Kevin-Alice affair was getting ever more frenetic.

Kevin had been forced to skip the after-work meet-up – a family trip to Melbourne to see an aunt who had notched up her ninetieth. It had turned out better than it sounded – the old stick was on good form, several glasses of *medicinal* sherry partaken! Her nursing home had produced a cake, and staff and family sang her happy birthday. Still with enough puff to blow out her candles in one. Nine candles, mind you, not the full ninety!

So when Kevin and Alice hitched up the Friday after they were once again ravenous for each other. Unwisely, taking an indolent punt, they met up in the *office pub* ninety-nine per cent sure none of the rest were heading there, and snogged their tonsils out – no inhibitions. Once more laughing and joking like a young couple in love – which they weren't.

The sex was still all-pervading. They loved each other as friends but they were not yet in love and in truth neither contemplated being so albeit sometimes it seemed to be headed that way. Hard to say why. It just didn't have the smell of the long term. Like being on a merry-go-round where eventually when you go too fast someone gets slung off.

They ordered a second drink – he toasted her beauty; she toasted his virility. "So," she said mysteriously … and he wasn't sure what was coming.

"We've done it on the 'Kangaroo Club' table, your balcony has lost its virginity, where do you think we should make love tonight?"

They both knew this was a wind-up.

When at last they had half-composed themselves Kevin put his thinking cap on. As he sought to string her along and she told him wickedly that he had better match up to her expectations, he announced: "I know – we'll go to your place and make love in the lift!"

It wasn't a serious proposition – she smacked him in the chest as though shocked while he held up his hands and claimed she should be grateful.

"It could put a whole new meaning on going up," he said.

"Or a whole new meaning on going down," she said.

They were in stitches.

One or two of the tables around them glanced oddly at them.

"Shush," she cooed. "People are listening." And once more faked offence.

Silence. Who was going to take this on and where was it going to lead?

She spoke up first and deadpan asked: "So what are the rules for this shag-a-lift?"

He fell apart and almost losing it herself she hushed him into some sort of composure before the whole bar fixated on them.

Finally pupated into an aura of being proper, his estate agent persona took over. "How many floors are there in your block of flats?"

She shook her head in disbelief.

"Thirteen," she said, playing him at his own game with not the hint of a smile.

"OK," he said, putting on his studious professional voice. "Right to the top, back down to eight, time up whether we manage to go all the way or not, and into your flat."

She tried to hold it together without cracking up.

"Fine. You're on."

Neither had the remotest inclination to do anything of the sort. Yet they could not have been more enthralled and liberated in each other's company.

A bite to eat, a brandy apiece, and then a taxi to her place.

They got out of the cab in good humour – they had been holding forth about holidays, *Mr and Mrs Smith*, and where they might go. As the meter racked up the charge, the suggestions had become more expensive and outlandish.

They walked arm-in-arm to the block entrance and thence to the lift. She pressed the up button and their eyes met. They could hear it rumbling down from whatever floor it had been on. It came to a stop and the doors parted. It was empty and they got in.

She looked at him, he looked at her, and almost as one, they started discarding clothing in all directions.

By floor four they were into each other in an upright position in all respects.

By seven they had sidled to the floor going for it as though an Olympic medal was dependent on the outcome.

Ding! The bell for 13 sounded.

The doors opened and suddenly she screamed, pulling away from him just as he was on countdown to launch.

She turned away in shame. There stood a woman in her sixties, mouth ajar, jaw on the floor, unable to move, incapable of taking in the scene in front of her. What was she doing there at this time of night?

His reaction was immediate. "Sorry," he said. "Won't happen again. Have a good evening." And pushed the button for floor 8.

The doors closed, she screamed again at the pornography of what they had done, clothes frantically being gathered up.

They burst out of the lift and raced for her flat.

Oh God, where were her keys? Who had her handbag?

It turned out he did.

She fetched out the keys, dropped the keys, picked them up, floundered with the lock, got the door open, and their foolhardiness propelled them into the front room. Clothing like a paper trail along the hallway, a flesh fetish on the sofa, histrionics riddled with sin. Creased up, body parts contorted, until they came apart in a medley of claim and counter-claim.

"How could you? You're perverted." She was trying to sound as if she meant it.

"What! It was your idea," he insisted.

"How dare you – I was brought up a nice girl," she exclaimed. "Anyway, it was your idea, don't pin that on me."

He burst out laughing once more. She gave him a smacking. Next they were on the floor again and thinking of making love.

Yet they held back.

"What if she calls the police?" said Alice.

"The police have better things to do than respond to some old granny who maintains she's seen two naked people having it off in a lift," he retorted. "At least I bloody well hope so."

"But what if there's some comeback with the agents who look after the block?"

"We will just say we know nothing about it," he said. "Will she remember what we look like – there's hardly going to be an identity parade! It sounds so fanciful. Who's likely to believe her?"

There was logic in what he said.

He hammed up being the presiding judge hearing the case. "Mrs Jones – was this knob, belonging to the defendant Kevin Jackson as before you naked in the dock, the knob you saw in the lift?"

It was back to laughter as she tried to visualise the revolting scene.

"How could you tell her to 'have a good evening'?" chortled Alice. "What are you?"

Now he was laughing too. "It just came into my head," he squirmed.

"I'm going to run a mile if the doorbell rings," she said.

That doubled him up.

"What's so funny?"

"No, it's nothing."

"Tell me."

"I just thought of nipping to the loo, then using my mobile to order a pizza delivery. Just to see your face."

"Swine," she shrieked, hit him with a cushion, and jumped on top of him.

He let himself go loose to *take the punishment* until she ran out of energy. The play-fight over, he feasted on her body, and then their lips met.

"Come on," she said. "Let's go to bed."

"This time, no hurry," he said.

"Definitely no hurry," she agreed.

Under the sheets they made it slow, deliberate, intimate, profound, meaningful and very much together.

It was as if their affair had gone to the next level!

42

Too good to be true? Something had to go wrong.

True to form next week in the office it all went pear-shaped.

Within half an hour he sensed something was up. It was clear the Kevin-Alice cat was out of the bag.

How had that happened?

They should never have gone to the office pub – someone must have popped by as an afterthought, their eyes had almost popped out, and he and Alice, otherwise engaged, never noticed.

They'd been snitched on, this was great gossip, and it had clearly done the rounds. There were knowing sniggers. Somebody asked him whether it had been a satisfying weekend – they never normally said anything like that.

In the lunchtime queue at the sandwich shop the office wag Freddy ripped into him. "What's this about you and Alice – you dirty dog?" He nudged him in the ribs. Kevin tried to look blank, but Freddy was on a roll. "Wow, Alice is a stunner. How did you manage to pull her?"

Kevin feigned nonchalance. "We're just friends – nothing to it."

Freddy was one of those people who never knew when to let go. "Oh, the old just good friends line," he chirped. "Come on, Kev, spit it out – are you bonking her?"

Freddy knew Kevin hated being called Kev.

"That's very insulting," growled Kevin.

Now Freddy knew he was getting under Kev's skin. "Buying butties for two, are we? I bet she's really tasty in bed."

Kevin said nothing, took his sandwich, handed over the money, and was out of the door without another word.

Inwardly he was fizzing.

He'd felt like punching the slime ball's lights out but – staying with feline metaphors – that would have really put the cat among the pigeons.

As the afternoon wore on Kevin and Alice took to *social distancing* as though a virus had broken out in the office. Another giveaway? Or was that too Machiavellian?

Even Daniel and James – his friend Sako had moved on some while back – were in the loop. Alternatively, maybe Kevin was imagining it. He shrivelled at his desk. Slunk away at close of play.

That night he phoned Alice – what were they to do? Agitated, he spelt out his doomsday scenario – it was known that the bosses loathed office entanglements, it could jeopardise their careers, it would be easy to dream up some excuse to fire them, this was a disaster.

"Hold on," she said. "What's all the fuss about?"

That saw him hit the roof.

"How can you say 'what's all the fuss about'," he repeated, voice rising. "We're in big, big doo-dah land."

"Don't talk rot," she insisted. Honestly, men could act like babies. She paused. "Look I'll meet you tomorrow night after work and we'll talk it through."

"How can we do that," he gulped. "We can't exactly walk out one after the other while proclaiming nothing's going on."

She started to get angry. "Well, if you want to play James Bond I'll turn left out of the office and you turn right. Is that dramatic enough for you?"

He began to feel a bit soppy. Perhaps he was over-reacting. "OK," he stuttered unhappily. "Where shall we meet?"

"We'll meet in the Botanic Garden."

Not exactly an ultimatum but no room for argument either.

"All right then," he moped. "See you there."

The phone went dead.

It was a restless night. How had he ended up in such a pickle? She had seduced him – that was what she had done. It was unacceptable.

Oh, God.

He was ill at ease at work next day, concentration skewed, back to not knowing where to look, suspecting they were talking about him under their breath.

Unusually for him, he was among the first out the door when the 5pm stampede sounded.

By Botanic Garden she had meant the Royal Botanic Garden Sydney. For those who don't know it, it dates back to 1816 and holds a formidable position on the harbour front adjacent to the central business district and Opera House. One of the city's top attractions covering 30 hectares. Flowers, shrubs, trees, lawns, ponds … it is … enchanting.

Except that evening its beauty was lost on Kevin.

He found her seated on a bench near the main entrance.

They greeted each other in a ridiculously formal manner and he sat down – there was no kissing.

"What are we going to do?" he garbled, an opening gambit that sounded so limp.

She went straight onto the offensive. "I don't know what you're whining about. What could be normal than two people going out with each other."

He was daggers drawn. "It's the office – it could wreck everything I've built up there. You know I'm quasi-management."

She wasn't having it. "So?" she asserted. "If office attachments were somehow banned half the country would never get themselves hooked up."

There was more to it than that, he told her. In offices like theirs colleagues had to get on whether they liked each other or not, where small things could become big things, where work and private lives could rarely co-exist without issues. It was a thesis shot full of holes, he hadn't put it at all well and it was a mile off being a knock-out blow.

"If we're transparent about it there won't be a problem," she said. "Only if we're devious might they justifiably have concerns. We do our job, to the best of our ability as always, and we go home at night having put in a shift. You're building barriers where there don't need to be any."

It was a good speech. He was losing the argument.

"I just see a soap opera developing," he insisted. "I mean … what if we bust up and decide we can't stand the sight of each other? One way or another there's going to be bad blood."

She still wasn't buying it. "Why would we bust up?" she asked. "It's going well, isn't it? I don't hear you complaining."

It put him on the spot. "Well, yes," he concurred. "It has been good."

"OK then," she said. "Stop being so namby-pamby, find some backbone and let's see how it pans out. I'll see you on Friday."

He'd been beaten. "I suppose so," he grovelled.

"There," she said. "That wasn't so hard, was it?" She kissed him, announced she had to be on her way, patted his leg as if to say everything would be fine, and, with a toss of her hair, was gone.

He sat there a long time, deflated, insignificant in a vast park. He'd gone into it hoping he could crowbar himself out of what was fast becoming suffocating, and had simply ended up deeper in the mire. She had twirled him around her little finger and he had no answer.

43

He trudged home – this could easily get on top of him, bringing the old doubts and demented memories back from the crash.

The rest of the week he wasn't in the office much. Houses to inspect; clients to see.

Even so, he was not himself.

The more he got his head round it the more determined he became that Kevin-Alice had run its course and it was time to quit. He had to steel himself and tell her it was over. She was being dumped.

They went to the office bar, reasoning that, now things were out in the open, it was neither here nor there. He got the drinks and they found a corner to themselves.

Like tasting salt on the wind ahead of a storm, tension was in the air.

She beat him to the punch.

"Look, the week is over, freedom until Monday, I want to chill, let my hair down, and how am I going to do that if you are in a bloody mood. I thought we'd settled all this nonsense on Tuesday."

Her aggression put him on the defensive – must fight fire with fire he told himself.

Smash her.

"I want out," he said. "I've had it. It's been fab as far as it's gone. You're an outstanding girl, but I can't deal with the office fall-out. We're done."

She flew into a rage. "What fall-out?" she yelled. "There has been no fucking fall-out."

"Keep your voice down, for God's sake."

She didn't.

"I've invested plenty in you," she charged. "You may be a fucking wimp but you're my fucking wimp. There is no way we're splitting up. Have you got that?"

He reeled back in his chair. "I am sorry if this is upsetting for you," he said. "But it takes two to tango and I'm no longer tangoing." He got up to leave. He had barely taken a sip of his drink.

"Sit down," she screeched at him.

The whole pub turned and looked at them. Disconcerted, rattled, he wished the ground would open up and swallow him.

He sat down.

But she was just getting going and with lethal venom. "Now listen to me," she barked. "It would be most unfortunate if Daniel and James were to find out that we did it on the *Kangaroo Club* table, wouldn't it?"

Rather like the granny in the lift, his jaw hit the floor and he sat there gob-smacked.

"How you raped me when all I was doing was innocently returning to the office to find my purse. Do I make myself clear?"

He sat there, wiped out, unable to think. This was like something out of a lurid novel.

"You wouldn't," he rambled. "That's not on – you know that's not the way it was."

"All I know," she hissed frostily. "Is that you took advantage of me – they are going to fire you on the spot … at the very least suspend you. It will be your word against mine and who do you think they're going to believe? The police will likely be alerted. I will tell them I didn't report it at the time because you pulled rank on me. You could go down. Do you think you could survive a stretch in jail?" She glared at him. "Don't fuck me about, sunshine, or I will make sure you get fucked over big time."

His marbles seemed to be out of sync – his spark plugs misfiring. "But that's blackmail," he gabbled.

"You bet," she said. "And you'd better believe it, hunk."

He sat there, trashed.

Like the spider and the fly.

Or, perhaps more pertinent, both of them knew she had his goolies in a vice-like grip. His thought patterns were all over the place. Surely, she wouldn't tell the bosses – would she? If she did, he was finished. He could make a clean breast of it (not the ideal choice of words) but then he would be finished anyway.

What a cold-hearted, vicious, witch.

He was to be her prized specimen, kept in a cage and let out once a week when she wanted to play.

Still speechless, he sat there mouth open like a dead fish.

"Oh come on," she chided, flicking a switch. "Drink your drink. Now we've got our little misunderstanding straightened out." Her face broke into a wide smile. "Consider yourself blessed. You have a pretty girl who is mad for you. Sit back and enjoy the sex."

He sat back. But, as a performing sea lion from now on in, how was he going to enjoy the sex? He took a long swig from his beer, then decided to do what many men do when cornered – get drunk, it might all go away, and, if not, put it off until the morrow.

Another swig.

"That's the way," she told him. "Lighten up. What about going to a club later – I feel like dancing."

What the fuck, he thought. In for a penny, in for a pound. He smiled back, hand on her thigh, they kissed – might as well make the most of it. Started chatting away as if nothing had passed between them, he bought another round, and the trademark giggling started.

They went round to an all-on-one-site commune of café restaurants. Out of a wide menu of international cuisine, they chose Chinese, and sat at a table in the square. The food was delicious.

Then along to a club.

It was hot, her jive bunny was intoxicating – intoxication on top of intoxication – and the blend of perspiration and perfume was like an aphrodisiac. They danced lots and then found seats at the far side where the light was dim.

They embraced one-another.

"You're a super dancer."

She soaked up the compliment then allowed her fingers to tip-toe over his credentials with delicate daring. "Ready for some yet?"

He stroked her thigh. "Balcony, lift … let's do it here."

Unlike the lift, they both knew this was not on – the club was busy and there were too many people close by. Besides, they had already pushed their luck once

They hailed a taxi and left for her flat.

She joked that she was going to put him in chains and do what she wanted with him – it seemed an appropriate analogy given the way things had gone.

They may have had the row to end all rows but the sex was as climactic as ever.

Given that had he had real balls it would not be taking place, a bit of him hoped that his libido would disappoint her. But she was so good at getting him going. He had to admit yet again, that office complications or not, she was a fantastic lay.

What is it the Poms say? *Lie back and think of England.*

It didn't happen very often but the Poms sometimes got things right.

44

And so, as the weeks and months ticked by, the partnership spluttered along, driven primarily by top-down sex albeit it had become more than that – knowing each other's likes, idiosyncrasies and much more besides turned them into something of a girl/boy fixture.

The office, seemingly at first hostile, mellowed. One or two even said they were happy for them. Kevin didn't see it that way, growing more and more to resent becoming her sex slave. Gradually it began to eat him up, though he sought to hide his unhappiness from her. Anyway, he reasoned, why cut off his nose to spite his face by failing to wallow in her voluptuous offerings – the typical selfish male's take on these type of *problem* choices.

However, he found that letting things lie affected him at work – he was less driven, tetchy, prone to day-dreaming.

Alone in his flat there were times he felt worthless.

What was he doing? Where was his life going?

He had to escape from under Alice, however nice a position that was. Maybe it was time for a complete break – from Alice, from Sydney, from Australia, from the whole schmozzle.

Unlike many Australians he had never travelled out-with the south Pacific – Bali, Fiji, New Zealand was a country and a half … and that was about it. He had never been to the United States, England, or mainland Europe. Time to widen his horizons perhaps. England continued to fascinate Australians. He could do the tourist bit, soak up the sights, scout links to the Mother Country, tour the Houses of Parliament. He had a vague recall of mum and dad paying an ancestry specialist to research their family tree and that some long-forgotten relative had apparently emigrated from Tamworth back in the nineteenth century, some place near Birmingham. He wasn't sure where.

Might be a laugh to go and see what Tamworth was like today.

He took a week to mull all this around but gradually it became an increasingly appealing proposition.

Sydney was insular; he knew everything there was to know about it. He would miss it – that was for sure. What a lifestyle.

He'd be exchanging that for the English weather – not a fair swop.

And the old jokes came flooding back – while Australians bathe in endless sunshine, the English are confounded by that mysterious yellow orb in the sky when it makes its annual cameo appearance each *summer*; Australia boasts more than 10,000 golden strips of sand, meaning you could take in a new swimming spot every day for almost three decades – which is roughly how long it's been since the sun shone on one of England's pebbly excuses for a beach. Ho, ho, ho.

But this was a turning point.

Australians of course usually go *walk-about* in their early twenties – Kevin was nearly forty.

It might seem an odd move abandoning everything familiar for a land he knew little about apart from what he had gleaned from school, literature, the media and pals who had gone and done it. However, it would mean he could extricate himself from the clutches of Alice and the very real danger that the toxicity of their pairing was slowly, ever so slowly, tipping him back into what he referred to as *crash mode* – the low esteem and negativity that had plagued him when he had first returned to the sports agency.

At all costs, he must fend off the shakes.

They hadn't been bad for a while – it was only on stray nights he still woke up in a total stupor. Which was why he always took a glass of iced water and a book to bed – put the light on, take a drink, read a few chapters, turn the light off, and, saints preserve us, next you knew, in the words of Cat Stevens, *morning had broken*.

So, a plan was hatched, but how to implement it?

He wasn't going to tell Alice – that was for sure. He hoped he could so contrive it that after sex on the Friday he simply wasn't there on the Monday. Absolute secrecy would be imperative.

To that end too he would tell his family just a week or so beforehand. He hoped they wouldn't take it badly.

First, he would outline his thinking to the estate agency. They had been good to him.

By coincidence, or maybe not a coincidence, just as Kevin was about to approach the bosses, they approached him. Called into a meeting, there was the usual pleasantries, some tippy-tapping around whatever was to come, and then they were biting into the kernel.

It had been noted that Kevin hadn't been his normal self of late. His business performance had tailed off. He seemed a little morose. Was there something troubling him that they didn't know about? A work issue. Something in his private life. He was a key player and they didn't want any disruption – could they assist in any way?

The stance took Kevin aback.

They were right in their assessment though it was a surprise to him how they had zeroed in on it so quickly. But then they were smart cookies.

Still, get it out into the open.

He had thought about what he was going to say.

He was definitely keeping all mention of Alice out of it, not only because he wanted a clean break but because he liked her and it would be vulgar to tarnish her reputation.

He told them he had become a little stale, was finding it difficult to crank into gear every morning, was taking clients for granted, and believed a change of scene might be beneficial to all parties. He had loved working for the partnership, he had always tried to give of his maximum, but it was the end.

Now, they were the ones out on a limb.

They had only ever intended to nip in the bud anything that was festering behind the scenes.

His resignation was not on the agenda.

So they sought to dissuade him. His vitality would be missed. If money was at the root of this then they would look to incentivise him further. If it was greater responsibility he wanted then they had been assessing whether Brisbane represented a gap in the market – they would put him in charge of launching and running the new office.

He said it wasn't money or responsibility, the remuneration was good and they had always allowed him his say. It was more that the job had run its course, he wanted to travel, then would chew over whether he should return to estate agency or look at alternatives. It was in the firm's own interest to bring in new blood. He had stayed way past what he had ever envisaged – seven years. He would stultify if he remained. They would get fed up with his face, he joked.

Don't do anything rash, came the reply. Think about it. Take a week off. He'd perhaps been over-doing things. Had they been putting too much on him?

He felt like saying he had been over-doing Alice, but obviously didn't. He would definitely think through what they had put to him, and reflected in private that he should not be dismissing Brisbane out of hand. It was promotion and might be just far enough away to put Alice on ice.

He didn't tell them he had already applied for a visa that would allow him to live and work in the UK – it was a plus that his grandfather on his mother's side had been born there.

He would let them know his decision on the Monday.

It was convenient because it would allow him to first break the news to the family and no doubt another grilling.

So he did take two days off – a week, he felt, would have been taking the mick – and drove up into the Blue Mountains. He loved them and, if he was off to the other side of the globe for a protracted period, he wanted to lose himself in its renowned natural environs. Do some walking. Listen out to the call of the wild. Marvel at this wilderness region from cliff top lookouts. Waterfalls, valleys and rugged sandstone tablelands, the Jenolan Caves, see the Three Sisters Hanging Rock. Diverse flora and fauna; centuries-old Aboriginal culture.

It re-invigorated the soul. He was glad he had gone.

And he had a cunning plan for when he got back.

45

Having savoured the Blue Mountains, he would savour the delights of Alice just in case she suspected something was up.

She did indeed query what was behind his vanishing act – the bosses had been generous, he told her. She sighed and said she wished she had been able to go with him. It made her sound clingy and dependant. Definitely time to knock it on the head.

Rejecting Brisbane – a clean break was called for – when he told his parents he was giving up the job to tour England and wider frontiers, he got a mixed reaction.

His mother was against it – when would she ever see her *baby* again? How could it be wise to throw away such a solid and rewarding job? He seemed so chipper at last – where had all this come from? Why the hurry?

Dad was more measured. He had travelled in his youth.

It was all well and good but Kevin was doing this as a middle-aged man. Would he fit in? Could he adapt? The grass wasn't always greener on the other side of the hill.

Vicky who had been backpacking told him simply. "Go for it!"

Hardly unequivocal, but overall he felt he had their blessing – mum would come round. Anyway, they could visit him. Yes, it was a long way but it wasn't like he was blasting off to Mars.

Kevin went in on the Monday as agreed and told them his mind was made up.

They said they were very sorry to hear it.

As to his shares in the business – they were willing to buy them back at a premium, which was magnanimous of them.

They set a date – the end of the month, just three weeks away.

He told them he did not want anyone to know he was off, there was to be no announcement, no leaving bash, he would simply walk out on the Friday and be absent on the Monday when they were then at liberty to reveal all. They said that was most irregular. He said that for personal reasons he'd rather it was done that way … wouldn't want there to be any ill will or unpleasantness.

They cottoned on – so the rumours about Kevin and Alice were true.

And they reluctantly agreed to his request.

He worked his socks off in those last weeks not wishing anyone to accuse him of winding down or slacking.

The visa came through, he paid for his plane tickets, Vicky was to take over the flat and the car.

So, it came to the final Friday.

He spoke with the partners, they shook hands, wished him well, told him to let them know how he was getting on, and if he ever came back and was needing a job to give them a call. He thanked them once more for all they had done for him and thanked them in particular for keeping his departure under wraps.

That evening he took Alice out as usual. She remained completely in the dark.

Whatever their differences she was a belter and he wanted to treat her with dignity.

He wrote a long letter which he planned to post on the day he flew out. It told her she was gorgeous. It had been wonderful. He was extremely fond of her but that was as far as it went. He felt claustrophobic being unable to take the relationship forward or backwards. He apologised for not saying this to her face but wanted to keep it civilised. He trusted she would understand. He hoped she would find happiness.

It was the best he could do.

He had also chosen to buy her a *going away* present to in effect say thank you for her largesse in ministering to his needs. It was a gold necklace cum pendant and he had spent a fat sum on it. He was honour bound to do right by her. Disgracefully he had never given her a present in all the period they had been going out.

He took her to the office pub, then they carried on to what would be their Last Supper. It was a posh restaurant because he wanted to put on a show.

She was in her element.

When they got back to her flat, he brought out the necklace.

He knew it wasn't her birthday but it was grossly remiss that he had never bought her anything, so had decided to rectify that. He hoped she would like it.

She was made-up by the gesture.

She removed the wrapping, opened the little presentation box, said the necklace was ever so pretty, tried it on, admired it in a mirror, took it off, thanked him and said she would always cherish it.

She put her arms around his neck, and kissed him slow and smutty.

So much so that his knees began to shake.

Part of his being told him he was acting crazy. Any self-respecting man would desire such a delectable woman. When she wasn't threatening him with rape, she was a stimulating playmate. She was intelligent. She was a goddess under the sheets. He was very much wanted. Maybe he should stick with Alice. It wasn't too late to abandon the Great Escape.

He teetered on the cliff edge.

No, he had to go through with it. He had to be free.

The lovemaking was out of this world and he left the next day, emotionally and physically eviscerated, but glad to have known her.

Finally, there was conclusion.

As they say, all's fair in love and war. When Alice went into work on the Monday there was no Kevin. It didn't immediately strike her as out of the ordinary – maybe he was on a job.

However, mid-morning the bosses called them together – Kevin had left. He had long wanted to go travelling. They were sad to part company. It wasn't at their instigation. They had tried to persuade him to stay. It wasn't to be. He hadn't wanted a going away party, nothing … there was an apology for keeping it from them but Kevin was insistent.

That was it. They went back to their desks and got on with it.

Alice was wounded but she was resilient. There were no tears – she didn't pale. When she got back to the flat that evening, there was the letter on the mat. She read it and this time there were tears.

She was furious at having been duped, she would have liked to have given him a piece of her mind, she would have liked to have taken him home for a spanking session.

For ten days or so she was below par – until Kevin's replacement Rikki turned up in the office. He had French origins, was tall, athletic, blue eyes, a snazzy dresser. Rikki never had a snowball's chance in Hades. She was on him before you could say ooh la la.

And so Kevin was cancel-cultured.

46

In Normal, Suzi took things steady, no need to speed her recovery, simply try and do a bit more as each day passed.

She helped her Gran around the house, took an interest in cooking, pottered about the garden, made it up with old dog Lady. She went for walks, having stated hand-on-heart there would be no bunking off. She began jogging, read books, worked on her suntan, tried to solve the newspaper crossword.

This was going to be the new Suzi.

She discussed going back to school – that is if they would have her back – and subsequently she, Sara and Jeb met with the principal.

Finally, said Suzi, she had fathomed out how crucial it was to study – it was probably too late to salvage all that she had missed from her truant past, but it would be good to start somewhere.

Perhaps not surprisingly, the principal vacillated – leopard and spots came to mind. Mindful though how young people do go off the rails and you shouldn't deny them a second chance. He would give Suzi the benefit of the doubt – he urged her not to let him down. They talked about her dropping a year and seeing how she got on. She agreed that would make sense. The next week she went in and grafted from the outset, much to her teachers' incredulity. The new Suzi was applying herself.

In particular, boys were off limits while she got herself firmly grounded.

She grafted at home too – decrying television, computer games and social media in favour of long hours in her bedroom, catching up on the many missing gaps in her education.

Months went by and Suzi kept at it.

She had turned into a model pupil – both the school and her family were over the moon.

Grateful, she herself felt her life was being re-booted.

Volunteering for demotion had one *out of left field* consequence. Her new classmates were mostly unknown quantities and in turn knew little about Suzi's fractured history. Therefore, she had something of a clean slate. Children tend to take people as they find them and so fitting in was straight-forward. Indeed, she was popular. Scarcely coming into contact with her old friends was a bonus – kept her from roguery. Being streetwise was sometimes an advantage – convoluting for sure, but she turned into a bit of an agony aunt. Younger ones making their own mistakes increasingly used her as a sounding board. You couldn't have made it up.

Yet she knew that, rather like a caldera, the old Suzi was bubbling under and had not gone away.

Would her volcano blow its top? The cynics would have said it was a question of not if but when.

And when *when* came around it was so disappointing for all concerned and so avoidable.

Her resolve withered on the vine one Saturday as she returned from shopping – T-shirts, jeans, shoes. Didn't buy anything, had already blown her monthly allowance, but keeping up with evolving tastes.

Yes, she had become fashion conscious.

In hindsight, she ought to have been alert to the possibility of being led astray when one-time "awkward squad" member Emma strode into view.

"What ya, Suzi," hailed Emma. "Heard you'd had a bit of bovver with them bikers. Horrible that. Back on the scene now though, are we?"

"Actually, no," replied Suzi. "Trying to steer clear."

"What?" sneered Emma. "You haven't gone all boring on us, have you?"

Suzi bristled. "No, just other stuff to do."

Emma cackled. "Never thought you'd be one to sell out."

Suzi blushed. "It's not like that." She felt tongue-tied and defensive.

"Well," responded Emma. "You go off and play with your dolls – we're going to the race."

"What race?" said Suzi, falling for it hook, line and sinker.

"Baz and Mickey are lifting a couple of motors," said Emma. "There's a hillbilly straight a few miles outside of town where they're going to have a face-off. Should be a hoot."

Suzi felt her heart pounding. "Na, don't want to fall out with the cops."

"Don't be a baby," snorted Emma. "Smokey know nothing about it." She could see Suzi was torn. "Come on," she insisted. "We're only going to watch – what's wrong with that?"

"OK," said Suzi. "But if there's aggro I'm gone."

Emma flicked her eyes back with disdain. She was wearing a T-shirt emblazoned with the words *Hot Chick* strategically ripped to expose a bra strap. The top button was open on old jeans that had been cut down into shorts complete with a badge stating, *Press to Enter*. She also had on leather boots rising to her thigh.

All for one thing – to pull.

Emma had first arranged to meet Anna and Anna's boyfriend Jez in a nearby bar. The mostly male clientele did a double take when the pair walked in. Anna and Jez were seated at a centre table. Every eye turned as Emma flounced over.

"You two up for it then?"

"Yeah," said Anna. "Half the cool cats in Normal will be there. It's going to be mind-blowing."

Jez ordered bottles of lager for the newcomers.

They sank them slowly, basking in the eroticism from burning eyes.

Emma liked to put it about.

Jez ran a battered Chevrolet Impala and they all piled in.

When they got to the meet, there was already a gathering host. Horns honking, engines blasting, music blaring. Windless conditions, bright evening. Just right for showing off. The majority congregated in the pit lane but there were a sprinkling of spectators dotted along the one mile route.

"Cheers," said Suzi, slamming the Impala door.

"Magic," said Emma.

They mingled with the crowd as they waited for the action to get under way. Every type of outfit. Every type of hairstyle. Baby-faced teenagers feigning the hard man. A host of Sandys out of Grease.

A ripple ran through the hundred and twenty-plus renegade band. Arriving at a chalk-marked *starting grid* were the two protagonists.

47

Baz was in a Ford Mustang, his mate Joey in the passenger seat, and two glamorous girls sending out *look who I ride with* boasts, one concertinaed in the back, the other draped over Joey in the front.

Mickey was in a Porsche 911 with pal Ben. That meant there were vacancies. They were auditioning the girls in the crowd. And didn't the girls in the crowd know it, posing and flaunting as if in a beauty contest.

Mickey's eyes honed in on Emma and Suzi. "You two – get in the car."

Legs alluring, tits titillating, Emma strutted her way to the Porsche, stuck out her bum, a bottoms-up salute to her fans, and squeezed herself in.

Suzi gave no thought to backing out. Revelling in being a sex object again. Anyway, she would have lost too much face. This was like out of the movies – power, spice, studs, let's get racing. She never seemed to move a muscle but there she was beside Emma, hair thrown back, chin out and her *this is for big girls* face on.

Mickey turned to look at Baz, and nodded.

Baz indicated he was ready.

A lad with a Ferrari flag had been designated as starter and was milking it for all it was worth. His twin brother was on the finish line with a chequered flag – very chequered as it turned out.

Finally, engines revving, dust flying, screeching tyres, screams from the crowd, they were off. Instinctively Suzi put on her seatbelt – nobody else did.

Premonition? It was to save her.

Occupying both sides of the road the cars were racing wheel-to-wheel at over a hundred miles per hour.

This out-of-the-way stretch was invariably empty of traffic and they had reasoned that, it being late evening, nothing would be using it.

Wrong call.

Two hundred yards up an ancient, mud-spattered, pick-up edged out onto its side of the road, and into the path of the Porsche.

Mickey had two seconds, maybe three, to do something about it.

The farmer surveyed death bearing down on him brought his vehicle to a shuddering halt. "Mickey," he said later, "...had, like me, terror writ large stamped into his features."

The Porsche swerved to avoid the collision, but clipped the pick-up's wing. Now out of control, it slewed into the roadside gravel, took out a bush, bounced end over end perhaps five times, hit a tree, did another three revolutions, all the time metal fragments being thrown about like confetti, and crunched to a halt, steam and fury, threatening to explode.

It was carnage.

Mickey died instantly – so mangled was the corpse that his parents couldn't recognise their own son. When they found Ben, a branch was protruding from his chest. Emma's torso was spotted twelve feet off the ground – it took them three hours to discover her head buried in foliage.

Suzi came round, at first not knowing where she was, beyond bewilderment. In a trance. She couldn't remember how she had come to be there.

Prisoner of a wizard's spell.

As her senses cleared, and smouldering hit her nostrils, the risk of fire electrified her. She had to get out of this car – had to get out.

Releasing the seat belt, she realised that the door no longer existed.

Face in the dirt, every movement an agony, she crawled away from the vehicle.

She managed maybe fifteen feet before the Porsche torched itself.

The fireball burned her eyebrows away, seared her face, singed her clothes and left her unable to hear.

Somehow, she had to get back to the road – sheer willpower pulled her through. When they found her comatose, she had nearly made it.

The crowd splintered, heading for the hills, no longer wanting any part in the fiasco, nothing to do with them.

Baz raised the alarm.

The girls were screaming and screaming and screaming. Joey was ashen.

The farmer had survived but was badly shaken, sat in the roadway, head hunched, completely gone. The pick-up had been spun round. A write-off. Hens, which had been busted out of a cage in the rear, were all over the road, some dead, others clucking and squawking.

Baz began thinking fast. He turned round and told the girls in no uncertain terms to shut it. Red eyed and quaking, they obeyed. Then he took his phone out and dialled 911. When it answered he provided the basics – road traffic accident, location, multiple injuries, and then he turned his mobile off.

It was time to save himself – if he could – from the possibility of a hefty prison sentence for his part in the affair.

Aware there was a deep lake about three miles away, he turned the car and ordered Joey to keep a watchful eye out for the law. Yet more screaming from the back seat. Baz put his foot down and sped towards the spot. When he got there, he navigated the Mustang onto a slope close to the water. Everyone out.

"Right," said Baz to Joey. "She's going under – get ready to push."

He leaned back in, let off the handbrake, and the two of them gave the thing a shove. Seemingly reluctant, it began to move, accelerated and plunged into the lake. Spray everywhere, it sank fast, bubbles peppering the surface, one last gasp, and it was gone.

One of the girls was sobbing. The other was yowling that she needed her mother but so beside herself she kept on hitting the wrong buttons on her phone.

"No way," gobbed Baz and smacked her full in the face. Depositing her crumpled on the grass. Tore the mobile out of her hand and hurled it into the water. "What I say goes, or you follow your fucking phone."

His victim stayed prone; her friend, stung by a Baz stare, cut the racket.

This was the date you wouldn't wish on your worst enemy.

He took hold of the whimpering girls. "The first thing we're going to do is get out of sight of the fucking road – move it, slags."

He part pushed, part booted and part dragged them into cover and threw the girls onto the ground.

"Now listen to me all of you. I ain't going down for no fucking road race. We was never in a road race – have you got that?"

They looked petrified.

"We ain't going anywhere tonight – we stay here, hunch down and make sure nobody finds us. I'll have someone pick us up in the morning all things being equal."

Misty eyes stared back at him.

"Behave and you won't get hurt. Normally, you being attractive babes, I would happily give you a good rogering but not tonight, you'll no doubt be ecstatic to know. I've got enough on my plate."

Their faces were plastered with foreboding.

He stubbed a finger into the chest of the one whose phone was now being dialled by King Neptune.

"You tell your fucking mother when you get back that you was out camping with friends." He gave her another slap though not as vicious as the first. "You fucking sort it, or I'll come for you and when I'm finished that pretty face won't be pretty no more."

Miserable, a weal coming up on the side of one cheek, she sought to make herself small while her friend tried to console her.

Baz marched them into a section of thicket, undergrowth and serried ranks of trees well away from paths through the woods.

Nobody slept much that night, particularly the girls. It was uncomfortable, there were rustlings in the undergrowth so loud they convinced themselves that wolves were on the prowl, and they kept being bitten by insects.

The next day Baz made some calls and around mid-day a Toyota Sequoia sports utility vehicle trundled to a halt in a forest clearing.

They all got in – nobody spoke much as they processed the previous evening's slaughter.

They made it back to Normal without attracting suspicion.

At the grizzly crash scene police, fire and ambulance, though battle-hardened, were grim-faced at the gruesome sight.

Paramedics were around Suzi.

She was unconscious, bloodied, pulse and heartbeat steady, but breathing erratic. Given the potential for neck, spinal or internal injuries, they took their time, plenty of padding, eased her onto a stretcher and into an ambulance. Oxygen mask on, drip set-up and it was onwards to hospital, lights flashing, siren blaring.

Others were assessing the farmer. He wasn't making much sense, still very shocked, but no physical injury apparent.

They got him into a wheelchair and a second ambulance, thence to the same hospital. His condition would need monitoring.

The fire brigade had been hosing down what remained of the Porsche.

The chickens were making the most of their freedom.

It was obvious to all that nothing could be done for the other casualties.

From there it was a long slog – removing the bodies and body parts and, with the vicinity taped off, investigating what had caused the accident.

At first, it demonstrated all the characteristics of car-on-car, but the farmer had spoken of two vehicles bearing down on him. Could that have been the case or did the man, in his haze of confusion, have himself muddled?

At the hospital trauma department staff were working on Suzi to ascertain the extent of her injuries. Collapsed lung, broken arm, depressed fracture of the cheek bone, severe concussion, superficial second degree burns, but nothing internal and nothing life threatening.

She had been fortunate.

48

Sara and Jeb were mystified – Suzi hadn't come home.

They thought she was over all the disappearing acts and let-downs. With heavy hearts they phoned the police and reported her missing. The police took down her details, sought a description, requested a photo, said they would keep a lookout and get back in due course.

Just another entry in the log.

Until someone churned the brain cells – the description matched the female in the car wreck, didn't it? They ran a check on Suzanne Elizabeth Duthie – the computer displayed an extensive file on her – and put two and two together.

An officer was despatched to inform Sara and Jeb there was a possibility their grandchild had been in a car accident. He ran them to the hospital.

They were taken to the girl's bedside – Sara started sobbing, Jeb looked like a ghost.

There was no doubt. It was Suzi.

So began another family vigil at Suzi's bedside though emboldened by the medical opinion that she should make a full recovery.

Suzi woke up on day two – she was lying in a bed, with white sheets, white ceilings, white walls, and a white curtain.

She knew what that meant – she must be in a hospital.

Then it all came back to her – oh, yes, the race. What a stupid thing to do, why was she such an idiot, how did she allow others to ensnare her in such pranks.

At which point she noticed Sara and Jeb. "I'm so sorry, Granny, I've betrayed your trust again."

"Don't be silly, we need to get you better," said Sara.

Suzi smiled. Her whole body protested, she knew what it meant, she had been there before. "What's the damage?"

Sara tried to be matter-of-fact. "Oh, you've broken a few things, nothing too serious, the doctors and nurses have been ever so diligent, however you're going to be here a while."

She had cheated death for a third time.

A nurse requested they pop to the waiting room while she changed a tube. They could return as soon as she was finished.

When they did so Suzi was back among the sleepy heads.

Abby flew in on day three and went direct to the hospital.

"What have you done to yourself now?" she said, her impish aside designed to counteract the gravity of Suzi's situation and lift her morale.

Suzi tried to laugh but couldn't. "It's good to see you," she responded, in turn lifting Abby's morale.

After all the times when she had been called a 'cow' and more besides.

As had become the custom, they stuck to the banal and talked about Normal, Toronto, the family, the weather.

Until Suzi became more earnest. "I tried so hard not to get into that car. What's wrong with me, Abby? Trouble seems to follow me around."

She clasped Suzi's hand. "You were doing so well. This is just a blip – an aberration. Nobody is annoyed. We know there is so much good in you. We love you lots. You're going to get over this. We got the real Suzi back once and we're going to get the real Suzi back again. You'll see."

Suzi began to cry. "I'm so flawed. I'm forever having regrets. But I promise one day I'll make it up to you."

The pep talk worked – soon she was improving by the hour.

At which point, the police came round to take a statement from her.

Show willingness by all means, said Abby, but don't mention anything that might incriminate yourself. Astute advice, but Suzi felt she had little choice – she owed that to the dead. She had to take her medicine.

Yes, there was a second car, Baz was driving, she didn't know the other three with him.

Were they racing?

Yes, they were racing.

She could remember a vehicle pulling out in front but had no recollection of the crash itself. She could dimly recall dragging herself from the mangled heap.

What was the make of the second car?

She thought it was a Ford Mustang.

They were still trying to locate it – a Mustang had been reported stolen that day. Did she have any information as to its whereabouts?

No, she hadn't.

Was money being bet on the race?

She didn't think so.

How fast were they going?

Bending the truth, she replied: "I honestly wouldn't know – maybe eighty – eighty-five miles per hour."

Could the cars have been going even faster?

They could, she acknowledged.

It really must be the last time I give way to the dark arts, she thought to herself. Never again.

That applied to the newspapers too where she was now being termed a *wild child* and "the plane crash survivor who keeps trying to kill herself".

The ignominy she was heaping on the family sucked.

She wasn't the only one to identify Baz – there had after all been over a hundred witnesses. And despite Baz's threats, the girl who had seen her mobile hurled into the lake was *clapped in irons* by her parents, and then made a present of to the police, ordered to cough to her part in the crime.

The police did Baz for aggravated reckless driving and motor theft, his hopes of staying out of jail dashed.

The funerals for the victims were chilling – what a waste of three young lives.

Suzi left hospital to recuperate at home.

It was back to tidying the house, smartening up the garden, idling in front of the television and, when she felt up to it, walks around the local neighbourhood.

There was also the poser of – what next?

Another interruption in her schooling. This time they probably wouldn't want her back. Anyhow, she didn't think she could face the teachers. It would be too humiliating.

As her strength returned, at Abby's instigation, and once OK'd to fly, she travelled to Toronto for a holiday. Spending time with her cousins and being pampered by Abby was not to be sneezed at.

They did the tourist thing – boat trip around the harbour, went up the CN Tower, walked the Toronto Islands. The highlight was a day trip to Niagara Falls. A scenic drive there, cruise to the base of the falls, mist in your face – it was unforgettable. It brought back so many recollections for Abby – she and her John and that quaint little motel.

186

Abby and Suzi talked, but no ultimatums about sorting herself out, no harsh observations on where life was taking her.

The closest it came saw Abby simply advise her niece to lay down moral standards but otherwise to go with the flow. After all, how insane was it that she should fall in love with a man in a country she had never dreamed she would ever visit – and it was all down to Suzi. Someone overarching had surely been mapping a path for her. So, you never knew what twists and turns life would bring. She was sure Suzi would find herself.

Wise words deserving of serious contemplation.

When the holiday was over, she thanked Abby and John for their kindness and hospitality. It had been brilliant. She didn't deserve an aunt like Abby. It had taken her time to *get it*. Abby had done so much for her – thrown up her career in Dubai, gone all that way to Bali to look after her, brought her to Normal so the family could care for her, never failed to fight her corner despite her own trials. In turn, she had been so beastly to Abby. She could never repay her.

Requited, Suzi flew back.

The trip had been beneficial. It had enabled her to find an equilibrium. It had transported her from the goldfish bowl that was Normal. It had sowed the seed for the vast possibilities out there. It had captured her imagination.

It set her thinking that perhaps the time had come to abandon Normal – there would be no hasty decision but it had to be an option.

Normal was home and would always be home, but it was small, keeping a low profile was pretty much doomed, and she was now one of its most notorious figures.

Could she ever be free of her chaotic lifestyle while still living in Normal?

Probably not.

But where would she go? What would she do? How would she put food on the table?

Questions assigned to the backburner for now, but which she would have to deal with in due course.

Perhaps Abby was right – play it by ear, don't over-complicate things.

No doubt, something would be coming round the track.

All these thoughts were pin-balling about in her head as she settled herself back into the familiarity of Sara and Jeb's.

Mundane and domestic.

Yet everything was about to be thrown high in the air and it came about quite innocuously.

49

On this particular afternoon Suzi was in her bedroom reading when Sara shouted to her from downstairs.

Winter had come, it was cold outside, in weeks there would be snow on the ground, sometimes several feet of snow. Sara and Jeb were heading out. Could Suzi find her black gloves and drop them down please.

"Go into our room – they're in the chest of drawers. Can't remember which one. Try the second down."

Suzi did as requested. It took a tug and a heave. It was jammed with letters. She opened the third. Ah, there were the gloves granny wanted. Called out, then tipped them over the banisters.

"Thank you," said Sara. "That's excellent. See you later. We won't be long."

She heard them step out. The front door clicked shut.

Suzi returned to the bedroom and first closed the glove drawer. Next, she shaped up to the heavy one. As it shifted something caught her eye – one of the letters was addressed to her, Suzanne Duthie. Intrigued, she shunted the drawer out wide again.

She probably shouldn't be doing this because this was her grandparents' room and their private domain. But Suzi being Suzi could not resist.

She turned over some of the other letters, all still in their envelopes.

And she got a shock.

It wasn't just the one that was addressed to her – it looked like they all were.

Who could they be from? What were they doing in the drawer?

She felt like a burglar, but she had to open a letter out and find out the sender's identity. Delicately she did so, taking care not to tear it, and spread the letter on the bed. It began 'Dear Hope'.

Well, that was bizarre for starters – *who was Hope?*

She looked at the envelope again.

Yes, the addressee was definitely Suzanne Duthie. So who was this Hope?

She read on.

It was a long letter and the thrust was definitely adult-to-adult rather than adult to child. The author, she quickly deduced was male, and it spoke of all that he had been doing in the period, the people, the setbacks, the victories such as they were, his inner-most anxieties poured out onto the page.

At the bottom it was signed Kevin.

Kevin? She didn't know a Kevin. Except, wait a minute, wasn't that bloke who rescued her from the plane crash called Kevin? That could be it.

According to the postmark, the letter had been written fourteen years previously. When she would have been just four.

Truly whacky. What was that about? She re-read the letter – what was she to do about all this?

Feeling guilty for *ransacking* her grandparents' room, it was only right to play this straight down the line. She would read no more of the letters … and she shut the drawer. However, when propitious, she would reveal to Sara and Jeb that she had accidentally stumbled on the hoard when searching for the gloves – that, after all, was the exact truth. Then she would quiz them on what it meant and ask to be able to read them all. She wasn't sure why, but she felt that this was a fork in the road.

Half an hour later Sara and Jeb had returned.

"Hi, we're back," shouted Sara. "Everything OK?"

"Yes, good," said Suzi.

She said nothing about the letter cache.

Sara cooked dinner – home-made burger, with lettuce, onions, tomato, cheese and fries. Suzi emptied the dishwasher and then stacked it with the dirty plates and cutlery.

Jeb went into the computer room – said he wanted to catch up on emails. Sara sat down in the lounge, reading a magazine.

Suzi asked if she would like a cup of coffee.

"Yes, that would be nice, sweetie. I could do with a strong coffee."

Suzi made the coffee, just a dash of white, and took the two cups through, giving one to her grandmother and balancing hers close to her chest so, as she gingerly levered herself into an armchair, it didn't spill.

She took a sip.

Sara seemed relaxed – it was surely as good a time as any.

"Granny."

"Yes, dear."

"You know when I threw you down the gloves when you were going out earlier."

"Yes, dear."

"And you said to open the second drawer."

"Yes, dear."

"Well, they weren't there – they were in one of the other drawers."

"Is that right, dear?" Sara was engrossed in an article and was only half listening.

"Yes," said Suzi. "And it was impossible to miss that the wrong drawer was stuffed full of lots and lots of letters."

Sara lifted her head out of the magazine and focussed on Suzi.

"And, by accident, I noticed that all the letters were addressed to me."

She now had Sara's full attention.

"I'm a bit flummoxed," said Suzi. "Perhaps you could tell me about them."

Sara sighed and hummed to herself. "There's no riddle to this," she began. "We told you about the plane crash, didn't we?"

"Yes," said Suzi.

"And we told you about the man in the water who saved your life."

"Yes."

"Well, ever since you were tiny, he's been writing these long letters to you. We read them just in case there was some observation within them that necessitates a response. Then we put them away in the drawer. In our estimation, they seem odd and we did not want you upset by them given the other problems you've faced. They have I'm afraid just piled up – out of sight out of mind. They come as regular as clockwork every two months or so."

Suzi chewed it over.

Her irascible side wanted to know why, if addressed to her, Sara had taken it upon herself to read them and then kept them hidden. Fair enough when she was a child but surely that no longer held true. Instead, she reined in the charging steed – she had provoked her grandmother enough. She was learning that you picked your fights carefully, standing fast only when it counted and letting the rest go. This was not a battle worth taking on.

"I'm afraid I couldn't resist reading one of them," said Suzi. "What I can't figure is why the letter begins 'Dear Hope'."

"Well, neither can we," replied Sara. "They all begin 'Dear Hope'. I can only assume that it is some sort of nickname for you. That was another element we thought dubious."

"It does seem strange," agreed Suzi.

She paused. "What else do you find odd about them, Granny?"

"Goodness me, the questions you ask," chided Sara. "It's more the general tenor. First, they're all constructed as if you were an adult, which of course you aren't, or rather you weren't. Secondly, they're almost obsessive. Thirdly, they're starkly confessional. Fourth, you could argue that they're unduly forward – the sort of material you might find in someone's personal journal. Maybe I'm being too unkind. This is not fair but he sort of comes across as a stalker. If you know what I mean. I hesitate to be too judgemental but one might suspect he's slightly unhinged. Do you see where I'm coming from?"

"Yes," said Suzi. "I understand how that perception could arise."

It prompted Sara to take a step back, concerned that she might have over-done the negative.

"On the flip side," she said. "You wouldn't be here without him and he clearly holds you dear. Having said that, these are not love letters or even redolent of love letters. Yet they predicate some sort of glue binding you together. Maybe there is; maybe there isn't. But, in a way that is hard to describe, we just felt the whole thing was unhealthy. You may think otherwise but for better or worse your well-being had to be paramount. I apologise if you believe you've been deceived. That was never our intention."

Suzi said there was no need for apologies. She accepted her grandparents had sought to shelter her and believed they were doing the right thing. She took a few seconds and mulled it over. There was much to process. Then, even if it meant irritating her grandmother, Suzi returned to the fray.

"I hesitate to raise this, Granny, feel free to tell me off, the last thing I want to do is make you cross, but would you have any objection to me reading the letters and making my own judgement in due course?"

What a mature question, thought Sara. "Not at all," she said. "That is your right." She went on: "It will take you days to get through them if that is what you want to do, but by all means. And you know we're here for you if, as I mentioned before, you find something untoward. We may be able to put it into context; we may not. But, I emphasise, we are here for you."

Suzi got out of her chair, kissed Sara on the cheek and gave her a hug. "That's really good of you, Granny," she said. "I know you and Grandad mean well. I love you both very much."

For Sara, it was vindication for never giving up. She swelled with pride.

"If it's OK, Granny," said Suzi. "I'll remove them from the drawer, and then make a start. It will give me something to do. I feel a need to work out what drives this man, Kevin. What is he at? Where's he coming from?"

"That's fine, dear," said Sara. "You do what you want."

"Thanks, Granny."

Sara returned to her magazine. Suzi fiddled with her mobile phone, but her thoughts revolved around the gold mine of letters.

Next day Suzi collected them all up out of the drawer – it took her several trips – and transferred them to her bedroom.

Positioned them on the bed.

Then began putting them in date order – it took her an hour.

She laid them out in neat rows across the top of a side table, each row representing a calendar year.

And began reading.

They were in turn compelling, trite, shocking, mystical and at points indecipherable. As Sara had indicated, they were certainly from the heart and she found her own heart going out to a brave but complex personality.

He was carrying an enormous weight of guilt.

It struck a chord, and her thoughts turned to the mess in which her own life had descended. Perhaps it too was all to do with the crash. Maybe they were both searching for answers which weren't there, trying to find outcomes where none existed.

The letters were in part narration of events – Bali, Sydney, the sports agency, estate agency. But they were far more than that, taking her along with him on the rollercoaster of depressive lows and small but defining wins. The pulverising of his very being in the confluence of the Indian and Pacific oceans resonated with her. The description of his break-up with Becky, his detachment from the opposite sex, and the extraordinary Alice saga mined deep feminine urges.

As Sara had portended it took Suzi a long, long time to get through all the letters.

Nevertheless, she read them religiously from start to finish.

It was a remarkable sequence of colour and comment, a portrayal which, once you had done some weeding out, threading them into a narrative, cried out for a wider audience ... and it was all written to her.

A work of fiction or non-fiction, either would be possible with clever editing. No natural storyteller, she had neither the patience nor the doggedness but perhaps she could go one better and get to know this *fellow-traveller*, some of whose prose could be so like poetry.

She had been bitten by a craving and a curiosity to find out yet more about Kevin, what drove him, and what over and above their sheer survival they might have in common. To take this to its logical conclusion would mean setting out to meet him. This would represent a huge leap of faith on both their parts. Would they click? Could they become friends?

Conversely, would it prove a grave error of judgement? Different ages and cultures.

Placing him on a pedestal as her guardian angel might set her up for a fall.

She would think this through. It was not to be rushed. Was she making a mountain out of a molehill?

Would this be a disastrous wild goose chase or could the two of them prove cathartic saviours of each other?

The one thing she must not do was place her grandparents in an invidious position. She had stressed them enough.

She would do nothing without their blessing.

50

Kevin got off the long and arduous Sydney-London flight, having spent much of it absorbing a guide to the capital city.

He had pre-arranged bed and breakfast at a reasonable budget hotel for a week – enough to wander round the tourist sights while assessing whether he could hack living in the midst of ten million people.

Transport would not be a problem – Shanks's pony and the Tube.

He had his bucket list – Houses of Parliament and Big Ben, Buckingham Palace, the London Eye, the Tower of London, British Museum, Tower Bridge, Hyde Park, Trafalgar Square, St Paul's Cathedral, Piccadilly Circus, Harrods, Soho, Portobello Road – and was itching to get going.

Mustn't dash round like a crazy man trying to tick them all off – better to take it slower and appreciate the finer points.

If some hit the cutting room floor then so be it.

Taxi to the hotel, check in, and then jiggle with the standard cheap and tacky key card (you can never be sure they're going to work). First impressions of the bedroom – compact would be the estate agency idiom. Take a shower, dying to brush his teeth and eradicate the flavour of airline catering, three beers in the bar – no more, put the phone on charge, crash out and hope the jetlag isn't too seismic.

Must remember to text his parents to let them know he had arrived.

So began the English adventure.

The tourist bit went well even if he was on automatic pilot the first few days – you're there in body but in mind you're somewhere over the Bay of Bengal.

Buckingham Palace was imposing. Stratospheric views from the London Eye. The Tower of London was monumental – from the Crown Jewels to the Tower Ravens, tales of lost princes, World War I spies, and the tragic story of Anne Boleyn, one of Henry VIII's many wives, through her imprisonment, trial and execution. Trafalgar Square and Nelson's Column lived up to the hype. He was like a kid in a candy shop at Harrods – not that he bought much. Jaw-dropping what you could purchase there and in many cases jaw-dropping prices to match.

He could have eaten dinner in his hotel but took himself out to salivate over the nightlife, scope the scene and sample the buzz. There were so many bars, restaurants and clubs.

Such that he felt somewhat inhibited.

He had beers in various pubs – mostly nobody spoke to him though he did share the craic with a couple of Irishmen and talked Down Under with an Aussie barman. He tried a nightclub, danced with girls, but, like pre-Alice, off the beat. Chat-up routine dated. Too long in the tooth for cradle snatching.

Now, you had to work at these things – to go to somewhere you had never been before and make friends was never a given.

However, he could vision how lonesome London could be despite its populace. After all, he had felt the same in Sydney.

There were other doubts.

When walking on pavements he forever had to dodge out of the way. Everyone seemed to be in a perpetual hurry, glued to mobile phones and not looking where they were going. There were hustlers all over the place. Lycra loonies on bikes abusing car drivers and pedestrians alike. Would anyone stop if you had a turn and pitched into the gutter or would they assume you were simply a dosser/druggie/waster and walk on by? He wasn't at all sure.

He made some desultory inquiries about jobs with estate agencies, handed in his CV, but felt age was against him – this was a young man's game.

Towards the end of his week, he located Regent's Park, had a wander around, sat down on a bench, got absorbed in the bird life ... and took stock.

London was a truly magnificent city.

He could probably walk into a job of some sort easy enough, lots of employment agencies around, but then accommodation was incredibly expensive.

Could he cope with buildings, buildings, buildings, stretching mile upon mile? Could he cope with the constant traffic, traffic, traffic? Could he cope with people, people, people at every turn?

His instinct said London would crush him.

Anyway, there was more to England than London however much Londoners – cocooned in their woke world of entitlement – believed otherwise.

Birmingham billed itself as the nation's Second City – did the title fit or not?

Checking out of the hotel, he got a taxi to Euston station and bought a one-way ticket to Birmingham New Street.

The busiest station outside London, New Street had been *done up*, had millions lavished on it and was now intertwined with a glitzy shopping centre. Albeit critics called it a shopping mall with a station rather than a station with a shopping mall.

The locals were friendly, the atmosphere was tranquil, it was a good first impression. At around one million people, nowhere near the size of London, it had a village atmosphere that appealed to him.

First stop was the tourist information centre where they put him on the right path. Identified a hotel – there proved to be lots of them – and he replicated his London approach with a week's bed and breakfast.

He obtained a map of the city centre. He had always been hopelessly dyslexic at map reading especially when it came to those giveaway tourist sheets that often lacked scale, but managed to get about without going wrong too many times.

You had to achieve a feel for a place, what it was trying to do, how it saw itself. He found Birmingham a curious ebb and flow – a mix of ethnic origins, a mix of manufacturing and professional, a mix of low paid retail and leisure jobs and yet seams of hidden wealth.

As for the sights, he had never before cottoned on to how tied in Birmingham was to JRR Tolkien, of Lord of the Rings fame, and how little it made of that in tourism spend.

The Jewellery Quarter was fascinating as was Birmingham's leading role in the Industrial Revolution.

About as far from the sea as you can get in England, its restored canals and towpaths were arteries for walkers, cyclists, the young and the old. He ambled along them – what history there must be beneath his feet.

Pity then that it let itself down with too many selfish types who thought nothing of dropping litter in the street while expecting someone else to sweep up. Birmingham was plain filthy.

Squeezed between a massively dominant London, which treated it like a tiresome country bumpkin, and jealousy for Manchester – better bands, better football teams. Remnants of an inferiority complex from decades of jibes about thick Brummies; defined and defiled by the grotesque Spaghetti Junction and the permanent traffic jam which is the M6 motorway. The architecture was all over the place – high rise, low rise, lots of new buildings though few of any great merit, some splendid old buildings, isolated survivors of 1960s bulldozers. However, warts and all, he would take it because friendly transcended its flaws. Plus it was going all out to improve its image.

From Birmingham, he took a train ride to Tamworth in the footsteps of his ancestors. A market town on the River Tame, it was once the capital of the Anglo-Saxon Kingdom of Mercia. In its day far bigger than Birmingham, now a satellite to the regional capital.

Kevin tapped up estate agents but the regional market was going through an iffy spell and nobody was taking people on. But they did put in front of him a good offer for a six-month lease on a pleasant enough two-bedroom furnished town house in a presentable area, and after being shown around he decided he might as well take it – he hadn't intended to but it was more cost-effective than a hotel room. No longer a wandering hobo. He was optimistic, he had plenty of savings to fall back on, but now he needed a goal in life.

Which is where it all began to unravel.

Initially, it didn't grate. He bought a second hand car, drove to a food store to stock up, and took trips out into the countryside.

There was a convivial day at nearby Drayton Manor, a massive theme park. Another at Twycross Zoo – billed as the largest collection of monkeys and apes in the Western World – brought back the times he had visited zoos as a child. Lots of goofing around and making faces like a chimpanzee. He toured the site of the Battle of Bosworth Field, the last major set piece of the Wars of the Roses, fought on the twenty-second of August 1485.

Then what?

He toured the Tamworth estate agents again – still no joy.

He hit a whole load of Birmingham estate agents – nothing doing.

Back at the house, over three days he pinged off letters to estate agents all over the West Midlands, inserted his CV, posted them off, and awaited replies – forlornly. In the evenings he tried several different pubs, went to the cinema, had a first unsuccessful go at skiing at the nearby *SnowDome*. There was the television, he read a book, he stared at the four walls.

With his sporting pubescence, he had in his locker the old adage that you could turn up at a rugby club anywhere in the world and get a friendly greeting. He took himself along to some Tamworth Rugby Club games, cheering them on from the side-lines. People did speak to him and the jars of ale went down a treat. It was a novelty having an Australian around, provoking the usual wisecracks. Yet he felt a bit of a fraud – too old for serious combat. He was invited to wear the jersey of the veterans' side, but he hadn't trained in years. Would be pulling muscles he didn't even know he had.

So, something of a square peg in a round hole.

The solitude was getting to him … and alarmingly the yips were returning.

Maybe it had not been such a good idea to take the Tamworth house after all. Something of an ill-considered decision, he should have been more circumspect. Had he been young, thrusting and driven, like he once was, maybe he would be making a better fist of England. As his Dad had warned, there was a mountain to climb if you were middle aged. He should have held his nerve, told himself that it took many months to acclimatise to living in a new place, resolved that persistence would pay off. Instead, he began drinking over lunch, all afternoon, at night … until it merged into savage benders.

Next day he couldn't remember where he had been or what he had done.

Sometimes there were cuts and scrapes on his face, bruises down his body, trousers torn, hangovers like no tomorrow – must have tripped. Clot!

Eating junk food or no food at all.

He knew it was tearing him down, the old afflictions ensnaring him. There was just no reason to do anything about it.

Getting out of bed about noon, brunch was the liquid variety down one of the cheap pub chains – scruffy locals, jumpers full of holes, stained jeans, only one up from winos.

It culminated in the bender to end all benders – a twelve-hour session and he wasn't done even then.

51

As drunk as a skunk, slurring badly, careering from side to side, bouncing off street furniture, for some reason he knew not what, he asked to be taken to the rugby club.

Paying off the driver, head spinning, he halted at the main entrance. It was way after midnight and unsurprisingly the place was in darkness.

Empty.

He thumped on the door, he shouted for all he was worth … he cursed the club, he cursed England, he cursed his lousy life.

Held his head and gave into despair.

Felt in a pocket for his mobile but it wasn't there.

Had he left it at the house? Had he lost it on the pub-crawl? Had it fallen out in the taxi?

He let out another volley of expletives, prompting hooting from an owl hidden somewhere in the trees. It sounded as though it were mocking Kevin, and well it might.

The rugby club is way off the beaten track – it would be a long walk back to civilisation.

Then it all got dangerous – very dangerous.

Tamworth Rugby Club play on Wigginton Park, next to the clubhouse.

Totalling forty-five acres, the park is well used – dog walkers all year round, children sledging in winter, footballers, and cricketers. The fast West Coast Main Line railway borders one side of the park. Trains thunder past parallel to the rugby club's pitches. In his inebriation, the solution came to Kevin like a bolt from the blue. He would end it all there and then.

Bye, bye, cruel world.

While attending games he had observed how easy it would be. All he had to do was step onto the rails and it would be over.

He probably wouldn't feel a thing as his body was mashed.

To his sozzled self it was the final curtain call.

Exit stage left.

Maybe the owl was Satan's prophet.

Somewhere he had read that in most Native American tribes, owls were regarded as a symbol of death.

Hearing owls hooting was a bad omen among other peoples too, with numerous *bogeyman* stories told to warn children to stay indoors at night or the owl might carry them away.

Probably codswallop but a sinister thought.

Bugger the owl – time to act.

He lurched to his feet and weaved his way down the grass slope into the main expanse of the park.

However, he had forgotten how slippy it could be and pitched forward into the mud. He got himself back upright, plodded onwards, but then arms went one way and legs another and he took another header. There was mud on his face, his hands, his clothes. A shoe was missing. But, hey, what did any of it matter. Where he was going there would be no need of clothes and shoes. He lumbered on, patted the rugby posts one last time for posterity, trees eerie in the night air, a fox padding across the grass in search of prey.

At last, he was almost there, but looming before him was the perimeter fence that barred his way to the tracks.

This wasn't part of the equation, he was cognizant of its existence, but he'd thought it would prove a doddle. No chance. It was high, substantial, metal-linked and well-constructed. Had he been stone cold sober it would have represented a major barrier. In his exceedingly well-oiled state, it was virtually impassable.

He could not bring himself to concede that he might be thwarted.

But there it was looming as large that night to Kevin as the Berlin Wall at the height of the Cold War.

Heading left, he tagged alongside it, hoping he might find a gap where vandals had been at work, or perhaps an overhanging branch – shin up the tree, onto the bough, leap across … to no avail. He turned back on himself and tried to the right, yet still unable to fathom any way of scaling it.

Until finally, on his knees, he admitted defeat, and began convulsive retching. What a useless, pathetic, creature – so useless and pathetic that he couldn't even kill himself.

As if goading him a high-speed train sped on its way, casting further censure.

Hunched up, he must have dissolved into some kind of alcoholic blackout.

Whatever, when reality dawned, dawn was breaking. Cold, bedraggled, covered in gunge, ponging like a tramp, there was nothing left but to head home.

Much later, in a personal debrief, Wigginton Park stood out as some sort of watershed. However, caught up in his own self-pity he could only regard it as the most God-forsaken place on earth. He never found the missing shoe even though he tried to backtrack the way he had come. It was excruciating, limping along as stones punctured the sole of his foot and blood was drawn.

He never found the mobile phone ... until hours later back at the house. It was sitting on the kitchen table.

A passing workman stopped his van – "Whoever shat on you, mate?"

Kevin felt the red mist descending, but bit his lip. Good job too because the driver proved a decent sort and gave him a lift most of the way. Windows fully down to mitigate the smell.

However, by the time Kevin turned the key in the lock the commute was underway and kids were on route to school. Producing countless snotty looks – half of him recoiled at the discomfiture and the other half was too pooped to care.

Almost falling into the house, he kicked off the remaining shoe, with the last of his energy mounted the stairs, and tottered onto the bed, fully clothed – oblivious to the mud, oblivious to the dank and damp, and oblivious to the odium.

It would have made a pitiful sight had anybody been there to witness it.

52

Back in Normal, Suzi had been building up to breaking the news to Sara and Jeb that it was time for her to venture forth.

Signing on to the internet, she entered 'Kevin Jackson' in the search engine and thought the computer was going to blow up. Doh! She should have twigged that there would be many, many people with the same name. Inputting 'Kevin Jackson air crash survivor' produced a more sifted response.

She was after anything in-depth which would give an insight into his makeup and character. However, with hundreds of articles out there, it was difficult. Perhaps because there were very few which stood out. A man in the public eye about which much had been written but a man who liked to preserve his privacy. Words galore but illustrative of not much. She got a few steers but only a few. Indeed, she felt she knew far more about him from his letters.

She also sought to bone up on England – her ignorance about the country was manifest.

The American War of Independence had been against the English; World War II had been in alliance with the English. London was the capital. The place still had a monarch. Queen somebody or other. Tennis was still played on Wimbledon grass. The Beatles came from England, didn't they?

Er, that was about it.

Once again, she was paying for her school truancy. It had left gaping holes in her knowledge base.

When next Suzi found herself alone with Sara she once more turned the conversation round. She told her grandmother that two things were coalescing in her thoughts.

First, she believed she must meet Kevin face to face and get to know him. She had found the letters riveting, he had saved her life, the very least she could do was thank him personally. Letters or emails would never cover it. Second, she had come to the conclusion that she had to flee the Normal nest. She was a marked woman in her home town – everyone had an opinion of her. She had blown the trust of good people and was still a target for the baddies. She had to get out or one way or another she would be brought low once more, like with the road race.

Sara poured over the words – she didn't want to lose Suzi albeit there was an argument that they lost her mentally in that appalling plane crash, in body in Normal but in spirit with Robert and Rose.

Suzi was her own person, her misfortunes had in some ways taught her more about life than school ever could; ultimately she deserved to find the answers to whatever it was that was gnawing at her entrails.

Sara would have liked to have gone backpacking abroad when she was young. As for Kevin, if it would put Suzi's mind at rest then do it. A week in his company and the two of them would have run out of things to say, she speculated. Their story would have come full circle and hopefully both could go their separate ways and re-ignite their lives.

She and Jeb gave their approval.

There was one proviso – before Suzi did anything else they wanted to talk finances with her.

Finances had been the next item on Suzi's 'memo pad'.

All three sat around the dining room table on which were spread banking and legal documents.

Jeb did the talking.

In the aftermath of the disaster, people around the world had been touched by the plight of this orphaned baby.

The family had been so appreciative for the outpouring of love and, while reticent to do so, had fallen in with the clamour that a trust fund be set up to safeguard Suzi's future. Years on, they were still uneasy at having allowed themselves to be swept along with the flow … but there it was, money matters even though it cannot buy you happiness.

It was decreed that the huge sum amassed would be kept invested for Suzi until she was twenty-one when she would gain access to it and do what she wanted with the cash. An absolute fortune, sufficient that after years of compound interest Suzi was an exceedingly rich young heiress.

With Suzi going off the rails so badly they had never seen fit to put this to her as it might have done much more harm than good. Now she seemed to be on the cusp of turning her life around it was time she found out. After all, it would be hers to do with as she wished in a couple of years anyway.

On top of this donated money, Robert and Rose's savings had been kept for her including the proceeds of the house – it had been reluctantly sold when Abby and John moved to Canada. They accepted that if she was bound for England she would need ready cash. The trust fund should be left intact – it would be too difficult to unravel and there could be tax implications. Suzi saw reason in their argument. Jeb said he and Sara would pay her air fare – money from Robert and Rose could be utilised for living expenses. They would all go down to the bank, fix for her to open an account, if necessary put in place an arrangement with an English counterpart, sort debit and credit cards, and regularise any financial loose ends.

Did she think she could take on such a responsibility? Managing your financial affairs was fundamental. At one extreme you heard of kids blowing their inheritance on drugs; at the other extreme every variety of crook and internet shark was out there and would try and find ways of fleecing you. She should never reveal her worth to anyone.

Suzi absorbed it all like a sponge and, as over several weeks the various elements conjoined, she did take it seriously – very seriously.

The revelations had left her flabbergasted. The trust money, stressed Jeb, was meant as capital – to purchase a house or establish a business. She should try to respect this.

She gave her word.

Next, it would be for her to approach Kevin.

While she knew he was in England because that was where the latest two letters had been sent from, recounting the trip and his hopes for it, she didn't have address, phone numbers or email for him. Maybe Abby would – she had once told Suzi they had exchanged such details when meeting all those years ago in Bali. Perhaps he had updated them since.

She spoke to Abby on the phone. As always, Abby was supportive. Of course, given John's parents lived there, she had visited England most years since their marriage. Now very much an anglophile, she filled in some of the gaps for Suzi – the Munros would be keen for her to call by. No pressure, but, assured Abby, a bolthole if she ever needed one. An opulent bolthole at that. In a very upmarket, Kent village. She also expounded all she knew of Kevin's character, adding that he was a good person. A man of principle, a man who had standards, but someone who had been badly warped by his plane crash wounds.

Abby said she was glad Suzi intended to meet him – the two of them might find they had a lot in common. She wasn't explicit as to exactly what she meant by that, but she didn't need to be.

And just the job, Abby did have up-to-date phone numbers for Kevin – she had kept her pledge to keep him in touch with the family, and it had been reciprocated.

Suzi wrote them down.

"I want lots of postcards," said Abby. "And, if you go native and put down roots, I want an invitation to Buckingham Palace to meet the Royals."

They both laughed.

"But seriously," noted Abby. "Keep me posted – it sounds very exciting and I'm envious. The right age to be doing it too – I wish I was eighteen again."

"Nineteen," said Suzi. "You sent me a birthday card the other week – don't you remember?"

"Golly, yes," said Abby, bluffing that maths was not her strongest suit. "Have a great time."

"I'm sure I will."

They said their goodbyes.

Bolstered by Abby's enthusiasm, Suzi told Sara and Jeb she would make the call to England the following day when the time difference was more favourable.

She gave some thought to what she was going to say. He would be caught on the hop. She didn't want to startle him. She came up with a form of words and various alternatives but wasn't entirely convinced by any of them. Maybe play it off the cuff. Surely, the morning would bring clarity.

Except it didn't. Was she digging a bigger and bigger hole for herself?

A pensive, clipped, inconclusive conversation would do nothing for them. Making the phone call was what it was about – they would find middle ground. It was bound to be testing for both of them.

She dialled the number, and it began ringing out.

53

Kevin was awake but far from restored after the shambles of trying to do himself in, and still not compos mentis.

Could have been taken for a down and out, not even got round to a shower, hadn't eaten for two days, hated himself.

Brrr, brrr.

Initially it didn't register.

Brrr, brrr.

It was the landline.

Fuck, probably another of those scam callers who needed their heads seeing to, preferably by someone wielding a baseball bat.

He bolted down the stairs, raised the receiver to his ear, and summoning every ounce of malice, spat: "Yes."

Nothing at the other end, usually a giveaway, and he nearly slammed the thing down.

The woman who had begun to speak wasn't the typical foreigner with only a basic command of English. Nor was there the spurious background noise alluding to be a call centre.

"Is that Kevin Jackson," she enquired.

A more cautious "Yes," this time.

"My name's Suzanne Duthie."

He almost dropped the phone. He had long given up on hearing those words.

"Hello," she ventured, unsure whether they had been accidentally cut off.

"The Suzanne Duthie?"

It was all he could come up with.

She laughed hesitantly. "Well, I'm not sure about that. This is the Suzi Duthie you rescued from the water all those years ago. Don't tell me you've forgotten."

It was now his turn to feel chastened. "No, no, no," he burbled. "I remember it like it was yesterday. It's just … it's just … it's just that after all these years it's hard to take in that it really is you."

The American accent should surely have given him a clue. But, hold on, what was she doing calling now? What did she want off him? Was this some sort of stunt?

She had been well aware it might prove a shock. Must disarm his apprehensions before springing the news that she was intent on flying to England to see him.

"Don't think ill of me. I understand your caution. This is purely a social call – no more and no less. I recently read your letters, they spoke volumes, and I felt I had to contact you. I know it's been a long time. Forgive me."

It shook him, but in a good way.

Berating himself for being rude and mean-minded, he apologised for his reticence. It was special to hear her voice. He told her so.

Then, rat-a-tat-tat, questions streamed forth. How old was she? Was she still living in Normal? What news of Abby?

Another one of those hesitant laughs and it struck him how it must have sounded like a burst from a machine gun.

More apologies.

She was nineteen, she was still living in Normal, though maybe not for too much longer, and Abby was tip-top.

As she had intended, he pounced on the *not for too much longer*.

Thence, with no apparent ulterior motive she was able to reveal that she was keen to do some travelling, and was coming to England. She would look him up while she was there. If, that is, it fitted in with his plans. She didn't mention that meeting him was her prime reason for crossing the Atlantic.

He said it would be fantastic to see her but his response was perhaps more defensive than she had hoped, betraying doubts as to whether she would in actuality make it over or rather this was one of those fanciful whims which never come to fruition. These things are easier said than done.

She admitted she was yet to finalise dates never mind airline tickets but added firmly that it would happen within the next three months. He was in the middle of the country – right? Some village outside Birmingham?

Not so much a village, he told her – nearly 80,000 people. Reflecting to himself in passing that it was the same size as Manly – he had never correlated the two.

There was more small talk as they fenced around trying to get the measure of each other. However, in conclusion both were ebullient at the possibility of catching up.

She would be back in contact once arrangements had been formalised. He responded that the house was rented, was small, but quite presentable – she could take the spare room. Stay as long as she liked. "There is a vacuum cleaner – if I can find it," he joked.

"I want fresh sheets and clean towels," she told him gleefully.

By the time they broke off the call they were almost bosom buddies. She blew out her cheeks – it had gone well, as well as she could ever have hoped.

Now to get on with organising the visit. Regularising US passport status – she assumed there must have been documentation of some description covering a child to enable her parents to take her on the ill-fated Bali trip, though whether that was still relevant she didn't know – booking her flights, sorting a tourist visa.

Go to a store and purchase a large backpack.

Make a list of everything that had to go in it, ruthlessly culling anything that was non-essential. She could buy jeans and tops in the UK as and when.

Thank God she had told him three months. It would take at least that to get all her ducks in a row.

He was seated in his favourite chair, astounded.

That had to be the most unexpected phone call he had ever received. How a little baby had grown up. She sounded very adult. He tried to visualise her – Abby had sent the odd photograph but nothing recent.

Bound to have a social media presence. And there he found the new Hope – he hadn't called her Hope earlier (could have been off-putting) but would definitely do so if she made it over. The woman whose profile shone back at him was pretty, yet older than her years. Lots of earlier images of a teenage rebel.

Well, doesn't everyone rebel in their youth?

He could only guess at how much the plane crash and everything surrounding it might have taken out of her. He knew how much it had taken out of him. He would have to tread warily at first but he would love to ask her about it.

Kevin was day-dreaming away, detouring here and there in his analysis.

Come on – snap out of it. Stop second-guessing yourself.

He looked himself up and down – a light bulb moment.

His clothes were filthy, he needed to shower and shampoo his hair, his bedroom was a pig sty, there were piles of clothes to wash, loads of dishes in the kitchen, the house required cleaning from top to bottom – what would she think being introduced into such a dump?

Mortified, he vowed to get cracking ASAP.

As host it was down to him to make her stay as accommodating as possible. It had to be pristine. He had let things slip; he had let his personal standards and hygiene slip. Got to get back in the groove.

Daily shaving, monthly haircuts, deodorant, nails short, shirts which hadn't been worn for a week, shoes that hadn't gone into holes. Jogging every day, no more junk food, a ban on binge drinking, regular weigh-ins, compulsory waist measurements. He would get back to the Kevin who could do sleek and groomed so well.

She would come with expectations that he was somebody of stature and that's what she would get.

No more shabby bozo.

First stop the shower. He stripped out of his clothes and began scrubbing vigorously. Once dry, the Expedition to Find Clean Clothes took shape – few existed. Dressed in what you might call remnants, he gave himself another verbal sledging for letting that side slide.

He found some antiseptic cream and spread it on the sole of his bad foot, the one scratched and riven from the shoeless walk. It ached and he was still limping.

The next day he went to town – three loads in the washing machine and drier. Every utensil – cup, saucer, plate, knives and forks – cleaned. An initial vacuum of the entire house.

The day after that – wipe down the grease-spattered kitchen while putting the elbow grease into making the bathroom and toilet shine, eradicating disgusting male smells in the process.

Cut his finger and toe nails, using a file to remove any residual grime. Nothing so indicative than grubby hands resembling a potato patch.

Give the place a dust, remove countless cobwebs, a second vacuum.

She was still weeks away from turning up. He felt reinvigorated for having something to aim towards.

It took a week to get the flat, including what would be her room, up to standard. Just call me Mrs Mop, he told his diary.

Time to upgrade his wardrobe too – a train into Birmingham to mosey around the big stores. He came away with much-needed new shirts, three pairs of shoes, handkerchiefs to replace what were now rags, and some colourful sweaters.

His old leather jacket was staying – he couldn't bear to be parted from it. However, it was sent to the dry cleaners to remove years of alcohol stains.

OK, what next?

Stop getting into a funk. She was just a visitor. There was nothing big deal about it … except there was.

Got to get fit.

To supplement the jogging he joined a gym even though he hated gyms. Mindless, robotic treadmills where you tried to block out the turnip heads next to you by listening to the latest music on headphones.

Weights – but not the justification of a new rugby season ahead. The stink of perspiration. Gyms were both putrid and soulless.

He reasoned that he was improving himself on behalf of himself when he knew full well it was a vanity project for her.

Middle-aged man meets nubile young woman.

Abashed at the thought and not wanting her to perceive him to be a slacker, he would have another go at finding work. He would hit that other treadmill again, the estate agency circuit. Make himself out to be an ace Aussie salesman, give them the full treatment.

Hallelujah, he caught a break.

There was an element of good fortune – some poor sod had been sacked for failing to hit his numbers and Kevin cold-called the next day.

It took three weeks to tie it down – the boss had done a professional job, two interviews, a probing of his CV, even called in his Oz references. He never twigged about Kevin and the plane crash but then he was the sort who probably wouldn't have cared anyway. So, level playing field, three-month trial. Perform and the job would be his.

He walked out of the meeting, an impulsive hop, skip and a jump, bought a bottle of Champagne, took it home, toasted Hope, and drank the lot.

It was the first alcohol to pass his lips since Suicide Night.

The weekend was coming up and he would be starting on the Monday. He was in employment and it would keep him occupied.

54

Suzi was trying to banish lingering blues.

She had done a lot of reading up on England, its history and people. Was in awe of an island nation that was smaller than some US states – three times smaller than Texas – yet had once ruled the largest empire known to man. Under a mountain of debt – the price of victory in World War II – it had stalled in the 1950s, been at war with itself in the 1970s and '80s, but had rebounded. So inventive and creative. Constantly re-imagining. She would have to hold off diving in at the deep end. No brash American. Humility would be her password.

Sorting the red tape was a pain, but it had to be done.

There was time after all for John, Abby and the children to come over from Toronto – rather than flying, they drove, stopping off on the way. And where were they bound to make that stop? Why, Niagara Falls of course. Had to be. It was tradition.

While there, they stocked up on some bottles from the famous wineries. More than twenty nestle below the Niagara Escarpment amidst a landscape of vineyards and orchards. The family celebration to mark Suzi's great leap forward saw her toasted in Niagara's finest.

It was moving, full of affection – it dawned on Suzi how much she would miss Normal.

Nevertheless, she was sticking with the plan.

She was going to dazzle Sara, Jeb and Abby by making a success of England.

Ruminating on how to play it on arrival, she made a perhaps surprising call. She would head direct to Tamworth via Birmingham rather than experience the London hot spots. From the Normal frying pan into the London fire – not good! She wanted a firm base from which she could find her feet, and initially, though he didn't know it yet, Kevin's place would be that base. Later she could figure out what parts of England would be a gas to see.

It seemed most sensible to fly Normal to Chicago and then Chicago to London Heathrow. From Heathrow she could take a National Express coach to Birmingham.

Kevin was to meet her in *Brum* – speaking slang like a resident, she joked. She texted him provisional dates and later the definitive ones.

Both times she got an effusive reply saying he was very definitely up for seeing her.

There was just the one spanner in the works – he had got himself a job so could she try and arrive either in the evening or at the weekend.

No problem, she replied. And passed on her congratulations.

She got a bit wistful ahead of her departure and, incongruously, homesick when she hadn't even left home.

Something else to overcome.

However, come the morning she was buzzing, bent on being mistress of all that lay ahead.

Sure, there were bound to be setbacks. She knew all about setbacks. Overall, if things went well these would pale into insignificance. It would be her own fault, nobody else's, if she blew it.

Sara and Jeb ran her to the airport.

There were tears, hugs, make sure you phone, we're going to miss you terribly, don't let the Limeys grind you down. Cups of coffee. More tears and hugs.

Again and again, she could only say "Thank you for all you have done for me."

Two generations removed but family counts for everything.

So to the desk, a final wave goodbye, on to security and then the gate. The comparative short hop and then the big flight, Chicago to London.

Leaving the United States proper – Canada didn't count – for the first time since the baby trip, the enormity of it all struck her. What had she let herself in for? Far too late to do anything about it. At 35,000 feet over the Atlantic the die was well and truly cast.

The US offered certainty; there was nothing certain about the undertaking upon which she was embarked. England had been home to the Pilgrim Fathers – they had set out into the unknown. But, still in her teens, this was a big judgement call. What if it went wrong? What if Kevin did turn out to be unhinged?

Come on. You can do it.

Well used to catching forty winks at odd times and in odd places, she spent much of the flight snoozing.

A routine landing at Heathrow; would she quickly find her own routine?

Heathrow is so large that getting to and from gates is time-consuming. But the signage is good. So exiting was plain sailing. To be on the safe side she had factored in being delayed when deciding what bus to catch. Had read that at full capacity, which was always, planes were often stacked in holding patterns waiting for a landing slot. However, hers had been on the money.

She found the National Express office. Was there anything any earlier? There wasn't, and, had there been, they would have billed her extra, while she would have had to mess Kevin around.

Time to kill.

She bought a sandwich and a cup of English tea, the first of many she presumed, then wiled away an hour or so studying people and their habits, playing a game of trying to guess what they did for a living.

Rang him but he must have been busy because she was unable to get through and he never replied to the missed call.

The bus was prompt and soon she was amidst the English countryside. Very green and she got why when a sharp twenty minute rainstorm struck.

A few stops on the way so plenty of time to prepare.

Her only mild concern was recognising Kevin when she arrived at the terminus and it kept nibbling away at her. What if she approached the wrong person – that would be the pits. She would be mortified.

It was mid-evening and the motorway wasn't too congested. The route in via Birmingham Airport weaved through the sprawling outskirts. At last, they were turning into Birmingham coach station. Wearily, she negotiated the steps down, collected her monster backpack from the underneath lockers, hung it over a shoulder, thanked the driver, and passed through the gate into the main concourse.

55

Glancing about her she spotted a well-dressed man with the lean look of the clean-cut *Neighbours*-style Australian, far removed from that other Aussie stereotype, the big belly and beer-sodden loudmouth. The wide-brimmed leather Outback hat – presumably deliberate on his part – was the giveaway.

There was a tentative acknowledgement.

Kevin?

Hope?

They smiled broadly at each other.

He relieved her of the backpack. That was nice of him.

"You must be bushed?"

"I am, to be honest. It's a long way. Trust I'm not too dishevelled."

"No way – it's magic to meet you again. You've grown a bit!"

More smiles.

Did she need the rest room? No, there had been facilities on the coach. Was she starving? No, a sandwich at Heathrow had topped up the plane fare.

Anyway she didn't want to hold him up – he'd put himself out by driving into Birmingham to meet her. Much easier by train, but no knowing how loaded with paraphernalia she might be.

There was a small drop-off and pick-up car park on site.

"Ready to go?"

"Yes," she said, putting on a composed air that was entirely false.

"This way," he indicated.

Backpack on the rear seat, ensconced in the front, she was soon getting a spin around the inner city. A bigger place than she had thought. Strikingly industrial. A bit like the Rust Belt back home. She felt sure she was doing Birmingham down.

Onto the motorway network, he told her they were now negotiating the famous Spaghetti Junction. She'd never heard of it.

Next stop Tamworth. Impossible to make anything out now apart from the lights of the cars and lorries.

"If you're peckish when we get there then there are likely to be a few fish and chip shops still serving. Unlikely you've ever tasted a fish supper before, but it's something of a local delicacy in these parts."

She professed that all she wanted was to get her head down.

"No worries."

Someone had told her that this was the catch-phrase of all Australians – she expected to hear it plenty more … and she wasn't to be disappointed!

They turned off for Tamworth, wound their way through town, and pulled up beside a modern semi-detached. For sure, far smaller than Sara and Jeb's place in Normal. But, she guessed, he didn't need a whole lot of space.

He turned the key in the lock, inserted the code to shut off the bleeping burglar alarm, and ushered her into the lounge.

"Have a seat – I'll just get your backpack. Do you have a coat – there are pegs in the hallway?"

Which was when she realised it wasn't with her. Must have accidentally left it behind at Heathrow. Dolt!

He went back out to the car.

She surveyed her surroundings. It was basic but it was clean. She surmised he had been sprucing it up.

Her first impressions of him? Polite, genuine, and surprisingly good-looking for someone in their forties.

He returned with the backpack, left it by the stairs, and re-entered the room.

Would she like a drink?

"A glass of milk, if you've got enough to spare."

"No worries."

There it was again!

He'd done a *big shop* with two four-pint containers among the many items on the list.

He handed her the glass.

She was cute, even better in real life than in her photos; she was certainly all-American and would probably be bossing him about in no time.

Sleep in as long as she liked in the morning – he would be out at work and back around 6pm. He found her a spare set of house keys and quickly double-checked that they worked. He took her into the kitchen, indicated the main food cupboard, opened the fridge and told her to help herself. Finally, he wrote down the number for the alarm.

"Ring me on the mobile if you need anything," he said. "I'm sure you'll find your way about."

He suggested he show her the spare room, got hold of the backpack and began climbing the stairs, she hot on his heels.

It was functional.

He said he'd laid down on the bed and it seemed agreeable. If not, he would see what he could do about it.

She said "I'm sure it'll be comfy."

There was a chest of drawers and a wardrobe for her clothes.

"The sheets and the towels are all clean and spotless, madam."

It was her own bit of fun being thrown back at her.

They laughed.

He indicated the bathroom.

Not exactly spacious but it would do, and he had spruced it up too. If this dedication to housework was all for her, then she was privileged. She doubted he could keep it up, and nor should he. She must do her bit, and, as a guest, more than her bit.

Perhaps she would like to get washed and undressed first, so she could hit the sack. He had a few things to finish off downstairs.

She thanked him.

He left her to her own devices.

She got her wash things out of the backpack and her makeup bag for morning. Removed a nightdress. Everything else could wait for the next day.

Bundling the backpack against the wall farthest from the bed, she next locked the bathroom door. Did her teeth, splashed water over her face, too exhausted for a shower – that too could wait until morning. Peeked in the mirror. Scowled. Determined she would be all dolled up for when he returned the following evening. After all, making her presence felt was a priority.

Called down to him that she was out of the bathroom.

Got into bed and was soon dead to the world.

He gave it five minutes then went to bed himself. Already the bathroom had a slight female scent to it. Women ruled bathrooms.

The house lacked colour and comeliness – a woman's touch would make it more homely.

His dreams were about perfume bottles, nail varnish, hair spray and being lassoed in the bath by discarded tentacle-like hairs.

She woke with a start – sun streaming in through the window. She stretched for her watch and was startled to see that it was past 11am. Yet she felt threadbare – must be the jetlag and the travelling. The bed was warm and snug – a voice in her head was telling her to sink back into oblivion.

Instead, she forced herself to her feet and made for the bathroom. A refreshing shower was definitely going to be the highlight.

She eyed it suspiciously. When you weren't acquainted with the knobs and gizmos, it sometimes took an engineering degree to get the things going.

She fiddled around and was promptly hit by a jet of cold water.

Squealing, in that distinctive pitch only girls can hit, then cursing like a trooper, she diverted the flow away from her body.

Only then did it start to heat up.

Her mood improved and soon she was luxuriating.

Now, much more herself, she turned the tap off and stepped onto the mat.

The towel he had provided for her was big and thick – just how she liked them. However, he must have picked it out in the dark because it said on it *Big Boys Do It Better*.

Hmmm.

She finished drying herself. To start off on the right footing a cloth and bath cleaner would be handy.

Nowhere to be seen.

Men! He was going to need sorting out.

She swilled the ceramic down using a couple of tissues.

Then went to the bedroom, got herself presentable, put on her makeup. If he was at work all day there was plenty of time to beautify herself later.

Next, she spent thirty minutes emptying her backpack, putting her things away. The backpack itself went on top of the wardrobe. She smoothed the bed out and pushed open the window to provide some air.

Thence downstairs.

The letterbox clanged as some post tumbled through – what a fright she got. How silly. She collected it up, gave it a cursory perusal, being nosy, mostly junk mail, and left it on the side for him.

Through in the kitchen, she had a good trawl to see what was what. Many of the plates and utensils had seen better days, but, hey, it was a rented house. There had to be a limit on expectations.

She uncovered some cereal, and tucked in.

Spotting one of those corkboards where you pin *to do* notices as conscience salvers, she noticed there was an item with her name on it. No necessity to fix tea – there was loads of salad in the fridge, meat, cheese … leave it until he got back. Then it apologised for not asking about her likes and dislikes.

Sweet of him if a bit nanny state.

The back door key was in the lock, so she sauntered out into the garden.

Early spring and a bit chilly. He'd had a go at cutting the weed-ridden lawn but not got round to the flowers and flower beds. The compulsory garden tutelage of Jeb during her early teenage hissy fit years now came into its own. Nothing that a good chop back wouldn't sort. Many plants and bushes thrived on some harsh treatment to flourish and bloom. If she could find some garden implements, then, once she had her feet under the table, she would give it a go. There was a small shed at the bottom – might they be in there.

The door creaked open and she was assaulted by a mass of cobwebs – his big clean hadn't got that far – in what was spider heaven.

Yikes, she hated spiders.

What was it Sara used to say? Women only ever got married so there was someone to remove spiders from the bath.

Something else on her man-list.

Shivering, she went back indoors.

Wiped her feet – that was clever of her – and surveyed the lounge cum dining area in rather greater detail than the night before.

She turned the television on and played around with the channels – but it was mostly the afternoon dross programmes. She did find the twenty-four-hour news and caught up with what she had missed – it felt very odd to have this English take on everything and barely a mention of anything going on in the US.

She pressed the off button on the remote.

Boredom.

Despite only being on a tourist visa she would need a part-time job or go stark staring mad.

At last the clock ticked past 5.30pm, she went upstairs, a groom and polish, ran a comb through her hair.

Then waited for him in the lounge.

56

It wasn't long before there was the sound of a key turning and he walked through the front door. They greeted each other like old friends.

He was in excellent humour having tied up several house sales – the job was going well and he was getting on with the team.

How had her day been?

She told him she had slept in and felt much better for having had a laze.

"Good for you," he told her. "Travelling takes so much out of you." Overdramatising, he looked her up and down. "You scrub up well."

She turned brazen hussy. Flattered he had noticed.

Had she eaten?

A bowl of Weetabix. Lunch had gone by the wayside.

"You must be famished then."

The question prompted hunger pangs.

"I forgot to ask – do you have any dietary requirements – vegan, gluten-free, nut allergies … that sort of thing."

She didn't.

"Are you up for salad – lettuce, tomato, hard-boiled egg, onions, beetroot, cottage cheese, cold potato, a choice of meats?

"Sounds yummy."

She offered to muck in.

Why not, he thought.

She shelled the hard-boiled eggs and sliced up the onions and beetroot. He put a portion each of chicken breast and ham on plates, plenty of lettuce, washed the tomatoes, took the cold potatoes from the fridge, and prised away the seal on the tub of cottage cheese.

He poured two glasses of fresh orange and they took their meal through to the dining area.

He offered a toast – to her safe arrival. Not exactly quality crystal but the glasses made an acceptable *ching*.

They made small talk as they ate.

She couldn't find a cloth or bath cleaner. He apologised – the cloth had died and the last of the cleaner had been used up. He had made a note to get both when next at the shops.

The towel was large though the wording was a bit crude.

He gaped. "Oh Jeez, was that the one with the Big Boys motif?"

It was.

"Sorry," he confessed. "I never noticed. I'll find you another one."

Tickled pink, she said it could wait, but perhaps she could change it when next it went in for a wash.

"No worries."

She burst out laughing.

He was astonished. "What have I done now?"

How long had he had the catchphrase and had he copyrighted it, she jibed cynically. Oh, of course, he couldn't – every Australian owned it!

"Go on, slag off a poor Aussie transported to a foreign land."

"Surely the over way round – weren't the original settlers English criminals transported to Botany Bay!"

More banter until both stomach and facial muscles were affronted and chewing became a trial.

"I can see I'm going to have to watch you," he said.

Yet more broad smiles.

The jocularity was put to one side as they concentrated on finishing their salad – it was plain, but then she had been brought up on plain food.

They took the used plates and cutlery through to the kitchen – he washed and she dried.

Then they tootled through into the lounge with a cup of coffee each.

"What, no English tea – I thought it was compulsory."

"I'm not English."

She adopted a new slant.

"Your letters were an insight into how it must have been after the plane crash – it gave me a jolt." She told him again that they had been hidden away until she was older so it was all new to her.

He clasped his fingers, his face hardened.

Probably a bit early to talk it through in any depth, but he was pleased she had read them. She shouldn't take them too literally – he hadn't been entirely himself when a lot of them were written.

She silently kicked herself for probing too hard too fast.

"Hope, I'm more than willing to discuss it with you, but it's been a busy day."

"No worries." Goodness, now she was saying it.

They were both laughing again.

Once more, she ploughed ahead. "I'm thinking of having a walk around the local area tomorrow just to get my bearings," she said.

"Go for it."

"I know your time off work is limited but at some point could we go to Birmingham city centre – I could do with picking up a few extra items for my wardrobe." It came out sounding cringe-worthy and pretentious. She waited for a riposte but he didn't make anything of it.

"We'll definitely do that. Do you like walking in the countryside – there are some beautiful parts quite close?"

She said she loved walking in the countryside.

"Great," he said. "I'll hold you to it."

"And sorry," she said. "I know I'm rabbiting on but I do want to make my contribution to the house – shopping, cooking the dinner, tidying the garden. Don't think I'm going to be sponging off you."

"You're hired," he announced. "Just don't expect to be paid!"

She looked at him with dancing eyes – "You're a meanie."

She skipped the part-time job idea. That would be for another day.

It felt good between them. They liked one another. It had only been twenty-four hours but they were already comfortable in each other's company. Yet there was also an acceptance that both had so much baggage in tow that there was a steep learning curve before they could truly relax.

Things between them continued to blossom as the days passed.

She walked around the block, bought some bread rolls at a convenience store, and got her hair done at a local salon.

He took her in the car to the supermarket and let her pick and choose what she wanted. She cooked her first meal – pork chops, potatoes and peas. Keep it simple – poisoning him at the outset would not have been a good idea!

Still, there were times when she found herself twiddling her thumbs.

Until, on a shelf in a corner, which like the shed must have also evaded his spring clean, she spotted there were half a dozen dusty tomes one on top of the other – surely not Kevin's, maybe left behind by a previous tenant? She cocked her head to read the titles on their spines and pulled out *The Thirty-Nine Steps* by John Buchan – he was not known to her.

Nevertheless, she was soon inveigled into the plot – burying her head in the whodunit over the next few days while ignoring Kevin's slurs about her being the love interest for 'sleuths in dirty macs'. How about becoming a private investigator, he teased – she could bill herself as Sherlock Holmes' long lost sister, Hope Holmes.

"It's well known that Australians have no intellect," she told him. Anyway, when was the last time he'd read a book? He couldn't remember and she pounced on the admission. Books in Australia were for propping up wonky table legs, weren't they?

And so on and so forth the kidology continued until the book became a kind of totem.

57

Kevin often worked Saturdays but managed one off and took her through to Birmingham on the train.

As she tried on jeans and T-shirts she was in her element. Feeling sexy, she chose to flaunt her curves in front of him as she asked his opinion.

Tantalised by her aura, he egged her on.

She purchased various new garments but also took in some charity shops – amazing how you could sometimes get cool gear in charity shops. With summer coming on she spotted a pair of shorts that didn't leave much to the imagination. And she added a long, more formal dress – it was bound to come in handy. There was a light summery anorak screaming *buy me* on one of the racks. It would replace the lost coat.

On to a shop selling soaps and smellies. She could not resist. All her Christmases had come at once.

Except Kevin was hangdog, couldn't manage another step.

She made a pretence of concern, no further penance, gently stroked his face – evocative of sexual smoke and mirrors. It was the first time she had really touched him.

Ever so lightly his fingers converged on her hips, stayed there while he prattled on about watching paint drying, and then slipped away. She gave him one of her playful slaps in the chest.

To her he looked suddenly handsome.

She was for sure one hell of a girl, he reckoned.

"I need a drink," he pronounced. "Don't you see, you're driving me to drink?"

She slapped him again.

"Stop hitting me, woman." Adding: "Anyone would think I'm a battered husband."

Now he was being melodramatic, she asserted, twiddling a button on his shirt and playing the innocent.

He took hold of her hand, a masculine edge. "Fancy a pub lunch?"

"That would be lovely."

They spotted a place called the *Old Contemptibles*. The name venerated World War I servicemen. High ceilings, oak panelling, it was a classy watering hole and must have been really something in its Victorian heyday. Now restored, it had an old/new appeal, and the staff too were up to the mark. They ordered drinks – there was a choice of ales and ciders. He went for a pint of cider; she had a half of shandy. From the menu he chose steak and kidney pie – another English staple. She opted for fish.

Found a table and took in the ambience. People nattering away. Pints being pulled.

A placid pub scene … until she clumsily knocked over her drink. It slopped across the table – he just managed to jump out of the way of a stream of beer.

"Oh, I'm so sorry," she wailed. "Did it get you? Are you OK?"

He smiled wanly. Examined his trousers. Just the odd drop. Put a serviette to good use. Then went to get a cloth from the bar. One of the staff saved the day with a mop and bucket.

She apologised once more.

"Same again? … Or are you going to throw this one at me too."

He meant nothing by it though she interpreted it as a bit of a dig. Deserved too. "I'm not safe to be let out of the house, really I'm not."

"Forget it," he said. "You're allowed – it's just nice chatting away to a pretty girl."

She blushed. It was the first time he had given any indication that he might fancy her. She quite fancied him.

The food came. It was hot, it was wholesome, it wasn't cheap but it was worth the money. When they left to catch the train back to Tamworth they were definitely full.

She placed her bags on a spare seat and sat back as it trundled along, houses and fields rushing by.

To walk to the house would have been too tiring – not feasible with all they had to carry. So they got a taxi. She insisted on paying for it – he had got lunch after all.

They disgorged, juggling precarious purchases, which were in line to wobble and topple at the tiniest of stubbed toes. He resembled a packhorse; she told him his life depended on not dropping any. She deposited hers higgledy-piggledy on the lounge floor, plopped into a chair and surveyed the jig-saw puzzle patchwork with a furtive frown.

Having dumped his share on the pile, he told her "I don't intend to lift a finger for the rest of the day."

She got up, went over to him, and thanked him for the trip into town. For a second she thought he might kiss her. He shrank back. There was that other baggage again – the plane crash variety. They were definitely going to have to do something about it.

They had time on their side. She could wait.

For his part, in the words of Elvis, he felt *all shook up*. Increasingly, in line with the lyrics, he was *actin' weird as a bug*. But that was fine – he was glad to have her around.

The weeks were flying by and she was now one of the fixtures. With every passing day, she was growing on him.

Their walks in the countryside were a joy. Wind in her hair, birds flitting back and forth, farm animals in the fields. They ambled through woods, became kids again playing hide and seek. She claimed to have won. No way, he maintained. He lobbed a fir cone and it rebounded off her back. It instigated a chase, she was quickly after him and as she caught up he tripped and they landed on top of each other in the leaf litter, giggling like thirteen-year-olds.

This time he did kiss her. At last.

The clinch zinged all the way to her toes but was over as quickly as it had begun.

"I'm sorry – that was wrong."

And rose to his feet as she remained on the floor.

"No," she said. "I shall treasure it ... and hope it's the first of many."

He pulled her upright. Then, turning serious, he told her: "We need to talk when we get home."

Good, she thought.

They finished the walk in silence.

They drove home in silence.

She brewed mugs of tea – in silence.

They sat in the lounge ... and there was silence.

Finally, he couldn't stand it.

"Look," he said. "Forget about the kiss. I should never have. I was bang out of order. After all, I'm old enough to be your father."

Her blood boiled. Couldn't he have come up with anything better than the *old enough to be your father* drivel?

She flew at him without ever moving from her seat. "I'm a big girl now and I don't allow any Tom, Dick or Harry to kiss me. You should be bloody grateful I find you attractive and if nothing else that kiss was evidence that you find me attractive. Don't patronise me ever again. I go with who I want. Age doesn't mean a damned thing."

There – she had said it. The outburst subsided as quickly as it had flared.

She expected a response. There was none.

The last time he had been spoken to like that it was Alice. He hadn't figured Suzi for a spitting alley-cat.

Struck dumb, words simply wouldn't come.

58

Instead, it was she who spoke, softly but lucidly.

"This isn't what it's about, Kevin." She paused. "This is about the plane crash baggage we're both carrying on our backs. It's coming between us and it mustn't come between us. I want to talk it all through, I want to clear the decks, I want to tell you about the bad times and I want to hear from your lips how it was for you. Letters can only tell half the story. I want us to be open with each other – nothing held back." Again, she paused. "Are you up for it, Kevin?"

He looked at her like a little boy chastised. "Yes," he said, to her utter relief.

"I tell you what," she said. "I'll start."

She garnered her thoughts.

"I have no idea how much the plane crash, losing my parents, has warped my life but it's hung over me like a fog. So much has gone awry. I've been hateful to others. Most of the time I've been nauseating to my grandparents who have only ever wanted the best for me. I've treated my aunt Abby like a louse."

He interrupted. "I met Abby on Bali – she was brilliant. She cared deeply about you … a beacon of light. Bali was bitter-sweet, but mostly bitter."

She looked at him as if scales were falling from her eyes. "Abby has always been steadfast," she said. "Yet I've called her names, I've shrieked at her, I've treated her like dirt. Sometimes I think I'm pure evil."

"You're not evil," he said. "You're exquisite."

She smiled at him. It was what she wanted to hear.

She started running through her catalogue of sins. Being thrown out of nursery, playing truant from school, acting the bully, alcohol and drugs, falling in with a very bad crowd … and then the motorcycle morons.

He sat there perturbed as she outlined the atrocity that had been done to her, sparing only the most gruesome elements.

And then the big one – would she ever be able to have children?

At that, she broke down

Immediately he was kneeling besides her, holding her, telling her to let it all come out. Her sobs seemed to go on such a long time.

At length the convulsions came to a halt. She thanked him. Locating a box of paper tissues, he dried her face. She took a few herself and blew her nose loudly. "Not very lady-like," she submitted. "I'm sorry about that – the thought just wastes me. The doctors aren't sure."

"Oh, Hope," his face full of concern for her. "You mustn't. Bad things happen. Hold onto me. I'm here to look after you. You're safe with me."

He kissed her delicately.

"Now," he said. "On you go. If you think you're able to." He sat back in his chair.

"Nearly finished," she sniffed.

Then she went into the stolen car race, agonising over why, after trying so vigorously to get back on the straight and narrow and stay there, she had allowed herself to be talked into it. She was so easily led. She wouldn't even be here had she not on impulse put that seatbelt on. The families of those who were no more would never get over it. As a willing participant, she had to take some responsibility for the death toll. It was something she would have to live with for the rest of her life.

She told him how recuperating at home she had come across the letters – there were so many of them in that drawer. She had subsequently read every one. Having not thought that much about him before, it had affected her considerably. It had sunk in how much she owed to him. She was duty bound to meet face-to-face and thank him – the least she could do.

"And here I am formally thanking you for saving my life," she told him.

He got up and held her to him. When he released her she felt purged.

"Is that it?" he said.

"That's it."

He shuffled back into his seat. "Right," he said. "My turn."

They both knew this was important for her. Very important.

"First of all, I am formally thanking you too for saving my life."

She tensed – what was coming next.

"I was gone," he said. "I had given up. Had it not been for you popping up in the sea beside me, it was Davy Jones' Locker. You were the impetus which gave me the will to live." He told her how lonely and frightened he had been. "I think until now and you … that loneliness has stayed with me and in some ways blighted my life."

She could see how much it was crucifying him. She leaned across and held his hand. He had been there for her; she must be there for him.

He ran through as much of the rescue as he could recall, losing his hold on her, getting it back, would the next wave be his last, straining every sinew to haul himself into the life raft, the whole thing had taken so much out of him. He had so wanted to keep her alive and when his rescuers told him she was indeed alive he wanted to get up and celebrate. Of course, he was in no state to do so. Nevertheless, if that was the highlight of his life, it would do him. He could go up to the Pearly Gates and say – *Let me in, I deserve it*.

Everything about the hospital was grotesque, he told her. "Don't get me wrong – the medical care was excellent. The doctors and nurses were top drawer. I was mentally shot. I was in the middle of a whirlpool – this was a huge international story. It seemed everyone wanted a piece of me. Everything was closing in – I had been slung into a dungeon. I was in a prison called a plane crash – to some extent I'm still a prisoner."

Her hand roamed over his. This was tough.

"My parents were round my bedside with my sister Vicky. And then Becky was there. I treated Becky so badly." He was back there now – in a vortex of regret. Eyes screwed up. "She tried and tried, and I gave her nothing back. I was a brute."

"You're not a brute," she assured him. "You're kind, caring, loving – what more could anyone want?"

He fidgeted. "Oh, but I behaved so badly to her. Had it not been for the crash I think we would have got married. But nothing was the same afterwards. I couldn't think straight, I didn't want the burden, it was all too much. When I think of what I put her through … I behaved disgracefully." It was as if he too was about to break down.

She held his hand ever more firmly. "I'm here Kevin. You're not alone. You're never going to be alone again."

They were getting there.

"When I got home I was just not myself," he said. "Again, it was the mental thing. I couldn't concentrate. I couldn't look all those who had died in the face. Why had I survived and so many others hadn't? It just seemed wrong. It was then that I started writing those long and rambling letters to you. Possibly a mistake. I'm sure your grandparents must have thought I was loopy, but it really helped. I had to tell someone about my true feelings. The rest of creation was on a different pathway. You were the only other survivor. I knew I could confide in you. Now I know I still can." He halted. "Does that make any sense?"

"It makes every sense, Kevin."

It gave him the strength to go on.

"Then they had that memorial service – oh, my Lord." He lowered his head. "I couldn't face it. I told them I wasn't going. Then Dad lost his rag. It was just awful, awful. Emotionally, I was on the floor."

Now he was sobbing and reaching for a handkerchief.

She held him as the tears splashed onto her face.

"Sorry," he said, shaking.

"You can stop if you like," she said.

"No, I've got to do this. If you can manage it then I can too."

She so wanted to mother him.

"The service was beautiful but it broke my heart. I couldn't react, I couldn't empathise, there was nothing left inside me. Those poor people and I gave them so little of myself when they most needed it. I beat myself up about it all the time. I don't know how I got through – that was the bottom though I hadn't figured it."

He told her the aftermath. How the Becky thing had just drifted away on the wind. Gradually, ever so gradually, the line on the graph bottomed out and assumed a slow upward trajectory. There was the sports agency return. They had been more than good to him. But it seemed so inconsequential in the light of all that had taken place. He felt he was going nowhere. With estate agency, there was nothing to lose. He didn't think he would take to it, but he had. He wouldn't say he had exactly found his vocation but it was somewhere to put down roots. He had made money – lots of money. That was the lucrative by-product. Had financed the England trip and lots more besides

Then came Alice – Suzi was looking forward to this part.

He told her straight out, nothing held back. "Alice was a class act in bed. The sex was incredible."

She blanched – how could she match Alice – and he noticed.

He gave her arm a reassuring squeeze. "It was different," he said. "She was a great girl, it was tremendous, but I wasn't in love with her."

This was the moment.

"Are you in love with me?"

"I'm in love with you."

She beamed. "Because I'm deliriously in love with you."

They embraced again, kissed again, she would have liked to have been swept off her feet and taken to his bed, but that would come.

He told her about the blackmail – she was outraged – how he should have been strong but wasn't, and the way it had gradually started boring into him like woodworm. To the point he had no choice but to chuck it all in – Alice, the job, Sydney – and flee abroad. Initially England had been a disaster. The plane crash depression reared its head, no friends, no job, nothing to look forward to.

Would he tell her about the suicide attempt? He had signed up to no secrets. He had to go through with it.

"It got to the stage where I couldn't stoop any lower."

She wondered where this was leading.

"I decided to end it all on a train line – wouldn't feel a thing, I told myself. But I couldn't even get that right." His voice broke.

She was shocked.

But he wasn't finished.

"And then, the phone rang, I picked it up and it was you." He smiled happily. "So, you see, you have saved my life twice – you're one up!"

Both of them were laughing.

"I'm not keeping score," she jibed.

They were worn out – emotionally exhausted. To their astonishment, it had been a three-hour session.

It was ten past eleven at night.

Too late to take anything further, but now there was an understanding.

It had all come out, everything had been said, a new day had dawned early. They went to their separate beds.

57

The next few days she wanted him so much but it wasn't happening.

Why?

They held hands, they kissed, but there was something missing … and there was definitely no sex.

It was baffling. If she wanted a guy she snapped her fingers and they came running. She was throwing herself at this man but couldn't seem to turn the key in the lock. She had departed America wondering if they might become friends; now she was desperate for them to become lovers. Her unhappiness was palpable.

"It's not what it seems," he said. "And I honestly thought I had got rid of all the baggage."

"Tell me."

"I'll get over this hurdle – just allow me to do it in my own time and in my own way."

"What hurdle?"

"Please don't shout at me."

She promised she wouldn't.

"This is irrational but I've got to rid myself of the notion that when we sleep together – because it is when and not if – it's like incest. Obviously not in its dictionary definition. But when we were in the sea and you were crying and I thought maybe your nappy was full and I got rid of it … and there you were, naked from the waist down. Now you'll be naked in an entirely different way in my bed. I'm finding separating the two an obstacle."

This time she was the one who didn't know what to say.

She started to tell him how he was sketching a picture that was bizarre and far-fetched. It wasn't comparable – this was the two of them nearly twenty years on and they loved each other.

"I know," he said. "It is far-fetched. I want to do you justice. Bear with me."

She said she would. She wanted to do him justice too. She would take him to heights he never knew existed. Anything Alice could do she could do too … and more.

She backed off.

Three days later and still nothing.

Enough. She would bring feminine wiles to the party.

The next night she went upstairs first, washed, called to him, went into her room, and closed the door.

She dabbed on her most expensive perfume, admired her bare nipples and put on the polka dot panties that had always sent men potty.

Then she waited.

Now his footsteps were on the stairs, he didn't take long in the bathroom, next the bed springs creaked as they always did, then quiet.

She counted sixty long seconds, got up, cautiously entered his room, nipped inside and tip-toed to his side as a shaft of moonlight through a gap in the curtains settled on her torso for the briefest of moments.

She wriggled under the duvet, and he was ready for her, arms open – it was like coming home. They stroked each other's bodies, kissed madly, gyrated in unison.

He breathed in her beguiling scent; she inhaled his manliness. She wanted him more than she had ever wanted anyone before and he was entranced by the sensuous curves of her body.

This was going to be no rushed affair, no fumbling in the park in Normal, no wham bam thank you ma'am with Honcho.

He spent ages kissing nearly every part of her body until she almost came. In turn, she nibbled his neck, licked his tummy button and accosted him lower still.

When he pulled down her panties he did so with the charisma of a mime artist – it made her feel like a princess. He slid his fingers through her pubic hair and indulged her wetness.

She squirmed deeper into his body as if to say *Now, I'm yours.*

He moved on top of her.

When he entered her the satisfaction went off the gauge.

It seemed to go on and on. She came first, then a whoosh and his sperm surged into her in a raging torrent. She had never thought that being in love could make such a difference.

And for him - this was what it felt like when you met the woman who was meant for you – Alice wasn't even close.

As they eased down, she told him she would want him for ever. He told her he had found the girl to make him happy.

They slept the sleep of the angels.

He woke up in a frazzle.

"Oh my giddy aunt, I'm late."

Panic in his voice.

"Late for what?"

"Late for work."

"It's Sunday."

He sank back. "It's Sunday," he sighed. "What a prat."

She looked at him with bleary eyes and an eyebrow raised as if to say *Yes, you are a prat.*

He wasn't having that, and tried to tickle her. She screamed in mock disarray and beat him off. The love-making started again. This time it was rowdy, him grunting like a top tennis star, she urging him on.

Game, set and match, they lay there panting, hot, fruity, but complete.

She was the first to speak. "You rotter," she wailed. "You've taken advantage of me twice – poor, innocent, me."

He tossed a pillow at her.

She hit him with hers.

Now, knees on the bed, it was a full on pillow fight.

He half pinned her down.

"I'll bite you."

It saw them chuckling away like children.

"I love you."

"I love you too."

This was how they categorised their commitment – fun, laughter, play, love. There had been too much darkness; they only wanted light.

He let her go. It was time for a breather. Then, still full of friskiness, he burst out with the banal. "I bags the bathroom first."

She hadn't come across the expression before.

"You can bags off!" she told him forthrightly.

He was laughing so much he couldn't move. "OK darling," he said. "I give in – ladies first."

She rummaged around the partly demolished room and found the polka dot panties – they had done their job. Now she whipped them on to cover her modesty.

Then, on cloud nine, headed for the bathroom. *His lover and his darling.*

She had her man.

58

He lay back and tried to take it all in.

They were so good for each other. There were no reservations. They were extricating their plane crash straight-jacket in harmony – no flight of fancy this. He was certain it would last.

For the rest of the day he couldn't keep his paws off her – she similarly with him.

When they went to bed that night – always his *place* now – they were tying each other in sex knots. Except that this time he did have to get up in the morning and go to work.

"You're a spoilsport," she moaned, as he threw on clothes and tried to metamorphose into vaguely respectable.

He put his tongue out at her. "See you tonight, Hope."

The words were erotica. It was like she couldn't wait. He was addictive.

The fun, laughter, play and love manifested itself in all kinds of obscure ways.

Cleaning the outside windows one day, Kevin accidentally on purpose flicked water at Suzi. From where it developed into a water fight and both got soaked. What in their own world became known as the Battle of the Buckets.

One weekend they finally got to attack the garden.

He swished his way through the spider webs guarding the shed – he had only investigated its innards once.

She was wearing a favourite top. Complaining that she didn't want to get it all mucky.

Noticing a scruffy old sweater hanging on a nail, he gave it a good shake. It might do the trick.

She held up this moth-eaten man garment dismissively – catwalk it was not.

"Well, come on, give it a go," he entreated, knowing how ill-fitting it would likely prove to be.

Unwillingly she tried it on

He nearly wet himself at her doleful appearance. The sleeves hung over her hands in swathes and it was so bulky you could have fitted two of her within its vast circumference. A picture of dejection.

Arms wide, devilry in his eyes, he scoffed: "Come here my scarecrow baby doll."

She was having none of it. "Scoundrel! Don't soft-soap me with your baby doll bilge." Then pushed him so hard that he tipped over and they ended up rolling around the grass, him telling her it was today's fashion chic, she telling him that as soon as his back was turned he was going head first into a bed of nettles.

With a wicked smile, he undid the top button of her jeans and twirled a finger in the direction of her sweet spot.

Her turn for the wicked smile.

She allowed him to suppose that he just might get away with taking this further … and then cut him off at the knees (or should that have been balls). "I'm very happy to do it in the great outdoors," she said. "But it is probably not a good idea to put on a peep show for the neighbours."

She furrowed her eyebrows, daring him to object. Wisely, he didn't. That was him told.

Going back into the house to see what else he could come up with, he disinterred a light sweater he had shrunk in the wash. He had an unfortunate knack of shrinking sweaters. It more or less fitted her. It would have to do.

They cracked into several hours of cutting, trimming, weeding, hacking … until they could hack it no more.

He made the tea; she produced the biscuit jar.

Then there was the instance when walking beside a children's play park which they passed regularly she had a penchant to regress. "Last to the swings is a scaredy cat," she cried, and took off in dynamic style.

He couldn't catch up with her. But at least there were no kids there to rub his nose in it. She was on one of the swings and sailing through the air with the greatest of ease. He tried to follow suit but the sides were too tight to his hips and he had to write it off as a bad job, much to her glee.

"Ha," she gloated. "The trouble with you is that you're far too fat."

He let the insult pass as she flew past his nose yet again.

Knowing he'd been done over, he ogled that slinky waist so glorious whether it be on a swing or in polka dot panties. She had to be a contender for *Rear of the Year* too.

Now she was waving to him and blowing raspberries. What a bundle of energy. He blessed the day that this stunning woman had set her sights on him.

And she wasn't finished.

As she allowed the swing to slow, she hurtled off spectacularly, did a cartwheel, and sprung into his arms smothering him in kisses. It was quite a finale. Almost out of the circus.

They had a go on the roundabout – his favourite – until they were both dizzy. All he knew was that he was as dizzy for her as any man could be.

They had also taken to going down their local pub twice a week and were becoming familiar faces there. It made them feel they were part of the community. He had got into dry Somerset cider and she had become partial to a gin and tonic.

One evening they noticed the landlord had a sign up – 'part-time bar staff required'.

There was no mention of how many hours were on offer or the length of the shifts. It transpired he wanted someone three days a week, mostly at lunch times and afternoons, but it varied.

"That's a job down my street," she told Kevin. "It would give me something to do while you're out at work."

He was fine with the idea but claimed tongue in cheek that she didn't have big enough knockers to be a barmaid, which got him a forty-eight hour sex ban.

Perhaps being too honest, she informed the landlord that she was only on a tourist visa and so had no permission to work, but he didn't bat an eyelid. Said he would pay her out of the till – it wouldn't go through the books. The black economy must be thriving.

They started her off under the supervision of one of the regular bar staff, but she was quickly up to speed – fill pints of cider to the brim but put a head on the lager, how to change a barrel, a crash course in some of the terminology like *snakebite* (lager and cider) and *black velvet* (champagne and stout).

The job suited her; she flirted with the punters, laughed at their jokes, however tame, put them in their place when over-excitable. From time to time she got called in to work in the evening if they had a busy night on – a big football match on the television, the darts team in action, a function in the back room.

Then, Kevin might tag along and keep her company.

They developed a 'comic' routine, designed to astound strangers – like in a TV *soap*, he would chat her up, stoking the smut and shenanigans, and she would be dead cheeky back, the locals who had seen it all before taking bets on how many times the newcomer choked into his beer.

When they got home, it would prompt *extras* – further suggestive naughtiness and corresponding spicy put-downs. Usually a prelude to *rumpy pumpy* later.

59

It was now four months or so since she had turned up on his doorstep. They were effectively living as man and wife, and it was all good. No, more than good, sensational. The demons had been driven away, hopefully forever, and they were both fully conversant with how only they could have achieved the turnaround because only they knew what agonies the plane crash had wrought.

Yet there might still be *hungry bears* – stretching it a bit but Tamworth being half in Warwickshire, which boasts a bear and ragged staff heraldic motif – out there keen to scavenge on scandal. In particular should the media stumble across the pair of them in flagrante. Here were the only two survivors of a ghastly plane crash, and he was *shacked up* with the baby he had saved from drowning. In anyone's book that was one helluva story.

He might come in for a lot of stick, with stirrers hinting he had taken liberties, even groomed a child – the letters being the so-called evidence. She was far more sanguine, seeing no reason why anyone should want to trawl the dirt after so long and betting on it being manageable even if somebody did.

Both knew there had been no grooming but if you had to could you prove there hadn't been?

He knew how resourceful the media could be and to put it mildly did not relish being hauled over the coals like in the aftermath of the disaster. He thought it wise to take precautions. Keep their skeletons firmly in the closet. For example, he would always call her Hope in public places, such as the pub. It might put someone off the trail should they be sniffing around.

There was just one other cloud on the horizon – the six month expiry of her visa.

The spectre of a grotesque balls-up whereby she was thrown out of England and sent back to the United States, while the United States blocked Kevin joining her there, kept her awake at night. The thought of being parted from him for months, perhaps even years appalled her.

Like Abby and John, this was the man she wanted to father her children, always assuming, of course, she could have children. Why had she been so incredibly stupid to hook up with that bunch of motorbike mobsters?

She didn't want to overdo the visa dilemma, but it bothered her.

It bothered them both albeit Kevin thought it unlikely that the worst would indeed happen. Would immigration even latch onto her having overstayed? Anyway, she was still legitimate for two months.

Nevertheless, it could not be side-lined for ever.

What to do about it?

Kevin had it all worked out. He was going to marry her.

Critics might say four months was simply not long enough to be sure and smacked of one of those C-list *wed one week; divorced the next* impetuous couplings which filled the gossip pages of the tabloid rags.

He knew she was the one, she loved him, he couldn't care less any more about the age difference, she would keep him young. For the record, it wasn't four months – it was nearly twenty years. All he had to do now was buy a ring and pop the question. But how to find the time during a busy working week – you couldn't just nip out in your thirty minute lunch break. It wasn't as if it was going to buy a banana or a chocolate bar. This was a ring.

He told her he had to work a half day on the Saturday, which was bunkum.

He would take her out to a posh restaurant for a late lunch to make it up to her.

All that week he was fidgety. She thought he was acting oddly but couldn't put her finger on it. He denied anything was amiss.

On the Saturday he made sure he was out of the house promptly and to keep his cover from blowing was wearing his work suit. A train into Birmingham and onto the city's famous Jewellery Quarter.

The Jewellery Quarter, where he had done a spot of sight-seeing on first arrival in Birmingham, walkable from the city centre, renowned for high quality, bespoke pieces and claimed to house Europe's largest concentration of businesses involved in the jewellery trade. Safe to say, Kevin knew he would find something ornate to seal their partnership.

He went into several shops seeking inspiration before his eyes alighted on a combination of diamonds and emeralds in art deco style, which, he hoped, would dazzle his prospective bride.

It cost a pretty penny but it was worth it.

He was well satisfied as he sat in the train back to Tamworth but then the jitters got going, butterflies in his stomach. What if she said 'no'? Oh, come on, don't be ridiculous. Of course she's not going to say 'no'. But, wow, hang about, she's only nineteen ... she might think it far too soon.

Stop it, Kevin. He was so caught up in this 'will she, won't she' that he almost missed his stop.

When he got back to the house, she was immediately agitating to know where he was taking her for the promised meal. All for rushing out of the door. He shepherded her into the lounge, saying he had something he wanted to show her.

What was it?

Be patient. It's a surprise.

60

Ostensibly in a huff at his keeping it back from her, she went from grumpy to open-mouthed wonder as he sank to one knee. He tilted the catch on a small jewellery box and angled it towards her. She could see it was a ring.

"Oh my God," she said, getting what this was about.

"Suzanne Duthie, Hope Duthie, will you marry me?"

She started crying and for an instant he wasn't at all sure of her response.

"Darling, of course I'll marry you." She was standing there, laughing, crying.

He placed the ring on her finger, and she loved it. This was the preserve of fairy tales, wasn't it? They kissed and then she was in his arms.

Before consternation set in – his body was going limp.

She staggered back, there was this opaque look in his eyes as though he could not believe what was transpiring, and, as his weight took him, he slipped through her fingers to the floor, the empty jewellery box somersaulting along the carpet.

He lay there motionless – didn't seem to be breathing.

This time her 'Oh my God' was of blind hysteria.

This couldn't be. What to do?

A voice was calling out, appealing to him – it was hers … "Get up Kevin, you must get up, Kevin, please Kevin, please."

She was on the floor beside him, imploring him. Slapping his cheeks.

Maybe he had had some sort of turn.

She ran to the kitchen, filled a jug with cold water, and splashed it onto his face.

There was no response.

She cradled his body, stroked his head.

Nothing.

She let out the most blood-curdling scream.

She must get help. That was it. She would go round to the neighbours.

More screams as she rung bells and hammered on doors.

She only knew the neighbours to say hello to in passing and that was it. A door opened on the latch and a querulous face peered through the crack.

"Please – he's on the floor dying. We have to save him."

It was a woman in her fifties. She went to get her husband.

Another neighbour, a man in his twenties, heard the racket and came outside to investigate. He raced round with her to the house.

Kevin was still lying prone.

Had she phoned the emergency services?

So flustered was she that it hadn't occurred to her. What was the number? 911? No, that was the United States.

"999," he told her.

She found her mobile. It was out of juice.

He rang from his phone. Then passed the operator to Suzi who was by now close to disintegration.

What was the address and postcode?

She rattled off the address but couldn't remember the postcode.

"Oh, you are such a trollop, what is the damned postcode?" she demanded, tearing into herself.

Leave it, said the operator.

What was the phone number she was calling from in case they were cut off – she could recall the landline digits, the mobile wasn't hers.

What was the purpose of the call? *He had collapsed in her arms. He was lying on the floor, not moving. He wasn't breathing.*

"Please, please he needs an ambulance urgently."

The operator said she was sorting it out.

The questions kept on coming as Suzi became ever more incoherent.

The patient's age, sex and medical history. Forty-one, male, healthy or so she had thought.

Was the patient conscious, breathing, any bleeding or chest pain? Her rancour boiled over – she had told them all this. No, he wasn't breathing and he wasn't conscious.

"Just get the bloody ambulance here. Don't you understand – he's dying."

She was now back on her hands and knees once more imploring Kevin to come round. Pleading with him to say something.

The neighbour took over the phone.

He explained who he was.

Was the airway clear of obstructions? He said it seemed to be.

She took him through the steps for carrying out CPR (Cardiopulmonary Resuscitation).

He said he thought he had the gist of it, told Suzi what he was going to undertake, and handed the phone back to her.

With hands interlocked he began pumping Kevin's chest in regular cycles – one, two, three, four, five, six, seven, eight, nine, ten.

Pause.

One, two, three, four, five, six, seven, eight, nine, ten.

On and on – it was energy sapping.

Suzi was just standing there dumbstruck, but, hang on, kiss of life, she had seen that in a television thriller.

She was down beside the neighbour now and every time he paused she blew air into Kevin's lungs.

From the control room the alert had gone out – cardiac arrest.

Both an ambulance and a rapid response vehicle were on their way, blue lights flashing, sirens blaring.

Suzi heard the whining noise first. She raced outside to direct them to the right house.

A small huddle of neighbours were in the street wondering what was going on, chattering awkwardly amongst themselves, unsure what to think.

The rapid response vehicle sounded its horn and they scattered.

The two occupants, bailed out, dashed inside, took over, asked for space while they worked on him.

Medical equipment, stretcher, defibrillator in a bid to electric shock his heart, but nothing seemed to be working.

Now the ambulance was here.

And at that Suzi fainted.

She came round as they were getting him into it, and begged to be allowed to go too. The ambulance crew relented. She grabbed her bag, the house keys and they were off, blue lights and sirens again warning traffic to get out of the way.

Every minute felt like an hour. Then they were there and he was being wheeled into A&E where a crash team was waiting.

It was hopeless. DOA – dead on arrival.

They took her to a side room – she looked terrible, face streaked by countless tears, hair all over the place, the floral dress she had put on for the lunch ruined.

Seated, they took it slowly, gradually weaving the narrative towards the brutal truth.

Cardiac arrests put lives in jeopardy, first responders and the ambulance crew had done their level best, battling all the way in to bring him back from the brink. Nothing had worked. He was very sorry to tell her, there was no way of breaking this gently, Kevin had passed away.

She rested her head on the table, and closed her eyes. She didn't cry – there were no tears left.

Until the consultant said he was afraid that there were other facets he must mention. The coroner was bound to order a post-mortem because of the sudden nature of the death. That would mean a delay in the body being released. Secondly, donation of organs – he would ask a member of the organ donation team to speak to her.

"Would you like someone to sit with you? The hospital chaplain perhaps."

She said she would prefer some privacy.

He said she should take as long as was necessary and closed the door.

She was alone; she had never felt so alone ever. She visualised his mannerisms, his kindness, his playfulness, how he had dedicated himself to her. The love of her life was gone – how would she manage, what would she do, it was so unfair.

There could be nobody else after him. She felt bereft.

Time seemed to stand still … until the knock on the door.

The first decision of many.

"Come in."

It was the organ team representative. She said her name was Gwen.

She ran through the technicalities about donation – organs quickly become unusable for transplantation but bone, skin, heart valves and corneas can be donated within the first twenty-four hours of death. Harvesting such body parts would mean he had not died in vain. Very ill patients would be the recipients.

In turn Suzi said she had been living with Kevin, they had planned to wed, but doubted whether she would be classed as next of kin. His family was in Australia. They almost certainly didn't know she was with him, they definitely would not know he was dead, she hadn't got the Sydney phone number on her. She had no idea what opinion the family might have on organ donation and she never recalled him raising the subject.

After which she lost interest in the whole thing.

If they could sort it out they could do what they wanted.

Tiredness all of a sudden overtook her. All she wanted to do was go home.

Gwen said she understood – Suzi was sure she wasn't even close to understanding. Nevertheless, the woman was sincere.

They would phone a taxi for her.

While she waited, it struck her how hospitals were such a sterile environment in every sense of the word. She had seen too many hospitals. Enough to last a lifetime.

Was there someone who could be with her once she got back – a friend or neighbour?

The neighbours had done what they could, she said. However, she would rather be on her own.

The drive back to Tamworth was laboured – Suzi knew the road ahead was going to be even more laboured.

At last, it pulled up outside the house. She retrieved just enough money from purse and pockets to meet the fare.

61

Eyes seemed to be on her as she walked to the front door – the neighbours were on watch from behind the cover of their curtains.

The lady whose bell she had rung first came out – there was no need to ask as to the outcome. She could see from Suzi's tear-stained face and bloodshot eyes. "I'm so sorry for you, dear," she said, and put a wizened arm around Suzi.

It set her off again as, retrieving the house keys from her handbag, she poked at the door lock, kept missing the slot, but finally managed to control the shakes sufficient to stop her hand from juddering.

"Would you like me to come in and make you a nice cup of tea, love?

Half of her wanted to tell this no doubt well-meaning busybody to take a hike while the other half longed to be hugged and told none of this was happening.

They went inside and the woman put the kettle on.

"Sit down on the sofa – you must be wrecked," she told Suzi.

She got the tea brewing and kept her company as they drank. It transpired her name was Mrs Wilson.

"I'm sure he was a good man," she said. "I feel for you. How old was he?"

"Forty-one."

"Oh, dear, that's no age at all. How very, very, sad. And the medical people did their utmost."

Suzi had had her fill of this. "You're being very decent," she told Mrs Wilson. "All the neighbours have been marvellous. But I feel completely exhausted."

Mrs Wilson stood up. "Got you, dear," she said. "You have yourself a good night's sleep. Maybe take a paracetamol or two. Remember, I am next door. If you need anything just knock – doesn't matter what time it is."

She was a gracious old duck.

"Thank you – you've been an enormous comfort," said Suzi.

The door closed – it was closing on a chapter of her life.

She sat back down in her misery. She had gone from fiancé to 'widow' in a mere thirty seconds. It was scarcely credible.

She turned to the picture of the two of them, which she had insisted went centre stage on the mantelpiece. They had been so happy – you could see it in the portrait.

The jewellery box was still lying where it had fallen. She couldn't leave it there. Picked it up. Looked at the engagement ring on her finger. The ring, the framed picture and her memories – that was all she really had of him. Not much to take away from such high passion.

What day was it? Oh yes, Saturday still. The pub bar would be humming with lively and jocular exchange. In contrast, here she was, isolated and broken, in a room that now seemed contaminated by tragedy.

There was no evading the calamity – she kept on going over and over the day's events in the vain hope that they may have a different ending. It was the same each time.

Could she have done more in those critical minutes before brain damage sets in? There had been no warning that he might be ill. Why had she never taken a first aid course? She must put that right sooner rather than later in case she ever found herself tending to someone else at death's door. She must not feel it was somehow her fault – that was the way, like him, to an early grave.

What about Kevin's family – she should be phoning them, but it was late, she hadn't the strength, it would have to wait for the morning.

She thought of phoning Abby – the ever-reliable Abby who had done so much for her. Abby would know what to do. Abby would try to console her. Abby was so together.

She toyed with all the duties she would have to take on – contact the hospital and the coroner's office, apply for a death certificate if she was allowed, funeral arrangements. And where would that be – not Tamworth as they were in effect just passing through. Probably the body would have to be repatriated to Australia. Or cremation perhaps.

There would be much, much, more – that was for sure.

How would his parents take it? Would she be able to cooperate with them? Would they marginalise her?

She couldn't stand it.

She must have dropped off because when she woke up with a jolt her watch said 1am. For her own good she must get herself to bed. Shut everything out if only for a few hours. She slowly raised herself, legs stiff, got a glass of orange and water, and heaved her way up the stairs while leaning hard on the banister. She would do her teeth – she hated going to bed without doing her teeth. She put her clothes into the laundry basket (it was so automatic) and then pulled the sheets over her. She would pretend he was making love to her one final time. Then, pray God, allow her rest.

It took a while but then she was walking through California's Death Valley vainly calling to him.

From there, the next she knew was that she had left the house, undertaken a long hike, the main rail line was in sight, and she was yomping across Wigginton Park.

With her nimble frame, it was nothing to scale the guard fence.

This was it. No more need to grieve, no more need for undertakers, red tape, family, and the rest, she probably wouldn't feel a thing.

A train was approaching, she stepped onto the line, turned towards it, denied the tortured face of the driver, and … obliteration.

She woke up screaming the rooftops down.

It had been so real she could barely accept that she had never left her bedroom. She thrust her head into her pillow and sobbed, and sobbed, and sobbed.

It took her many minutes to take hold of herself.

She knew what this was all about. As the nightmare unfurled it had taken the exact same pattern as the failed suicide Kevin had outlined when they made their confessionals to each other.

Was this the underworld, that mythical abode of the dead, casting her out? A shiver went down her spine – it was almost paranormal. Macabre. She sat there rigid with fear. Until eventually she sussed it.

She could not remain in this house a moment longer. This house that epitomised the very best and very worst, this house which had now become a vampire, sucking the life from her. To hell with funeral, body, possessions, rent, bills et al, she was quitting. From now, it was all on his parents. A callous way to act perhaps, but she was gone, it was finished.

She set about her mission systematically.

Wash, shower, toilet – she wanted to be prepared for what she was about to embark upon. She wasn't sure where this was taking her. Probably train to London and flight across the Atlantic. Where else could she go but Normal? Or maybe Toronto. Yes, Toronto would be the place. She could ring Abby from Heathrow.

Now where had she put her big backpack?

It was where she had left it on top of the wardrobe.

She gave it a wipe with a rag. It needed a comprehensive clean but that wasn't going to happen.

Going into her bedroom, she packed as many of her clothes as she could carry, folding them neatly rather than tossing them in willy-nilly – that way more could be accommodated.

For protection, she symbolically packaged the polka dot undies around the portrait picture of the two of them, then placed it carefully between a sweater and top. She got her wash things, her makeup bag. She religiously checked off – shoes, socks, panties, jeans, dresses, tops, shorts … until she was almost befuddled. Must not leave anything behind that was sacred to their union.

She went into his room. Wanted to see whether there were any further mementos she might salvage to remember him by.

She took a belt from around his trousers – she would wear it with her jeans – and found the Outback hat he had worn when first she arrived at Birmingham coach station.

To remind her she remained his.

She remembered the laundry basket. All inter-mingled, she had to separate her clothes from his. It was like a vulture picking the bones of a zebra carcase.

Tugging the backpack down the stairs, she hoiked it on the table where they had so often sat, be it breakfast, lunch or dinner.

Ah, food.

It would be wise to line her stomach. She toasted a couple of slices of bread, put some butter on them, poached an egg, placed it between the slices, cut it in half, and ate carefully – had always hated yolk dripping down her chin. All finished off with a hot chocolate. Even cleaned the pan. Then in an act of lunacy – the stress had made her irrational – she tidied the house. Didn't want the landlord to think of her, or indeed Kevin, as devoid of social graces. Swept the kitchen floor and put the vacuum over the carpets. Poured disinfectant down the toilet.

What else?

Hold on, there was that John Buchan novel staring at her, the one which had triggered such repartee between them.

Oh, forget it, just another thing to carry.

And, almost as she thought it, an involuntary shudder ran down her body as though someone was walking over her grave.

It freaked her out.

She would be cursed for the rest of her life if she didn't take the book with her.

Perhaps there was just enough room to cram it into a side pocket of the backpack.

Cautiously, picking the book up with tips of fingers so as to avoid the wrath of the spirits, she quickly shoved it into this last available space and pulled the zip across.

Outside it was raining … and raining cats and dogs. Some hail in there too. Wind rattling the kitchen window. Not a day to be out and about. Suzi would have to brave it.

She found the anorak bought during the Birmingham shopping spree – it wasn't fully waterproof. She had intended purchasing something heavier and harder-wearing but had never got round to doing so, too late now. Would have to get on with it. She was ready though she didn't feel ready.

Something was missing. It was all too sanitised, too regimented, she could not abandon this poky little hovel they had both been so taken with, a home from home, without saying a proper goodbye, acknowledging all that he had contributed.

She did not care much for religion – it was all tosh. But, just as he had said a prayer in the water, putting trust in a higher power, she felt she too must offer up a gesture of sorts, a testament to their union.

Suzi made the sign of the cross, knelt down, put her hands together, bowed her head, and closed her eyes.

She told God to look after Kevin, give shelter to a good man, spoke about his devotion and their love, and asked him to bless her as she journeyed into the wilderness. It made her feel a fraud – if God did exist, where had he been?

But then he worked in mysterious ways, didn't he?

She struggled into the bulging backpack, opened the front door and, immediately battered by rain and wind, forced it shut again.

It was as if nature was wreaking its anger on her.

However, the house was now dark and brooding in its emptiness. The place had served its purpose and that purpose was now on a slab in the hospital mortuary. It was time to depart.

She assaulted the door for a second time and braced against the ferocity of the gale.

Once outside, she tugged the handle, got the thing closed, locked it, put the keys back through the letter box and contemplated a long, wet, dreary walk to the rail station.

Trees creaked, twigs and leaves flew through the air, the wind blasted her ear drums. Her hair was being dragged all ways. Her nose started streaming.

No dawn chorus in these conditions – had things been different she would have appreciated some bird song to cheer her path.

62

She strode out onto the road.

Then, very deliberately, measured out exactly thirty-nine steps.

And looked back.

Tears were pouring down her face, rain was pouring down her face.

She turned and despondently headed away. It was done.

FICTION FROM APS BOOKS
(www.andrewsparke.com)

Davey J Ashfield: *Footsteps On The Teign*
Davey J Ashfield *Contracting With The Devil*
Davey J Ashfield*: A Turkey And One More Easter Egg*
Davey J Ashfield*: Relentless Misery*
Fenella Bass: *Hornbeams*
Fenella Bass:: *Shadows*
Fenella Bass*: Darkness*
HR Beasley*: Nothing Left To Hide*
Lee Benson: *So You Want To Own An Art Gallery*
Lee Benson: *Where's Your Art gallery Now?*
Lee Benson*: Now You're The Artist...Deal With It*
Lee Benson: *No Naked Walls*
TF Byrne *Damage Limitation*
Nargis Darby: *A Different Shade Of Love*
J.W.Darcy *Looking For Luca*
J.W.Darcy: *Ladybird Ladybird*
J.W.Darcy: *Legacy Of Lies*
J.W.Darcy: *Love Lust & Needful Things*
Milton Godfrey: *The Danger In Being Afraid*
Jean Harvey: *Pandemic*
Michel Henri: *Mister Penny Whistle*
Michel Henri*: The Death Of The Duchess Of Grasmere*
Michel Henri: *Abducted By Faerie*
Laurie Hornsby: *Postcards From The Seaside*
Hugh Lupus *An Extra Knot (Parts I-VI)*
Ian Meacheam: *An Inspector Called*
Ian Meacheam: *Time And The Consequences*
Alex O'Connor: *Time For The Polka Dot*
Peter Raposo: *dUst*
Peter Raposo: *The Illusion Of Movement*
Peter Raposo: *Second Life*
Peter Raposo: *Pussy Foot*
Peter Raposo: *This Is Not The End*
Peter Raposo: *Talk About Proust*
Peter Raposo: *All Women Are Mortal*

Printed in Great Britain
by Amazon

79485599R00159